RUTHLESS MAFIA DADDY

KIRA COLE

1

————

LILA

WHY AM I EVEN HERE? WHY DO I KEEP LETTING OTHER people make the decisions for me? Rule my life? Hurt me?

Like Sam.

It's been a while now, but the wound is still there.

I'm not ready for this at all. I'm not ready to get back out there. Not ready to open myself up to love again. Because love will chew you up and spit you out.

Again, like Sam.

I thought I'd be engaged to the man of my dreams by now. Maybe even happily married.

The joke is on me, I guess. Who knew that dream would turn out to be the nightmare of all nightmares. And after this long, I'm still waiting to wake up.

What's the one good thing to come out of what happened?

I wish I could say this date, but unless the dude sitting opposite me has a personality transplant in the next twenty seconds, this is a colossal waste of my time.

As I knew it might be. As I told my best friend it would be.

But did she listen? Did it stop her from forcing me to be here?

No.

His nasal voice pulls me out of one bad place and into another.

"It's fun because people consider the game a slightly more complex form of rock/paper/scissors. But in actuality, it is more like chess. You get a team preview, and you have to determine how your team matches up against the other and you control a handful of the stats so there is a lot of ways you can throw off your opponent by making a Pokémon more defensive or faster or something along those lines."

Pokémon? All I know about Pokémon is that there is a cute little yellow rat that shoots lightning from its cheeks and has Ryan Reynolds's voice.

Do I even care?

Apparently, it doesn't matter either way. He doesn't need my input on it anyway because he doesn't even stop to look at me.

"Did you know speed is an important stat in Pokémon? So, training them to be just the right speed to out-speed one of its weaknesses can be a major boon in a battle." He takes a sip of his beer. "At least for a best of one battle. If it is best of three, then you might want to preserve some of those secrets for a later game if you think that will give you the upper hand."

Speaking of speed, I can't believe I spent a good three hours getting ready for this. Cassi owes me big time.

And it feels like I've been here forever. I look at my phone. Two minutes to eight. Almost one hour into this date, and I've been ready for it to end from minute one.

"And now with newer games, there is a thing called

"tera" where you change your Pokémon's typing in the middle of a battle. You can only do it once per battle, but if you have a Pokémon that might be quad weak to a fairy move and then have it tera-steel, then it suddenly resists fairy moves."

I smile and sigh. I wish *I* had a tera thingy or even a fairy move, whatever that is, so I could just fly out of here or poof out of thin air.

"Oh?" I check my phone. *Again.*

Come on, why is time all but frozen?

My best friend, Cassi, is the reason I'm on this shitty date, and she better keep her end of this deal and give me an out in...one minute and forty-three seconds. She promised.

Then again, she also assured me the guy was nice, and that we had a lot in common.

So far, he's not living up to my very low expectations.

That's okay. I can endure one minute and... thirty-six seconds.

God.

"Lately, I really like Weezing. He got a new ability last generation called "Neutralizing Gas" that removes the abilities of all other Pokémon on the field. So, you can negate some beneficial ones from your opponent. Or negate some negative ones from your side." His smile is all for himself. "There is also Ogrepon. She's adorable and wears a mask but is *super* powerful. Her stats are just really good and her ability and typing change based on which mask she is wearing."

Breathe. You have only...

My eyes fly to my phone again, and I have to swallow a groan.

How is it that there is still one minute and eighteen

seconds to go? This thing has to be broken. There is no way time is moving this slowly.

Can I wear one of those magical masks and teleport out of here? Or maybe have him ooze back to where he came from?

"Back in 2016 when I was in the tournament, I was able to predict how I could lose if a certain Pokémon went down. So, even though I was about to go down to one Pokémon, I was able to preserve the ability because the big thing was weather control that year. And since I preserved that Poké-mon, I made it to where I still won the game one V. two because I had won the weather war."

"Uh, that sounds..." I have no idea how to finish that sentence, so I just glance around the bar.

Is there a clock around here somewhere?

I don't find one.

"So, the big Pokémon back then were Kyogre, Groudon, and Rayquaza and they all had the ability to mega evolve. Kyogre's ability was called Primordial Sea and summoned the rain on the field for as long as it was out. Groudon had Desolate Land which summoned the sun, which usually weakens water and powers up fire, you know, but Desolate land negates it. Those were cool."

Man, I'm the desolate one. Why me?

I need a drink. Or ten.

My eyes find the glass of red wine in front of me, untouched after that first sip.

It tastes like paint thinner.

Dirk insisted on paying, but only after confirming the cheapest option on the menu.

Can anyone say red flag?

Seriously, where did Cassi find this guy? Craigslist?

Do I really seem that desperate and alone?

The thought makes my stomach churn.

"But the weather wars would happen because if both players brought out their primal Pokémon in the beginning, the faster one activates their ability first, and then the slower one activates the ability. So, the slower one would win the weather war on turn one, because they get to keep their weather."

"That's, uh...nice." I force a smile.

Twenty-seven more seconds.

"Any time you're ready, Cassi..." I mutter, letting out a long breath.

Glancing around the bar, I can't help but notice the dozens of happy couples drinking cocktails and roaming their hands all over each other—not caring they're in the middle of a crowded bar. Because when you're in love, the rest of the world seems to disappear.

I thought I had that with Sam.

I was wrong.

I've been let down one too many times by the men in my life—each one leaving a crack in my heart—and Sam was the catalyst that finally shattered it. And no amount of cheap vino and Ben and Jerry's has glued it back together.

Work has been my refuge. Started there straight out of college and over this last year, I've managed to be promoted to executive assistant to the CEO.

Who needs a man when I have a laptop and a corner office with a view of the Hudson, right? That and a fucking good vibrator with ten settings.

That helps too.

One fleeting look at my phone shows me it's eight already, and the phone is not ringing.

What the hell, Cassi? Just call already.

"So, a general strat would be to bring out your weather

Pokémon to determine speeds of your opponent's primal, or to keep your primal in the back so your enemy doesn't know if they are going to be able to get off a fire attack."

Oh lord, please send a fire attack my way.

I listen to him drone for what feels like an hour more about Pokémon and wars and stats before I check my phone. *Again*.

How is it only nine past eight.

It doesn't matter.

I think it's safe to say that Cassi isn't going to save me from this date, so I'm going to have to do it myself.

"I'm sorry. I need to visit the ladies' room for a sec."

I move to slide off my stool when a warm hand cups my elbow as if to help me down.

Jerking, I turn to look over my shoulder.

My eyes land on the most gorgeous man I've ever seen.

"Sorry to interrupt." His voice is deep and rough as eyes the color of onyx flick to my mouth, and my breath hitches.

Who is this man and where has he been all my life?

2

ANDRE

Five years.

Sixty months.

One thousand, eight hundred and twenty-six days.

Forty-three thousand, eight hundred and twenty-four hours.

And each one has felt like a lifetime.

The pain of loss is as strong today as it was when I first learned about it.

A pain that shatters my insides every minute of every hour of every day.

And the worst part is I lost more than just her. I lost the whole life I had planned for us. Marriage, kids, grandkids. She was my happily ever after.

Now all I have is an empty ever after.

But every day I have to get out of bed because I have people depending on me. My men, my siblings.

I don't have time to break down. I don't have time to mourn. I have to be there for all of them. Because their survival, their well-being is my responsibility.

This day is the only day I allow myself to feel.

I gulp down my second double scotch on the rocks and wave a passing waiter for another. It's going to take close to a whole bottle to help my mind get fuzzy enough to not remember as clearly that my life is over.

Part of me hopes that with each passing year, the weight of the grief will lift, even just an inch. Enough where the world isn't clouded in darkness, where I might see past the veil.

But no amount of drinking or fucking or killing seems to help.

Death is everywhere. Except...

For five years, I've tried to get the man behind my misery. To make him pay.

For five years I've failed. Just like I failed to protect her.

And this need for justice, for vengeance consumes me.

At this point, I'm pretty sure if someone were to cut me open, darkness would spill out and all that would be left of me was an empty shell and a blackened heart.

The only thing that keeps this shattered thing somewhat beating is my family. Or what's left of it.

I lean back in the plush velvet chair and scan the room once more, my eyes finding the stunner sitting at the bar once more.

She's checked her phone six times in the past two minutes alone.

I clench the glass of scotch in my hand, watching as the fuckwit opposite her rattles on and on about god knows what, paying more attention to the beer in his hand than to the absolutely drop-dead gorgeous woman sitting opposite him.

And I mean *gorgeous*.

The way she's crossed her legs has made her short black

dress ride up, exposing tanned thighs that make my hands itch to run all over them.

Fuck, if I was sat opposite her, I'd find a way to have my hands on her immediately. To confirm that her skin is as warm and as soft as it appears to be.

Her long brown curls are loose around her slim shoulders, practically shimmering under the low orange lights of the bar.

She glances around. Her demeanor is tight, like she is nervous. Her back is straight ramrod-looking, her eyes wide and restless.

Shit, is this guy making her uncomfortable?

Why do I care? I should be drinking myself into oblivion tonight and stumbling home to my little brother and sister.

Speaking of, I check my phone.

Seven messages from Marco complaining about our sister.

I can't hold my chuckle in. Rosa may be the youngest at fifteen, but she is a force to be reckoned with.

I glance at the goddess at the bar once more.

Maybe I should indulge tonight. Let myself go. She looks like she could help me forget.

Before my brain registers what is happening, I'm out of my chair and crossing the distance between us.

As she tries to climb off the stool, I reach for her elbow, her skin as warm to the touch as I imagined it. My fingers tingle from the contact.

Her muscles tense under my hand, and eyes of the palest blue meet mine.

Fuck, she is even more gorgeous up close. I can't help but flick my gaze to those pouty red lips.

"I'm terribly sorry to interrupt," I start, letting the

corners of my mouth lift into a smirk, "but if I have to listen to this fuckwit talking about stats and battles and whatnot for one more second, I may just start killing people."

The woman lets out a nervous laugh, glancing sidelong at her date.

I lean in a little closer until her perfume hits my nose, and I bite back a moan. Vanilla and orange blossom. Delicious, just like her.

"You look incredible in that dress, by the way." I let my eyes fully take her in, appreciating the way her clothes hug her curves.

Her pale blue eyes widen, and she hides a smile as her date jumps to his feet.

"Hey, you can't talk to her like that," he growls, fists clenched as he confronts me. "We're in the middle of a fucking date, man."

I let out a long breath, letting my eyes flick to that sensual mouth once more before I turn to face the dickwad who thinks he has a chance against me. I scoff. "Are you?"

This gamer boy who looks like he's barely out of adolescence is at least half a foot shorter than my six-foot-four. It's pitiful at best.

"Because as I see it, you've been so self-focused that you haven't asked her a single question about her life or interests." I shrug. "If you're so happy talking to yourself about yourself, don't let us stop you, but the lady deserves a compliment and to be part of a real conversation."

He sputters, red in the face, but no words come out.

I shake my head. "No wonder you're still living with your parents, *Dirk*."

He blinks, gasping.

I ignore him. I'm here for the goddess, not him. Turning

my back on him, I get lost in the icy blue of her eyes. "What's your name, sweetheart?"

"L-Lila."

"It's a pleasure to meet you." I reach for her hand and bring it up to my lips.

I revel in the way her breath catches as I press my lips to her smooth skin. "I'm Andre."

I don't fail to notice the way goosebumps cover her bare arms at my touch.

Dirk's hand lands on my shoulder. "What the fuck—"

I round on him before he even has a chance to utter another word, grabbing him by the shirt and slamming him against the bar. "I wouldn't do that if I were you."

"And why is that?" His eyes spark with challenge.

"Because I own this place, and I will have you thrown out on your ass if you don't back the fuck off."

Dirk scoffs, rolling his eyes. "That's bullshit. You're lying."

"Does it look like bullshit to you, Lila?" I glance at her.

Lila is wide-eyed as she glances between Dirk and me, but she shakes her head.

"She's my date," he seethes, fists clenching, spit flying everywhere.

"*Was*. She *was* your date. You lost your chance when you acted like it didn't matter if she was even there. She's deserves better, so she is *my* date now."

Dirk's eyes flash as he looks to Lila, and I bite back a laugh.

Does this poor excuse for a man really think that she will choose to stay with him?

"What time was your 'out' supposed to call?" I ask Lila over my shoulder.

Those icy blue eyes widen. "Excuse me?"

"You've been looking at that phone of yours throughout the entire date." I smirk. "Not that Dirk here would've noticed. I assume you're waiting for someone to call. A call where you'll learn about an emergency that is sadly going to cut your date short. So, again, what time?"

She flushes, biting on her lip, eyes dropping to my chest. I like that a little too much.

"Eight," she mutters under her breath.

I chuckle, nodding. "I think it's time you get some better friends."

A ghost of a smile makes her pouty lips even more appealing.

I tear my eyes from her and aim them at Dirk as I tighten my grip on his shirt.

Holding tight and turning toward the door, I start dragging him toward the exit. "Now, I think it's time you leave Lila and me to *our* date."

I glance back to Lila who's clearly trying not to laugh at the sight of Dirk trying to bat me away. "I'll be right back, sweetheart."

"I'll be right here."

Her eyes flick over my body, and everywhere it touches, it leaves a trail of fire on my skin.

I can't help the feral grin that spreads across my face.

Holding on to my hands as he tries not to lose his footing, Dirk doesn't protest much as we reach the door.

Jerry, one of my men, is waiting right outside the door. When he sees me, he unfolds his arms and smiles at me. "Oh, hey boss. Taking out the trash?"

"Yeah, mind seeing to it? I can't stay. Have a gorgeous woman waiting for me at the bar."

"Sure thing, boss."

I toss Dirk at Jerry. "Enjoy your night, asshole."

3

———

ANDRE

As I head back inside the crowded bar, my breath catches at the sight of Lila waiting for me, her finger trailing the rim of her wine glass.

I instantly imagine those red nails digging into my back as I fuck her into oblivion, and I have to discreetly adjust myself as I approach the now empty stool opposite her.

"Sorry about that." I lean against the bar.

"It was very entertaining," she says. "Thank you for stepping in. I don't think I could've listened to one more minute of him waffling on and on about his games."

"Well, I would say you have extremely bad taste in men, but I'm hoping you prove me wrong in the next five minutes."

"Oh, really?"

"Why don't we start with something better to drink?"

Lila raises her eyebrows but seems to be content enough as I wave down a waiter and ask for a bottle of Don Perignon and a private booth.

"Is this only because you own the place?"

I take her hand and help her down off the stool, not

letting her hand go as I lead us across the bar toward the wall of booths at the back.

"Oh, I don't own the place."

"What? But you said..." Lila frowns.

"It's a little white lie, no big deal." I smirk. "I had to say something to stop your little friend from starting a fight he wouldn't win. We wouldn't anyone to get hurt, now would we?"

Lila shakes her head, a smile spreading across her face as she slides across the leather seat.

I follow.

A bottle of champagne on ice is already waiting for us, and I pour us both a glass.

"Well, this is more like it." She brings the glass to her lips. "So, *Andre*, if you don't mind me asking, since you don't own the bar, what do you do for work?"

"I have my fingers in many pies, so to speak." None of which I'm willing to share just now.

"I can only imagine." Lila smirks.

"Oh, yeah?"

This'll be good.

"Well, you're either a model—"

I bark a laugh, shaking my head at her guess.

"No?"

"Not even close." I chuckle.

"Well, that leaves my other two guesses."

"Hit me, sweetheart."

"So, it's a toss between finance bro and mafia boss."

I fake a snort, but my muscles tense up.

"Both wrong."

"Oh? So what, then?"

"I have a very, *very* rich sugar mommy." I try to keep my tone light even if my heart pounds in my chest.

Lila throws her head back and laughs, her smile wide and true.

"Well played." She laughs, nudging her knee against my own.

My body starts to relax.

My line of work is very much a need-to-know basis, and considering the fact that after tonight Lila will be nothing more than a fond memory, I will keep that door to my life firmly closed.

"So, tell me, was this a set up?" There is no way I want her to dwell on me, so the best way is to shine the light elsewhere.

"Huh?"

"Were you purposefully out with a waste of space to try and get rescued by someone who is actually worth your time?"

I sidle up close to her in the booth, my knee brushing hers, our bodies angled toward each other.

"You got me." She grins, then shakes her head. "No, in all seriousness, I went through a pretty bad break up a year ago, and my best friend was tired of me being stuck in a work and home rut. She thought it was about time I get back on the scene, so she set me up with Dirk, the dick."

I laugh. "She needs to be demoted to an acquaintance immediately if she set you up with that loser on purpose. And that name is dead on, just FYI."

"Oh, she's dead to me."

I laugh harder. There's an easiness to Lila which I'm finding intoxicating.

"What happened with your ex, if you don't mind me asking." I rest my left arm along the back of the booth, my fingers tangling in Lila's soft hair, idly playing with the strands. Each touch gets me more and more relaxed, and I feel better now than I have in... I don't even know how long.

"He...he cheated on me." She sighs. "With one of my friends."

I stay silent, not because I don't have words for her, but because the ones I do have are not helpful right now. No man worth anything would ever cheat on a woman. Any woman. But especially the one sitting right here beside me.

She fiddles with the hem of her dress, her face solemn.

"It really knocked my confidence. I mean, what is wrong with me that I wasn't enough, you know? Besides, after the pain of going through that, it took me this long to even think about going on a date."

My blood is boiling. There is nothing wrong with her and this prick made her feel less than. If I knew who this guy was, I'd pay him a very painful visit.

"I'm sorry you had to go through that. He was an imbecile to think he could do any better than you." I trail a finger down her cheek and tuck her hair behind her ear.

She instantly leans into my touch, her lips parting slightly.

My face gets closer to hers. "Because you are the most gorgeous woman I've ever seen."

Lila rolls her eyes, but from the way her cheeks heat, and a flush creeps across her chest, I know she likes what she is hearing. And if Dirk the dick and her cheating boyfriend are her standard, she needs to be told badly.

"Are you always so forward, Andre?" She raises her eyebrows.

Fuck if my name on her lips doesn't make my cock twitch in my pants.

"I'm just being honest, sweetheart," I say. "And trust me, this is not forward."

"No?"

"No." I lean forward. My right hand is still tangled in her hair, and I move my left one to her waist, squeezing softly. "Would you like me to be more forward?"

Her breath hitches, and my mouth twitches.

I glance down at her chest, reveling in the swell of her breasts as they rise and fall with each breath.

It's clear to me now that she's not wearing a bra as her nipples start to peak beneath her dress, and my fucking mouth waters.

I lean in further until my lips graze her cheek.

"Say the word, Lila," I whisper.

A choked sound escapes her, but she tilts her head back, exposing the smooth skin of her neck to me, a silent invitation.

I run my nose along her cheek and down her jaw, breathing deeply.

I want nothing more than to run my tongue over her entire body, but I'm all too aware of the very busy bar surrounding us. Not that it would bother me. I've done way worse in a booth than make out.

But from what little Lila has offered me, she's a little more reserved. She's been hurt and isn't quick to offer up her heart because of it.

That suits me fine. I'm not looking for anything other than a night of passionate sex.

I'd never seen her before, and chances are, after tonight, I'll never see her again, so I want to take my time and do things right by her.

I lick up the column of Lila's neck, moaning at the taste of her skin.

My cock hardens, straining against the zipper on my pants, but I have to play this right.

I don't want to scare her off, and I think I might need her more than she needs me tonight.

"Mmm, you taste incredible," I growl.

Lila lets out a breathy pant, and I squeeze her waist before letting my hand trail up the side of her body.

"Tell me, Lila. What sounds would you make if I were to lick other parts of your body?"

"Andre," she breathes.

I smile before pressing a kiss to her neck. "Yes, baby?"

"We're in a bar," she chokes out.

I smile again, grazing my fingers along the soft underside of her breast, the thin material of her dress leaving nothing to the imagination.

"I've noticed." I chuckle, running my tongue along her jaw.

She moans, shifting in place and squeezing her thighs together.

"Are you trying to find some relief, sweetheart?"

"No," she blurts.

"Hmm..." I move to kiss the edge of her mouth, my thumb still tracing the underside of her breast. "What about now?" I graze my thumb over her peaked nipple.

She gasps, clutching onto my arm as her body arches.

"I think we're going to have fun, you and I." I chuckle before dropping my hands and leaning back against the cold leather of the booth.

I watch as disappointment flashes in Lila's eyes at my withdrawal, and I know I have her right in the palm of my hand.

I smirk. "Shall we take the champagne to go?"

4

———

LILA

I was not expecting to be drinking champagne straight from the bottle in the front seat of a blacked-out Lamborghini when I took a seat opposite Dirk tonight.

Andre, unlike Dirk, is something out of a movie. There's no way he's real. From the way he swooped in and saved me from the worst date of my life to the way he has me throbbing between my thighs with one brush of my nipple to how he has me practically begging for him to take me home.

Fuck, I need to get laid.

"Where are we going?" I ask as Andre climbs into the driver's seat.

"I'm staying at the Ritz-Carlton."

Of course, he is.

I watch him out of the corner of my eye as he puts the car in drive, ignoring the thudding of my heart as he revs the engine. I still can't quite believe I'm going home with this guy, but people say the best way to get over someone is by getting under someone else.

And Andre made me feel something back there, he

made me get out of my head, and that is something that hasn't happened since Sam and I broke up.

My hand itches to rest on his muscular thigh as he races along sixth avenue. His eyes focused on the road, his hands gripping the steering wheel in a way I know has his forearms flexing beneath his suit jacket.

My mouth is actually watering.

If I want to keep my head cool and not make a fool of myself, I have to lay off the champagne, at least until we're at the hotel. Then all bets are off.

I look at his profile. God, he's beautiful.

"Are you staying in the city long?"

Andre doesn't immediately reply, and my stomach sinks, but I try to ignore the feeling. This is a one-night thing. Guys like Andre don't go for girls like me, so I should make the most of this one night of passion and make a memory out of it to warm me in the cold, lonely nights to come.

No getting attached, no feelings required. Just enjoy the night and move on. Before I get hurt.

"That depends on many different factors." He glances sideways at me, the corner of his sensuous mouth lifting.

I bite my lip, taking in the sharp angles of his jaw and nose, his chiseled cheekbones that most girls would kill for. A hint of a stubble covers his jaw, roughing up the edges.

Yep, I've definitely made the right decision here.

We're barely in the car ten minutes before we're pulling up outside the Ritz-Carlton, and Andre leans over to unbuckle my seat belt.

I move to open my door, but he reaches out to stop me.

"Sit tight, princess." He winks before climbing out of the car.

I do as I'm told, as Andre hands his keys off to a valet and strolls around to my side of the car to open my door.

Princess indeed.

I try to smother my grin as Andre takes my hand and helps me out of the car, which is obnoxiously low to the ground.

"I think I flashed most of the valets," I mutter as I take Andre's arm with my own, tucking my purse under my other one.

"Guess I didn't need to tip them, then."

I elbow him playfully and he grins as we climb the steps leading to the lobby.

Maybe it's the booze, but I feel more comfortable with Andre in the very short amount of time I've known him than I did with Sam for the entire year we were together. I know I shouldn't be thinking such things, especially as I know how this will go.

We'll have mind-blowing sex, that much is obvious just from the way my body reacts to the slightest touch from him, and then I'll leave in the night like it was all some fever dream.

The concierge opens the door for us. "Good evening, Mr. De Luca."

"Evening, Harrison." Andre smiles as we pass him. "Would you mind sending up some champagne when you have a moment?"

Andre's so polite. A rare quality to find in a man, let alone a man with wealth. He's not making it easy for me to stay detached.

It's all for show.

The thought hits me out of nowhere, but it clears the lust-induced fog just a little.

"Of course, Mr. De Luca."

Andre wraps his arm around my shoulder and leads us to the elevators. There're three main ones, and I frown as we walk right past them.

"Uh. Are we on the main floor? Or the second floor? Because much higher than that will be killer on my feet with these heels if we take the stairs."

Andre chuckles, running his thumb back and forth over my bare shoulder.

"I won't make you take the stairs., princess. Wouldn't even dream of it."

We round a corner to another elevator.

A bellboy is waiting beside it and at our arrival, he presses a button, and the doors ping open.

"Good evening, Mr. De Luca."

Andre nods and guides me inside first.

The elevator is small, giving me every excuse to stand close to him as the doors slide closed.

I glance at the buttons, and my mouth falls open as I see which one is lit up. "The *penthouse?*"

"Is that a problem?" Humor laces his voice.

"Uh, no."

Andre chuckles, placing a hand on my waist and drawing me close to him. Not enough where my body is plush against his, but enough where I can inhale his intoxicating scent of bergamot and sandalwood.

I let my eyes flutter closed for a moment, reveling in the presence of this man who towers over me. I'm five foot three on a good day, and even in ridiculous heels I barely reach Andre's chest.

I am going to climb him like a tree.

"After you," he says as the elevator doors open, and I step out into the penthouse at the fucking Ritz-Carlton.

"You know, it was hard deciding between a gamer boy's basement and a penthouse." I glance around.

The place is huge, with an open living and dining area with plush couches and paintings that likely cost more than my rent. There's even a bar stocked with every type of liquor, on top of which is a fresh bottle of champagne and a plate of chocolate covered strawberries. With the floor-to-ceiling windows along the entire back wall overlooking Manhattan, it's breathtaking,

"Oh, yeah?" Andre places a strong hand on the small of my back and guides me over to the bar area.

"Maybe you didn't know this but at some point tonight, I was told there were sour patch kids in the basement," I tease.

Andre narrows his onyx eyes at me before disappearing behind the bar and opening the fridge.

I bite the inside of my cheek as I hear the rustling of a packet, and he turns around, tossing a packet of sour patch kids onto the bar top.

"Baby, I can offer you a hell of a lot more than candy." His voice is deep and rough.

My cheeks burn as his dark gaze devours me.

"I—" My phone buzzes in my purse.

"Why don't you get that while I sort out some drinks." He smirks.

I toss my purse onto the bar and pull out my phone, frowning as Cassi's name flashes on the screen.

"Now you call?" I snap. "You were supposed to have called two hours ago, Cass."

"Where the heck are you?" Cassi demands. "Dirk told Andy that you guys were having a blast until some old dude interrupted and started a fight with him."

"Trust me, that's not what happened." I snort. "That

'old dude' just saved me from the worst date of my life—something *you* were supposed to do."

I glance at Andre, who's pouring the champagne, and flash him a wink.

He shakes his head, his dark hair falling into his eyes as he fights back a smile.

"Sorry about that," Cassi mutters. "I fell asleep."

"It's fine. It all turned out pretty well, actually..."

"You little hussy. You're with the old dude right now, aren't you?"

"Stop calling him that." I chuckle. I glance again at Andre, my cheeks heating as his eyes flick over my body. "I'll explain everything to you later, okay?"

"Fine, but take a photo of him and send it to me so I can show the police when you go missing—"

I hang up on her before she can finish.

Andre hands me a glass of champagne, his dark eyes sparking. "I assume I'm the 'old dude'?" He raises an eyebrow.

"What can I say, I have daddy issues."

Andre snorts into his champagne and comes around the bar, taking me by the hand and leading me over to the windows so we can look out at the city. "Have you always lived in New York?"

I hesitate for a moment, taking a sip of my champagne as I take in the New York skyline.

"I moved here when I was twelve." My stomach knots. "To live with my aunt."

I'm not sure why I say it. I know Andre doesn't *really* want to get to know me, it's just small talk before we both get tipsy enough to get naked. But I guess after a year of being on my own, I'm more lonely than I thought.

5

ANDRE

My eyes are on her, but hers are on the landscape.

"Are you two close?"

She shakes her head. "Cassi's really the only family I have. What about you?"

My jaw sets, eyes flying to the view in front of us. This is not the time or the place to talk about me. That is not why we are here.

"I'm a closed book, sweetheart."

I set my champagne down on a side table and turn to face her. Just like that, our 'get to know each other' session is done. *This* is what we came here for.

I slide out of my jacket and toss it on the floor.

"Getting straight to it, huh?" She smirks.

"I wanted to get straight to it in that fucking booth," I growl. "I feel like I should reimburse you for that dress, though."

"Why?" The vein on the side of her neck is pulsing, and her pupils are dilated as her chest rises and falls at a faster pace.

"Because I very much want to tear it off you."

"This old thing?" She glances down at herself, fighting a smile as she tugs on the hem, shimmying her body a little. Her breasts bounce, and she glances up at me, whimpering as her eyes meet mine.

I'm burning for her.

Her lips parts as if she is about to say something, but I cross the distance between us, my hands tangling in her soft curls as I crash my lips to hers.

I devour her, and she melts against me, moaning.

God, that sound shoots straight through me.

My right hand moves to her waist and guides us until she's pressed up against the window. I only break the kiss long enough to take her champagne glass and toss it aside, spilling the contents all over the carpet before devouring her mouth once more.

Tracing my tongue along her lower lip, I ask to be let in, and she lets me explore her. I'm greedy, taking everything she offers. And just like that, I'm addicted.

She holds my shirt and pulls me closer against her, my thigh moving between hers, finding her blazing.

I want her to grind up against me, know exactly how bad she wants me.

Gasping for air, she lets her head fall back against the glass, and I go for her jaw, her neck, kissing, biting, sucking. Marking. Claiming. Even if just for tonight.

"Would you like this better, Lila?" I move to stand fully between her legs.

Her dress has ridden up almost to her waist, and I lean in once more, blowing gently to tickle her skin, reveling on the shiver that makes her tremble in my arms.

"How do you like it, Lila?"

Her breath catches as my hips grind into her, forcing

her to feel just what she does to me. My hardness against her heated center, with only her panties keeping me from getting drenched by her.

"I... I..."

"Don't make me ask you again." I run my tongue along her neck.

She arches beautifully against me, her hips lifting, a moan escaping her lips as my erection grazes her clit.

"Hard," she gasps, gripping onto his shoulders.

"That's what I thought."

She bites her lower lip as I grind my hips, and I curse fact that I want to be the one biting those full lips over and over again. Not just for tonight, but for as long as she'll let me.

But that's not what this is about. We are helping each other tonight. After this, we are done.

"Oh god," she gasps.

"I haven't even gotten started yet, princess." I chuckle before stepping away from her.

Her chest heaves, nipples peaking beneath her dress, and she has all the telltale signs of a wet pussy if that darker spot on her panties is any indication.

I want to see her. All of her.

"Take off your dress."

Not needing to be told twice, she reaches for the thin spaghetti straps and pulls them down over her shoulders. My eyes follow every minute movement as I picture my mouth and my tongue following her hands as she slowly shimmies the material down her body until her breasts are exposed, heavy and calling for me.

Her thighs clench together when I lick my lips, and I growl.

I want to taste all of her. Kiss, lick, bite every inch of her skin.

And I will. Later. For now, I want a show. "Keep going."

Her dress gathers around her hips and she wiggles to get the tight material over her amazing curves.

A low moan escapes me as it eventually it falls to the floor, leaving her in nothing but a red lace thong and heels.

Beautiful.

"Were you planning on giving gamer boy a heart attack?" I shake my head. "He wouldn't have known what to do with you."

"Good thing you were around," she murmurs, her eyes trailing down my body, lingering on the bulge in my pants.

Her foot starts to lift off the floor.

If she comes near me, I'll lose it. So, I hold up a hand to stop her.

"Stay right where you are."

I take a deep breath, centering myself before stalking over to her, rolling up the sleeves of my shirt as I go.

As I get in front of her and kneel, her eyes widen.

A smirk blooms in my face as I dip my fingers into the waistband of her lace panties.

"Right here?" she gasps, glancing over her shoulder at the city below.

"Right here."

I pulling her panties down her thighs until they pool around her ankles. She smells delicious.

"Spread your legs for me, baby."

She does as she's told, her cheeks glowing an adorable shade of pink right before my eyes descend over her body to her glistening pussy.

My tongue darts out to moisten my lips.

"I think we'll keep the shoes on."

She is a vision.

I lean in and run my tongue along her wet folds.

She cries out, her hands sinking into my hair, the prickling of pain only adding to the pleasure of the moment.

I chuckle.

She is delicious all over.

Fuck. I could get addicted to her so easily. Part of me wonders if I'm not already.

I blow a gentle breath to tickle her sensitive flesh, and the goosebumps that erupt on her skin make me do it all over again before letting my tongue flick over her clit.

Her entire body shudders, and her head falls back to the glass.

I don't care in the slightest if the whole of Manhattan sees me pleasure the most gorgeous woman on the planet. I want them to know she is mine. All mine. I'm the one making her feel this wanton.

Even if it is just for tonight.

I take it slow. Painfully slow. Exploring her pussy as if I has all the time in the world.

I want to torture her, but it's fucking for me too.

I lick and suck and nip until I find just the right way to slowly lick the length of her core before flicking out her clit to have her writhing under my touch.

She is my instrument, and I'm the maestro bringing this show to its crescendo.

"I've got you." I take one of her thighs, putting it over my shoulder, my hands moving to cup her ass before wrapping my lips around her clit and sucking. Hard.

She moans so loud I swear the entire building shakes, but I don't care.

Her taste on my tongue is the purest ambrosia I ever

tasted. And the feel of her in my hands, her weight, her touch are driving me nuts.

As I look up to her face, her eyes are on me and shining with unshed tears.

"More," she gasps.

I'm more than happy to oblige, moving a hand to stroke up her thigh before running my index finger through the wetness pooled between them, teasing her entrance.

"Please," she whimpers. And it goes right to my cock.

I suck her clit once more as I push one finger inside her.

Her hips buck, and she moans, grinding against my hand as I start pumping it in and out. Fuck, if my *finger* feels this tight, what's my cock going to feel like?

At the thought of her squeezing me as I fuck her, I moan, increasing the pace.

When her hips keep up with me, I add another finger, stretching her so beautifully.

The flutter around my finger can only mean one thing. She is close.

Her breasts look tight and heavy, and I'm mesmerized as her left hand trails up her stomach until she's cupping her own breast, pinching the hard nipple.

"Fuck, Lila."

Her eyes clash with mine and I groan against her.

Suddenly, I'm ravenous, and nothing but the taste of her on my tongue will do, so I start lapping greedily at her pussy.

"So...close," she gasps.

"Keep your eyes on me." I nip her inner thigh before circling her clit with my tongue.

Her legs are shaking in my hands, and when I curl my fingers inside her, grazing that sweet spot, her body seems to give out.

I know the orgasm hits her hard by how loud she cries out my fucking name as I continue to pump my fingers inside her, my eyes never leaving hers.

Mesmerizing. Hypnotic. Addicting.

She clings to my shoulders, trying to keep herself upright, her breathy pants the only sound as she comes down from the high.

With one last kiss to her sensitive flesh, I slowly pull my fingers out of her and climb to my feet, my body towering over her as I take her gorgeous face in my hands.

"So beautiful." The most beautiful thing I've ever seen.

I reach down and lift her off the ground and into my arms where she fits as if she was made to live here.

She squeals, wrapping her bare legs around my waist as I carry her to the master bedroom, my fingers digging into her delicious ass.

"That was amazing," she sighs, resting her head on my shoulder.

I chuckle and growl, "Baby, that was only the entrée."

6

———

LILA

ANDRE LAYS ME DOWN ON THE BED BEFORE STEPPING away.

I know I should be feeling shy, seeing as I'm stark naked in front of a complete stranger, and yet... The way Andre worshipped me has me feeling *powerful*.

I push myself up on my elbows and watch eagerly as Andre removes his white shirt, revealing tan skin and rippling muscles that have my mouth watering. I glance up to find him smirking at me, and I scowl.

"Enjoying the view?" He reaches for his belt buckle.

"Aren't I meant to be asking *you* that question?" I counter, glancing down at my very naked body.

A guttural sound escapes Andre as he takes me in, and now it's my turn to smirk.

"That's what I thought." I chuckle before maneuvering myself onto my knees and reaching for him. "Let me."

Andre steps closer, moving his hands to cup my face and pressing the softest of kisses to my lips.

I sigh against his lips, breathing in his scent as I reach for his belt buckle.

Andre continues to trail kisses along my jaw and neck as I work to undo his trousers, eager to free his cock.

"Mmm..." As soon as I have room, I reach inside his boxers and wrap my hand around his thick length.

Andre hisses a breath as I pump him once, running my thumb over the tip and moaning when it comes away wet.

I bring my thumb to my lips and slowly lick the precum, moaning at the salty taste.

"Lila," he groans, resting his forehead against mine.

"I think it's your turn to shimmy out of your panties."

Andre tugs on my hair, forcing me to look up at him, and his eyes are heavy-lidded.

His mouth comes to my ear. "I'd be careful if I were you."

"Oh yeah?" I press, reaching for his cock again, but he steps back.

"I'm very good at torturing people." His eyes flicker to my breasts as he reaches for the waistband of his trousers and pulls them down, finally revealing himself fully to me.

A strangled noise escapes me as I take in his cock, hard and glistening at the tip.

I knew it was big seeing as I literally just had my hand around it, but to actually see it is another matter entirely.

I fight the urge to reach between my thighs as I imagine him bending me over and pounding into me until I'm screaming my release.

Andre seems to sense the very dirty nature of my thoughts as he reaches for his cock and starts slowly pumping himself.

"I'll ask you again, Lila, are you enjoying the view?"

Bastard.

"Yes," I grit out as my blood starts pounding.

My chest is flushed, my nipples hard and aching as I watch Andre work himself for a few painful strokes.

"I'm going to go hard, Lila." He strokes his cock.

I can't stop the moan that escapes my lips as I imagine riding a cock that large.

"I'm going to sink my cock so deep inside that delicious pussy of yours that you're going to scream with pleasure."

"Someone's very sure of their skills," I mutter, though there's no bite to my words. We both know I'm completely at his mercy.

"I'd lie back against the pillows if I were you." His lips lift slightly at the corners.

I don't need to be asked twice.

I shimmy up the bed, flushing at the slick feeling between my thighs and keeping my eyes on Andre as he works his cock.

"Spread your legs, baby."

I fight back the feeling of embarrassment that builds as I part my thighs, exposing myself to him.

A pained expression crosses Andre's face, as if he's trying to fight back his own building release, and the thought has me reaching between my thighs, not able to wait any longer.

"So needy."

I nod, my fingers brushing over my clit, and my back arches. "I need you."

"I'm right here, baby." He climbs onto the bed.

Taking hold of my wrist, he removes my fingers from my pussy and pins my hand above my head.

I whimper, and he only smirks as he takes my other hand and pins it above my head too.

"Much better," he murmurs. "Now keep them there."

Leaning down, he flicks his tongue over my right nipple.

I cry out, arching into his touch, aching for more.

It's like this man can read my mind. He takes my breast into his mouth and sucks, running his tongue back and forth over my nipple.

I'm writhing beneath him. "Please, Andre."

And now I'm fucking begging.

"I'm not sure if I'm done torturing you yet." His breath tickles my nipple, but then he moves his hips, and the tip of his cock teases my entrance. "There's so much more I could do…"

"I…I…need…" I'm barely able to get the words out.

"I know, baby." He cups my cheek. "But before I go further, I need to ask—"

"I'm on birth control."

"Do you still want me to wear a condom?"

Fuck, why is he so considerate too? He's making it so hard for me to stay detached. "I'm fine with not using one, I'm clean."

"Me too."

"Thank fuck because I need to feel every fucking inch of you," I grit out, wrapping my legs around his waist and pulling him closer.

Wrapping an arm around me, Andre pulls me flush against him as he slowly starts to thrust his hips.

I wince a little as he stretches me, and he responds by kissing me so tenderly that my body relaxes.

"You're taking me so well, Lila."

Burying my face in his neck, I run my hands through his hair as he enters me inch by inch until he's fully buried inside me.

I gasp at the fullness, my hips instantly moving against him, and my eyes roll at the sensation.

"Fuck," he groans as my body adjusts to his size.

He doesn't wait long until he pulls out, almost to the tip, before slowly thrusting back in.

We both gasp, and I pull away to watch Andre's face as he pulls out once more.

His teeth are gritted as if he's holding back, and when he thrusts into me again, his eyes widen as I clench around him.

"Lila," he hisses.

"I'm so full," I moan, arching against the pillows.

"You're so fucking tight," he grits out. "It's going to be so hard not to fucking blow my load too soon."

"No better than gamer boy, then" I tease as I circle my hips, whimpering at the feel of him inside me.

"We'll see about that," Andre murmurs before kissing me.

I instantly part my lips, letting his tongue explore my mouth as he starts to move inside me once more, a little faster now.

"You feel like fucking silk, Lila," he moans against my lips. "I need more."

"Take whatever you want."

He grips me beneath the shoulders and slams into me, his cock brushing my sensitive inner walls.

The pleasure is like nothing I've ever experienced, and I can't get enough.

Running my nails along the hard muscles of his back, I revel in the feel of Andre on top of me. Of the pure male strength that radiates from him as he pounds into me.

And from the sounds he's making with each thrust, I know he is just as close as I am to being sent over the edge.

"Harder," I gasp.

I dig my heels into his ass, driving him even deeper,

needing more. I meet each of Andre's thrusts, our rhythm desperate and hungry as my release builds.

"Oh fuck," I moan as my climax threatens to take over, my legs quivering around Andre's waist.

"Come on, baby. I need to feel you come around my cock as I spill inside you." Andre licks the spot beneath my ear that has me shuddering.

His filthy words have me toppling over the edge, not able to hold back any longer.

My entire body shakes as my orgasm hits me, my pussy clenching around Andre as wave after wave of pleasure radiates through me.

Andre continues to pump inside me, his movements sloppy as he chases his own release.

"I'm coming—" Andre grunts, thrusting into me so hard the bed slams into the wall.

I cry out, my hips bucking as I feel Andre spill into me. I watch in awe as he comes, his eyes locking with mine, so heavy with need as his body shudders beneath my fingers.

"Holy shit," I gasp as he eventually stills on top of me.

"That was...amazing." He buries his face in the crook of my neck.

"I could do that forever," I blurt out before I have a chance to stop myself.

Fuck.

I tense, waiting for the inevitable 'time to go' conversation, but Andre only nudges my jaw with his nose, his stubble ticking my cheek as he kisses the corner of my mouth.

"I'm game for round two."

After round three, we're both spent and lie tangled up together as we recover.

I'm exhausted but deliciously satisfied.

A phone starts ringing, and Andre is immediately out of bed.

I instantly miss the warmth of his body tucked up beside mine, but I try to act otherwise, sitting up and wrapping the sheet around me as I watch Andre pull on his boxers and go searching for his phone.

"Yeah?"

There's a muffled voice on the other end, a male, and Andre's shoulders tense.

I'm sensing that this may be my cue to leave, even if that's the last thing I want to do. I'd much rather stay put and take in every muscled inch of the man who just gave me the best sex of my life because, once I'm out that door, I'll never see him again.

But I know that's for the best.

Be the one to walk away, not the one left behind. Not again.

I make to move from the bed, but Andre glances over his shoulder at me and shakes his head, pointing to the bed.

Yes, sir.

"How urgent is urgent?" he asks, turning away from me once more. "Fuck, ok. I'll be there in ten."

I wait patiently as Andre hangs up the phone and moves to perch beside me on the bed. I let my eyes roam over his strong, muscular shoulders, feeling the phantom touch of his fingers all over my skin. I shiver as he looks at me, my cheeks heating.

"I have to go deal with something." He sighs, reaching out to cup my cheek, running his thumb along my bottom lip.

"Ok, I'll get my stuff."

"I'm not kicking you out, Lila." His eyes flicker to my lips. "Not when we've barely gotten started."

I clench my thighs together, already deliciously sore between them, at the thought of more sex.

"Order yourself room service, whatever you want, and there's a jacuzzi bath next door. I'll be back as soon as I can."

"Where are you going?" It must be past midnight by now, surely he's not being called into the office? Or wherever it is that he works. I didn't like the way he tensed at whoever was on the other end of the phone.

"Need to know, baby." He reaches forward to press a kiss to my forehead. "Don't do anything naughty while I'm gone." He smirks.

If by naughty he means ordering a ridiculous amount of ice cream and enjoying it in a tub big enough for six people, then I should be marched down to the principal's office.

There's even a TV on the wall, and I indulge in some reruns of *Real Housewives of Beverly Hills* as I tuck into my mint choc chip.

Oh yeah, this is a hell of a lot better than some gamer boy's basement.

Too bad my time here is running out.

7

———

ANDRE

"Why the fuck couldn't you deal with this on your own, Marco?"

My younger brother is on speaker as I drive away from the Ritz-Carlton, and a very naked Lila, toward my family penthouse in the Upper West Side.

"Because you would've been pissed as hell to learn about this after I killed the fucking snitch."

Snitch?

"Who?"

"Over the phone? Fuck, no. Just get here quick." Marco hangs up.

Grinding my teeth, I slam the accelerator.

It's almost one a.m., and I had hoped to spend a little more time exploring Lila's body before heading back to real life, except Marco's tone meant shit is about to go down.

I just hope he kept Rosa out of this. She's only fifteen and needs to be kept away from the gory reality of our world for as long as possible.

I pull into our underground car park, parking alongside Marco's blacked-out Hummer and Rosa's shiny red

Porsche—a present for her birthday a few weeks ago. Legally she can't drive yet, but 'legally' is not really our thing.

I roll up my shirt sleeves as I take our private elevator, bracing myself for who I might find in our living room.

But when the doors slide open, the place is empty.

What the fuck?

I check my phone.

Marco sent me a red pin, showing me he's on the fucking roof. Luckily for us, it's private so we tend to take a lot of our...*dirtier* business up there. Which means whoever is up there is likely not coming back down.

Hurrying across the open plan living space into my office, I open up the safe and pull out a handgun along with a six-inch knife, tucking both into the waistband of my pants. The champagne and sex high I'd been riding has officially evaporated, and one look around my office has me switching back into work mode.

I nod once to the picture of my deceased parents on the wall, as I do every time I leave, and head up to the roof to meet my brother.

"What have we got, Marco?" I step out onto the roof.

My brother glances over his shoulder at me. He is wearing an almost identical outfit to my own.

"You tell me." His expression is grave as he steps aside, revealing Tommy Munro, one of our most trusted employees.

What the hell? Snitch?

I fold my arms across my chest as I observe the man chained to a fucking garden chair on the top of a Manhattan skyscraper. "This is a new low, Tommy."

Tommy's already sporting a black eye which has swollen and completely sealed shut, and blood is crusting the corner of his lip. His own white shirt is wrinkled and blood-stained.

"Speak." Marco pulls his gun so fast from the waistband of his trousers that Tommy flinches as the barrel is pressed against his temple.

Teeth bared, he takes a swift kick to Tommy's shin.

"Marco," I warn.

"Fine." Marco takes a step back, keeping his gun pointed at a trembling Tommy.

The sight is pathetic, and I let out a long breath.

"I suggest you start talking." My voice is low and even.

Tommy squirms, but the chains around his ankles and wrists are too tight to give much.

"Nothing to talk about."

"Then why does my brother have you chained to a fucking chair, Tommy?"

"Because he's a fucking *psychopath!*"

Marco makes to strike, but I hold up my left hand, reaching with my right to pull the six-inch blade free of my waistband.

"That may be true, but he never acts without reason. So, I'm gonna ask you one more time, what did you do to get you chained to a fucking chair?"

Tommy turns his head and spits bloody drool onto the ground.

I wrinkle my nose at the sight, my patience starting to waver.

"I never told him nothing." He glares at me.

"Who's *him?*"

Tommy glances at Marco, who nods.

"Lorenzo Rossi."

A red mist clouds my mind as I fight the urge to run my knife across Tommy's throat.

"You've been speaking to Lorenzo?"

"Not just speaking. He's been passing him classified information about our drug shipments. He's the reason we lost those shipments from Mexico last week."

I take a deep breath, caressing the sharp blade with my thumb.

I wasn't lying to Lila when I told her I have my fingers in many pies, but the majority of our money comes from drugs, so when a shipment gets 'lost', or rather, stolen, I don't take it lightly.

"You cost me two million dollars, Tommy."

"I-I never said nothing, Andre. I *swear*."

I take another step toward him.

The sound of Marco clicking the safety off his gun fills the frigid air around us, but I shake my head at him. "Now, how do you think you can pay me back?"

"I-I have money—"

"So, you did it?"

Tommy flinches, realizing his mistake.

"You're not leaving this rooftop alive, Tommy, so you might as well tell me everything you know. Try to redeem yourself at least before you bleed out on the concrete."

Tommy's eyes widen, or should I say *eye*, as he starts shaking his head.

"He threatened my family." His voice quivers. "My kids."

"And?"

"And I had no choice."

"You could've come to me. To Marco. We would've dealt with it. You think you're the first person to work for us whose families have been threatened by the Rossis?"

Tommy stays silent, and I take another step until he's

looking up at my towering frame, reduced to a quivering, spineless piece of shit.

"We're going to have some fun, you and I." I reach out to trace my blade along Tommy's jaw.

He flinches at the touch of the cold metal, and I smile.

"You see, Tommy? This is just another thing that Lorenzo Rossi has taken from me. So, I'm going to make you a deal. If you want to ensure your family's protection, because I assure you Lorenzo Rossi will likely slaughter your family anyway, then I suggest you start giving me something in exchange. Something...useful."

I tilt my head to the side as I trail my knife down the side of his neck, pressing it against the skin, but not hard enough to draw blood. Yet.

"I don't know anything."

"Wrong answer." I flick my wrist and slash my knife along his cheek.

Tommy hisses as blood starts to trickle down his ashen skin.

He will die tonight, but not until after I get what I want. And what I want is to make Lorenzo Rossi pay. He is well overdue on his debt to me. Slithery bastard has been able to survive this long. But reckoning will come. I won't rest until it does.

"He has a s-shipment coming."

I slice my blade along his forearm. "When?"

"T-Two... W-weeks."

I nod to Marco who turns his back to me, pulling out his phone to start making calls.

"Who's running it?"

Tommy strains against his chains, blubbering like a fucking baby, and my patience finally snaps.

I could be losing myself in Lila right now. She was a

much-needed light on the darkest night of the year, and I wanted more of her. All of her for as long as I could have her.

Tonight was not long enough, but it was all I had. And because of this fucking coward, I'm stuck on a rooftop.

I only had the chance to spend one full night with her. And thanks to fucking Tommy I don't even get that.

Fuck this.

I toss my knife to the side, craving the feel of his flesh beneath my hands. So, clench my fist and send it crashing into Tommy's face, splitting his cheek along with my knuckles.

I grunt, flexing my fingers. "I don't like to ask twice."

"Sergio," Tommy splutters. "He could be...useful."

I tilt my head to the side.

"Why?"

"His loyalty to Lorenzo is wavering. He could be persuaded to switch sides for the right price."

Interesting.

"That's more like it." I take another swing at Tommy, sending his head snapping to the side.

Marco flinches. He hangs up the phone and glances at a now unconscious Tommy. "Andre?"

I'm panting, my knuckles screaming, but my head is a little clearer.

"Yeah?"

"He would've talked anyway. Was this really necessary?" Marco narrows his dark eyes at me.

"Says the person who chained him to a chair." I look to Tommy. His body is limp, pathetic. "He betrayed us, and I don't take that lightly. You shouldn't either."

"I don't." Marco folds his arms across his broad chest.

"Good."

"I can take it from here."

"No, I'm finishing this." I move to crouch beside Tommy's ankles to start removing the chains.

"Andre—"

"Stop."

Marco stays silent as I finish unchaining Tommy and drag his limp body onto the concrete.

I nudge his face with my shoe.

"You ruined my night." I land a swift kick to Tommy's stomach. And another. And another.

The darkness starts to take over, whispering sweet nothings of death in my ear.

And I oblige.

My body doesn't feel like my own as I grab Tommy by the shirt and land another punch to his already beaten-up face. Blood crusts on my hand, and I need more.

"Andre." Marco's voice sounds as if it's underwater, distant and muffled.

Tommy's face morphs into the face of Lorenzo Rossi. He's the one I'm killing, and I won't stop until his blood stains my skin.

My hands grab the collar of his shirt, and I lift his head off the ground before slamming it back down against the concrete.

Over and over.

Blood starts to pool. Bone starts to crack.

Death is near.

I can feel it, taste it.

"Andre! Stop!"

Hands are on me, hauling me away.

I round on my enemy, my hands ready to throw a punch, but it's not an enemy. It's Marco, and he steps back, holding his own hands up in surrender.

His eyes are wide and filled with concern.

What have I done?

I look down at my hands, bloody, bruised and trembling. My whole body is shaking, and I take a step back.

"Andre," Marco breathes. "Are you...ok?"

I blink, almost wincing at the sight of Tommy lying lifeless in a pool of his own blood, his skull smashed in.

"I'm fine." Lies.

"Was that because of what today is?"

My eyes snap to my brother, and I let my rage shine through, but Marco doesn't back down.

"A job needed doing, Marco, so I fucking did it."

"A bullet to the head would have sufficed, Andre."

I shake my head, moving to pick up my discarded knife and pocketing it.

"No, it wouldn't have. Send Tommy back to Lorenzo as a message." I run my bloody hands through my hair as I head toward the door.

"You heading back out?"

I don't bother to look back over my shoulder at my brother. "I have somewhere to be."

Washing the blood off myself in the shower, I watch it pool at my feet with no sense of satisfaction.

I would've thought that pummeling a fucking snitch to death would have released some of the rage within, especially given what day it is. But if anything, I feel more tense.

Of all people Tommy snitched to...

I bet Lorenzo was like a kid in a fucking candy store when he intercepted our shipment.

I grind my teeth together. I hate looking weak, and the fact that one of my own went running straight into the claws of my fucking rival rather than coming to me has me seething.

On any other day, having the blood of a snitch on my hands would bring me a sense of relief.

But instead, I feel empty.

Getting back to the hotel and finding Lila naked and asleep in the huge bed, the silk sheets draped over her lower half, gives me a sense of relief. It isn't a perfect solution for the long-term problem, but it will do for as long as I have her.

After taking off my fresh suit, I slide into bed beside her, letting my fingers trail up her thighs until her eyes start to flutter open.

My time with her is limited. I will not waste it on sleeping.

8

———

LILA

Calloused fingers tickle my thighs, and I start to stir. I wasn't planning on falling asleep, but the silk sheets were just too comfortable, and it seems the rigorous sex marathon wiped me out.

"You're back?" I snuggle deeper into the pillows.

"I am." His fingers trail up and down my bare thighs. "Did you have fun without me?"

"Mmm... You just missed all the other guys."

Andre chuckles, and his lips brush my cheek.

"Good thing they've gone because I don't like to share."

"Now, now, no need to get possessive..." I turn to lie on my back, exposing my bare breasts.

Andre takes the silent invitation and starts teasing my right nipple with his tongue while his hand palms the other.

I groan, reaching to run my hands through his slightly damp hair.

Did I not hear him shower? I must have passed out *hard*.

The way Andre is worshiping my breasts has my back arching, desperate for more, heat already pooling between my thighs.

"Andre," I sigh.

"Yes, baby?" His breath tickles my nipple.

I place my hand on his shoulder and push against him, silently asking for what I really want.

"Use your words, Lila."

This man is infuriating.

"You know what I want." I gasp as Andre grazes my nipple with his teeth.

"But I want to hear you say it."

I groan, rubbing my thighs together beneath the sheets, desperate for any form of friction.

"I want your tongue between my thighs."

"There." He chuckles, moving to position his muscular body over mine. "That wasn't so hard."

I glare at his beautiful face.

"You're an ass."

He smirks, dark eyes filled with mischief as he takes my nipple in his mouth and sucks.

I moan as he grinds into me, his erection nudging my entrance. My head falls back as I revel in the sensations that Andre awakens in my body.

He takes his time kissing his way down my body, running his tongue along the skin of my inner thigh until I'm writhing beneath his touch.

He kisses my thigh, so damn close to where I need him that I'm practically begging for his touch.

"Andre."

His tongue runs up my center and he sucks on my clit.

I cry out, arching off the bed as he teases my entrance with a finger as he works my clit. There's more urgency this time, as if he's desperate to get me off, and I'm loving every second.

His tongue is fucking magic, and the way he eats my

pussy like an ice cream cone has my orgasm building even faster.

"More."

He sinks two fingers into me, pumping them hard as he flicks his tongue over my clit.

My hips start grinding against his fingers, and Andre moans.

I look down, and his free hand is wrapped around his cock, pumping hard and fast.

A strangled noise escapes me at the sight—it's fucking magnificent—and the thought of that cock pounding inside me has me crying out with my release.

Andre groans as I clench around his fingers and that only makes me moan louder.

I love how much he enjoys getting me off, and he continues pumping his fingers inside me as I ride out my orgasm.

"Fuck," I sigh. "That was..."

"Mmm..." Andre slowly pulls his fingers out of me and moves to rest on his knees.

My eyes watch in awe as he takes his fingers into his mouth and sucks. "You taste incredible, Lila."

His right knuckles have a darker taint that definitely wasn't there before he left.

Is he hurt?

"Andre..." I gasp.

"I'm fine, baby."

"Was that the business you had to go and deal with?" I push, feeling uneasy.

"Need to know, Lila."

Those are the same words as before.

I shake my head.

"Are you in some sort of trouble? Because I have the right to know—"

"Lila." His eyes soften as he takes in the concern I'm sure is clear on my face. "Sometimes, you have to play a little dirty in my line of work to get the message across. It's no big deal. I promise. Now, let me finish what I started."

His bruised hand wraps around his erection.

I bite my lower lip, content to let the subject go. Ultimately, this is a one-night thing, so it's none of my business.

My eyes fall to his cock, and I spread my thighs even more.

Andre gazes at my slick pussy and starts stroking himself.

The ache between my thighs is unbearable as I watch him jerk off to the sight of me.

He groans, his eyes fluttering closed for a moment before he releases himself and moves to grip my hips, flipping me over, lifting my hips so my ass is in the air. "I want to be deeper."

I moan, burying my head in the pillow as he runs the tip of his cock along my ass before dipping between my thighs, lining himself up with my entrance.

"So fucking wet."

"Mmm..." I wiggle my hips against his hardness.

Andre places his hands on my hips, his fingers digging in hard before he fills me with one hard thrust of his hips.

I cry out as a moment of pain turns into the sweetest pleasure as Andre immediately starts moving inside me.

"Well done, baby," he coos. "You took that so well."

I sink my fingers into the silk sheets, gripping them as Andre thrusts so deep that his cock grazes my uterus, and my entire body trembles with pleasure.

I can barely hold myself up, but Andre keeps my hips in place as he fucks me so hard my eyes roll.

"Fuck, Lila," Andre groans. "Are you going to let me come all over that perfect ass?"

"Oh, yes." I push back against him.

"Good girl."

That sends a ripple of pleasure down my spine, and my climax builds once more.

I try to match Andre's pace, bouncing my ass against him as he thrusts into me, his cock brushing my inner walls so deliciously that my legs start to shake.

"I-I'm coming," I cry.

"Fuck yes, baby. Come with me."

His movements become more frantic and hurried, and I know he's close.

I want nothing more than to feel him spill onto my skin, to mark me as his one more time.

"Lila..." He pounds into me once more, so hard I scream as my orgasm hits me.

I clench around him, eager to send him over the edge too.

He thrusts two more times before pulling out and spilling all over my ass.

I let out a contented sigh, listening to Andre's breathy pants as he finishes.

I think that might have just been the best sex of my entire life.

"Look at you." His hands run over my hips.

I glance over my shoulder to the evidence of his release on my skin. I bite my lower lip before looking up at Andre under my lashes.

There's a faint flush to his skin, and his chest is heaving as he catches his breath.

Part of me wants to ask again where he went, what caused him to get so worked up. Because this sex was different than before. Harder, rougher.

Not that I'm complaining. It was incredible, but the shift in him didn't go unnoticed.

It's not my place. That's not what I'm here for. I'm not his girlfriend, I'm not his...*anything*.

In a few short hours, I'll be heading back to my apartment, and he'll be long gone.

"I think I might need some help in the shower," I murmur.

IT'S NO SURPRISE THAT ONCE AGAIN I PASS OUT IN THE sheets as the moon is still high above Manhattan, snuggled next to Andre, his arms around me, keeping me warm.

His soothing heartbeat lulls me to sleep, and I hope that, come morning, perhaps this might not be over.

But when I wake not much later, the sun still not yet up, the spot beside me in the bed is empty.

"Does that man ever sleep?"

I climb out of bed to use the bathroom. As I cross the room, I pass another door.

Andre's muffled voice comes from behind it.

I know I should just keep walking. I have no business listening in on his conversations, but curiosity gets the better of me.

What has got this man working at all hours of the night? Because he sure as hell didn't give me an answer when we were sharing a ludicrously expensive bottle of champagne.

I hold my breath as I lean against the door to what I assume is a study and press my ear to it.

"How many times to I have to fucking tell you, Marco?"

I can tell he's trying to keep his voice down, but there's so much anger lacing his words.

"Dispose of it, *now*."

Dispose of what?

"You only have a few hours before the sun rises." There's a beat of silence. "Well, it seemed to me that you needed reminding, seeing as you haven't disposed of the fucking body yet."

I blink, my blood running cold.

"I want Lorenzo Rossi to wake up to it on his goddamned doorstep."

Lorenzo Rossi.

I know that name.

It was in a news article I read a few months back. I don't remember the details, but I remember one word in the headline.

Mafia.

My feet are moving before my brain can fully catch up to what Andre is saying.

I step away, my heartbeat pounding in my ears, glancing around the bedroom.

The rustled sheets, the entire room reeking of sex. The evidence of what we did last night.

I let my body take over, moving around the bedroom in search of my clothes.

Dispose of a body.

I find my shoes and panties at the base of the bed.

I move into the living area and find my dress by the couch. Along with my purse.

Trying to stifle the strangled sob that is building in my throat, I find my phone safely tucked away inside it along with my wallet.

Without a second glance, I hurry to the private elevator and press the down button.

It's time I get the hell out of here.

The doors ping open and I rush inside.

The bell boy goes to speak to me, but I can't breathe.

I need to be outside. Now.

Why the hell is Andre dropping bodies on Lorenzo Rossi's doorstep? From the sounds of it, they're enemies, but what does that mean for Andre? Should I be grateful I'm even alive right now?

My stomach revolts, and for a second, I think I'm going to lose it.

Pulling out my phone, I ignore the dozen texts from Cassi and open up my uber app.

"Come on, come *on*." I keep one eye on the little black car on the uber app as it drives up to the hotel and the other on the hotel door.

Does he know I'm gone yet? Will he come after me?

As soon as the uber gets there, I throw open the door to the car and slide inside.

Only when we're far enough away do I look up at that wall of windows to where I know Andre will likely be standing.

"Here is fine," I say to the driver as he pulls into my street fifteen minutes later.

I need to change out of this fucking dress, to wash away this night. But first, I need my laptop and decent internet.

As soon as I'm home, I sag against the door.

When my legs can hold me again, I go to my laptop on the small desk in front of the window.

I toss my shoes and purse onto my bed and take a seat, my fingers trembling as I type in my password.

I could just leave this at the door, literally.

Andre has no idea where I live, and I can let the memory of our night together be just that. A memory.

But my fingers are typing into Google before I can talk myself out of it.

Andre De Luca and Lorenzo Rossi.

I hold my breath as the page loads, an image of Andre's handsome face appearing immediately. I try to ignore the dark eyes, the strong jaw, the perfect hair as I click the image and glance at the description beneath it.

My heart turns to ice as I read the words.

Fuck.

My stomach sinks.

I just slept with the don of the De Luca mafia.

9

ANDRE

The elevator pings as I'm on the phone with Marco, and I curse under my breath.

"What is it?" Marco asks.

"Nothing," I grunt. "Just get this shit sorted and head back to the main house. I want us all out of the city tonight."

"Rosa's already there. I sent her over as a precaution the moment I learnt about Tommy."

I let out a breath. At least my little sister is safe.

"Seems like you do have a brain after all, little bro." I hang up the phone.

I open the door to the study that attaches onto the master bedroom and curse when I find it empty. I go the living room, glancing to the couch where Lila's dress was, but it's gone.

She's gone.

And that can only mean one thing.

"Fuck!"

I ball my hands into fists, the knuckles still bruised, but that doesn't stop me from wanting to put a fist through a wall.

Pulling my phone out of my pocket, I dial one of the valets at the hotel, Alex, who also happens to be on my payroll.

"What can I do for you, boss?" Alex asks after one ring. It seems when my men know I'm calling, they don't hesitate to answer. Good.

"Do you see a girl in a black dress anywhere?"

Alex is silent for a moment.

Car horns and drunken cat calls come faintly through the line as I clutch the phone to my ear.

"There's some girl looking like she's waiting for someone. Maybe an uber," Alex says. "Long curly hair, killer body—"

"Alex, listen to me." I choose to ignore the surge of jealousy at Alex's appreciation of Lila's body. "Take my Mercedes and follow her uber. I need to know where she lives. It's essential I know, do you understand?"

Lila would recognize the Lambo, not that I'd let Alex drive it, but still. I need to play my cards right if I'm to keep this contained.

"On it, boss." Alex hangs up.

My fingers fly, dialing another number, and as it rings, I stalk over to the bar and pour a glass of whiskey. The packet of sour patch kids is still on the counter, and my gut twists as I look at it.

"De Luca," Kyle mumbles. "It's five a.m."

"So?" I down the liquor in one go, hurrying to pour another. "I have a job for you."

"It couldn't wait until the sun fucking came up?"

"Business doesn't wait for anyone, Kyle." I grind my teeth. "I need you to look into someone for me."

"That's what I'm best at." There's what seems like the

rustle of bedsheets followed by heavy footsteps. "Who pissed you off this time?"

"I need you to find out everything you can about someone named Lila."

"Last name?"

"Fuck knows. All I know is she graduated NYU three years ago and has a friend named Cassi."

Kyle lets out a long breath.

"That's more info than most of the fuckers you ask me to find." He chuckles. "Speak soon, Andre."

When the phone goes dead, I down my drink and stare out at the Manhattan skyline.

I should've known better than to take a fucking business call when Lila was in the next room. It's a rookie mistake, one I should have learned from a long time ago. And yet, here I am, having a fucking PI chase down a one-night stand so I can ensure she doesn't go blabbing to the police. Or worse, the press.

My hands shake as I pour another drink, the liquor barely taking the edge off my rage.

If Marco had done as he was told, I wouldn't have had to call to check up on the status of Tommy's body. But it seems my little brother isn't as cold-hearted and ruthless as I am.

I can blame Lorenzo Rossi for that too.

I lose count of how many whiskeys I drink before my phone starts ringing.

"Alex, what have you got?"

"135 West 19th street."

"Appreciate this." I hang up and shoot a text to Kyle with the address as I'm heading toward the elevator.

I can't stand to be in this penthouse any longer, not

when I'm surrounded by images of what Lila and I did last night.

It was probably the best sex I've ever had, and yet, what did it cost me?

It has the potential to cost me everything.

Despite the amount of liquor I've drunk on an empty stomach, my hands are steady as I get behind the wheel of my lambo and start the hour-long drive up to my family's main residence in Westchester.

I run through the conversation I had with Marco on the phone this morning over and over as I drive, trying to pinpoint every detail that Lila could have overheard.

Disposing of a body? Low priority.

Mentioning Lorenzo Rossi? Ding ding, we have a winner. Because where Lorenzo's name appears in the press, my name appears, along with many other shadows that like to follow me around.

I wonder if Lila laughed when she found out that her guess of me being a mafia boss was true after all...

The gates to my family's estate grow closer, and the sight of the perfectly manicured lawn and long gravel drive calms me just a little.

This place is where I feel the closest to my parents, where I have the most memories of them before they died. So, when I pull up outside the house, a little of the weight on my shoulders lifts.

It does so even more at the sight of my little sister sitting at the breakfast table, tucking into pancakes with one hand, a book in the other.

Marco is sitting beside her, nursing a cup of coffee, though knowing him, it's laced with something else.

At the sound of my footsteps, she looks up at me over her book and grins.

"Andre!"

"Hey, baby sis." I offer her a sincere smile.

At fifteen years old, Rosa is the spitting image of our mother, with her long, dark hair, tanned skin, and green eyes.

"Sit." She gets to her feet. "I'll get you some food."

"Thanks, Rosa, but I'm not that hungry." I take a seat opposite Marco, who offers me a small smile.

I ignore it, instead focusing on Rosa as she moves around the kitchen before coming to place a plate piled high with eggs and bacon in front of me.

"Which is exactly why you need to eat. Coffee is not an acceptable breakfast."

"We're Italian," I joke. "Coffee is always acceptable. Besides, shouldn't you be getting ready for school or something?"

"It's Saturday, idiot." She scoffs.

Right... I barely know what time it is, let alone what day or fucking year at that matter.

Rosa picks up her phone off the table, looks at the time, and curses.

I frown. "Language. Why are you up this early if it's not a school day?"

She rolls her eyes. "Like you don't cuss all the time," she mutters as she takes her now empty plate over to the sink. "And I promised Emelia that I would play tennis with her."

Marco mutters, "At seven in the fucking morning?"

"Language," I repeat, but Marco only responds by flipping me off, making Rosa chuckle.

"We want to get an early game in before heading to Hula for brunch," Rosa explains.

I instantly want to shut this plan down, to tell her to stay inside where I can keep an eye on her. But she's a teenager, and I want her to have as normal a life as I can offer her. So, I fight back every instinct that has me wanting to lock her inside this house.

"Keep your location on. And get Cal to drive you and Emilia. Those are my conditions."

"I know the drill." She sighs, rolling her eyes again before heading inside again.

Once she's out of earshot, I turn to my brother who simply raises an eyebrow at me.

He frowns. "You look like shit."

"Thanks, that's what I was going for."

"So, where have you been? Getting pissed again at some random bar?"

"Maybe you should focus on your own life instead of meddling in mine."

"Just making conversation." Marco mutters, pouring himself more coffee.

I take my coffee and get to my feet. "I'll be in my office."

As I enter my office, I close the door and lean against the wood, closing my eyes.

Lila sitting at the bar yesterday was a breath of fresh air I had no idea I needed. She was intoxicating.

I only hope that I won't come to regret our little rendezvous.

I have to wait for Kyle to get back to me with all the information he can find on my mystery woman. Until then, I have plenty to keep me occupied.

Taking a seat behind my large mahogany desk, I switch on my iMac and open up my emails. I groan at the sight of all the unread icons, the alcohol and lack of sleep finally catching up to me.

But then I remember why I'm so exhausted, and images of Lila's naked, writhing body flash behind my eyes.

I groan once more. But this time, for a very different reason.

I'm not a playboy by any means, but I do have occasional one-night stands.

Normally, I fuck the girl senseless and send her on her merry way. But Lila? Oh no, even three rounds wasn't enough for me to walk away. I needed more. I needed my tongue to touch every inch of her delicate skin, to commit the sounds of her moans as she comes to memory.

That's why, unlike any other time, last night I let Lila stay in my hotel room while I went to take care of Tommy.

And it's come around to bite me on the ass.

I was thinking with my dick, not my brain, and if Lila decides to go spilling anything to the press, my family is on the line.

The ringing of my phone snaps my attention, and I glance at the screen.

Kyle.

"What have you got for me?"

"Just sent it all over in an email," he explains. "She must be really good in bed if you've gone to this much trouble to find her because she's clean as a whistle boss. Nothing interesting about her."

"You have no idea how wrong you are."

Kyle chuckles and hangs up the phone.

I click open the email and download the file named *Lila Morano*, tapping my fingers on the mouse.

"What am I going to find, Lila?"

Instantly, a picture of Lila at her college graduation appears, taken from a newspaper clipping. It seems she was valedictorian of her class.

"Impressive." I zoom in on the picture.

Her blue eyes are shining as she looks into the camera,

her long, brown hair pulled over one shoulder under her graduation cap. Her cheeks are slightly flushed, and there's a small dimple in her left cheek which I didn't notice before. It adds an element of innocence to her face.

She's breathtaking, in a way no other woman has ever appeared to me before.

Yes, I've found plenty attractive, but Lila is different. Never before have I desired to learn what was on the inside.

And that scares the *fuck* out of me.

Kyle has composed a list of addresses—home, work, aunt's house, best friend's apartment. All useful but not what I'm looking for.

Finally, at the bottom, is a phone number.

Right now, my priority should be Lorenzo Rossi. But that isn't enough to stop me from programming Lila's number into my phone.

10

LILA

I can't tell which one is stronger, the fear that Andre will show up at my door one of these days or the fear that he never will.

He hasn't left my mind for one second since I left the Ritz-Carlton penthouse, and I have no idea if he ever will.

He gave me the most amazing sex of my life, but he is one of the most dangerous men in the country.

I will never tell anyone what I heard last night. I'd never do that to him.

Something about him makes me want to protect him. As if he needs it from me.

I'm lucky to have come out alive, but for a few moments throughout the last few hours, I've wondered if I wouldn't willingly sacrifice myself for another amazing night with him.

I'm so weak and pathetic. This is Andre De Luca we are talking about. Mafia boss and—

"Hello?" Cassi laughs, waving a hand in front of my face.

I blink.

"I was doing it again, wasn't I?" I run my hands over my face.

Cassi nods, smirking.

"Anything you want to share with the group?" Her index finger swings between us.

I roll my eyes and avoid the subject by tucking into my very overpriced avocado toast.

"No point in trying to deny it, Lila. You went back with the dude, so you obviously fucked, right?"

"Shh!" I glance at the tables on either side of us.

It's a Saturday, so *Smash!* is packed with tweens dressed head to toe in LuluLemon and women in their fifties getting drunk on bottomless mimosas.

It's a tradition Cassi and I've had since we were old enough to have our own money—every Saturday, we go for brunch and put the worlds to right.

Except this week, I want to do the exact opposite.

"Oh, come *on*, Lila," Cassi moans, leaning back in her chair and folding her arms over her chest.

"You know, Cass, you fit in well with all these tweens." I point to her half-finished matcha and athleisure wear.

"Fuck off." Cassi laughs, shaking her head, her ponytail swaying with the movement.

Cassi and I are exact opposites in looks. Where I'm short with dark hair, she's all blonde and legs.

Though we have joked since middle school that we should have each other's eyes. Cassi's are the richest brown, like melted chocolate, whereas mine are like an ocean.

"It's why we have to be friends," Cassi said to me on the first day of middle school.

I was petrified, having just moved to New York to live with my aunt after my dad bailed.

Cassi was wearing the coolest clothes and was even allowed lip gloss.

I should've been nothing but jealous of her and yet, it was like finding my other half.

She's been my rock ever since.

"You can't stop thinking about him." Cassi nudges some berries around her plate. "You've got that sex glow about you."

"First off, ew." I laugh. "And I'm allowed to think about him, but only for today."

"Why?"

"Because it was a one-time thing, so I have to let it go. I can have twenty-four hours, but then he's dead to me."

"Ouch." Cassi fake-winces. "If it was that good, why not just go out again?"

Because he might be a murderer who's mixed up with the mafia?

"Because I'm focusing on my career."

Cassi rolls her eyes.

"You've been doing that for a year, Lila."

"So? It's worked out well, focusing on work. Look at how far I've progressed since this time last year!" I take another bite of egg and gulp down the last of my coffee.

"A promotion doesn't keep you warm at night, babe."

"Am I not allowed to be single?" My temper starts to rise, but I do my best to keep the lid on it. "I'm just a little sick of everyone pushing me to date."

"I'm not pushing!"

I glare at her and clear my throat.

"Fine! Dirk was my bad. I had no idea he would be *that* bad." *Cassi* retorts, holding her manicured hands up. "Promise I will never do it again."

"Yeah, right. And chicken suddenly sprouted teeth, and pigs learned to fly."

"Look, all I'm saying is just keep getting some with mystery guy, that's all. You don't need to marry the dude."

I don't know whether to laugh or cry.

"We actually never swapped numbers, so even if I wanted to see him again, which I *don't*, I have no way of contacting him."

Cassi's mouth falls open as her eyes widen.

"It really was like a hit and run, just with sex." She laughs. "I'm surprised you even know his name. Wait, you do know his name, right?"

"Of course, I know his name!" Not that it rang any bells when he told it to me.

"Great. Here, let's go on googl—"

"Cass." I don't want to be mad at her, but if she doesn't stop this right now, I'm out of here.

She blinks, then sighs.

"*Fine.* But can you at least give me some details? Tell me again how he threw Dirk to the curb."

I can't help but smile at the memory of Andre dragging Dirk out of the bar by his shirt collar. It made my blood heat, the way he took one look at me and decided there and then that he wanted me.

It was something Sam never had, guts. He was, as Cassi liked to call him, a wet blanket, content to just sit back and let life pass him by, which is the opposite of what I am and what I look for in a man.

"He was staying in the penthouse at the Ritz-Carlton."

"WHAT?"

The tweens at the table next to us glower in our direction, and I mouth an apology to them as Cassi starts clapping her hands.

"Oh, my god, Lila. You slept with a sugar daddy?"

"Cassi!" I want to disappear under the table. Better, crawl under a rock and just die already. Why did I blurt that out? "Don't be crude."

"He's got some *money*." Cassi has a twinkle in her eye as she waggles her eyebrows at me. "Well done, Lila."

I shake my head, pouring myself some more water and taking a long drink to give Cassi time and chance to calm down.

"He bought us some nice champagne, and we talked a little."

"And then you knocked boots, didn't you?"

"Knocked boots?"

"Did the dirty, the horizontal tango, the dance of ages, the funny business, went for an afternoon delight, got dow—"

I burst out laughing. "Okay, okay, I got the idea."

"Well? Did you?"

"Well, yes."

"How many times."

"Uh..." Flashes of Andre on his knees, looking up at me as his tongue explored my pussy has my cheeks heating.

There is still a dull ache between my thighs from where he took me from every angle, fucking me so hard I screamed myself hoarse.

I'm surprised Cassi hasn't mentioned the croakiness to my voice, but if she does, I'm going to put it down to the bar being loud.

She is almost vibrating on her seat. "Oh, my god, really? You have to think about it? Was it that many that you have to do math?"

My cheeks burns. "Maybe four or five times?"

Part of me wants to relive the memories of Andre buried inside me forever, picking apart every detail of our time together. The way he murmured my name as he slowly thrust himself inside me. How he licked my neck, my nipples, the soft skin of my inner thighs.

It was magical, and I never expected to feel so cherished by a man I had *literally* just met.

Andre probably makes every girl feel like that—it's just part of his charm. How he gets you to come home with him by buying the fancy champagne and letting you relax in the enormous bed in a penthouse suite.

And yet?

Part of me thinks that last night was an exception for him.

"Five times? How are you even walking right now?" Cassi chuckles, finishing the last bite of her breakfast.

"Honestly, I have no idea."

"Well, I'm happy you got some, Lils. And if you change your mind about trying to find this mystery man, it would only take one phone call to the concierge at the Ritz-Carlton to find out who this guy is."

"No, Cass. I want you to promise me you won't go digging into this unless I say so."

"Sure, whatever." Cassi shrugs.

"*Promise* me."

I know she can see the panic in my eyes, but I need her to not go looking for Andre. I want to protect Cassi at all costs and keep her the hell away from Andre De Luca. Ultimately, I know he's dangerous and involved with some bad people, but I don't want to learn what he would do if he found out I overheard his conversation last night.

"I promise," she says.

I only hope it's enough.

Cassi is the only family I have except for my aunt, and I'm not willing to risk anything happening to her, no matter how badly I might want to see Andre again.

This time, my head has to win over my heart.

11

———

LILA

I love Cassi, but she can be stubborn sometimes, so I can only hope she respects my wishes.

As I head back, I stop by the grocery store to pick up a few things for dinner before going home to get some chores done around the apartment and catch up on some work emails to get ahead for the week.

I know most people hate New York in the summer months, but it's my favorite time of year. There's nothing I love more than walking over to central park and sitting on a picnic blanket with a good book and an iced coffee.

I make a mental note to take myself on a little date next weekend because in truth, I've spent too many of the past few either inside my tiny apartment or at the office.

I try to convince myself it's to make a good impression on my boss, but I know the truth. I'm too scared to be alone with my own thoughts because then I realize how lonely I've become since Sam left. I guess I just don't want to give him that power over me.

So, working on weekends it is, until I find a way to reignite my spark.

When all the emails are handled and I have nothing else I can do for work, I start cleaning around the apartment.

My phone starts ringing.

I groan at aunt Maria's name flashing, tempted to ignore it and continue on with deep-cleaning the toilet. I know her, though. She won't rest until we talk. So, I whip off my rubber gloves and hit accept.

"Ciao, Zia." I prop my phone between my chin and shoulder.

"You sound out of breath." Sharp and cold as always. I roll my eyes and shuffle across my living area to perch on my window seat.

"I was just cleaning my bathroom." I lean back against the wall and let my gaze drift upwards to look at the clear blue sky to try and ground myself. Speaking to my aunt always leaves me flustered and anxious.

"You should be outside. It's too nice to be indoors. You young people never go outside. In my day, our parents would send us out at seven a.m. and tell us to come back for dinner."

"Yes, well, my chores couldn't wait." I stifle my sigh. I love my aunt, I really do, but she can be an overbearing woman. Typical Italian.

"How is everything these past few weeks?"

"Fine. Work is good, all the paperwork for my promotion was finalized a few weeks ago."

"Hmm... And what about a man?"

"No man, Zia." My mind flashes to Andre, but I lock that out immediately.

"If you put all that energy into finding a man instead of getting a promotion, you could be married by now, bambina. Then you would have no need for promotions and corporations. You would be a wife, a mother. What a woman should be."

It's the lecture I've heard at least once a month since I was old enough to go on birth control. Though part of me wants to turn around and give the very same lecture to her.

Aunt Maria never married or had children, if by choice I'm not too sure, but I'm grateful every day that she was willing to take me in and raise me.

"I know." I tap my foot on the seat.

"What about Sam? You definitely don't want to see him again?"

"He *cheated* on me, Zia. Surely I deserve more than to be with a man who doesn't even have the decency to stay faithful."

"Men make mistakes."

"What, like dad?"

Fuck. Why did I say that?

The line is silent for a moment, and I cringe.

We rarely talk about my parents. My mother was Maria's sister, and she died giving birth to me. My father stuck around until I was twelve but then decided it was too much, so he dumped me on Maria's doorstep.

The rest was history.

"There was no decency in that man, bambina. I will not discuss him. What I do want to discuss is why you are single."

"Please, can we talk about anything else. I've already had this lecture once today."

"From who?"

"Cassi."

"Well, it seems Cassi and I are on the same page for once."

Maria has never hidden her disapproval of Cassi in the thirteen years we've been friends.

I'm almost tempted to tell Maria about my 'date' with Andre just to get her off my back, but it's safe to say she wouldn't let it go as easily as Cassi did.

If anything, Maria would go storming down to the Ritz-Carlton and bang on Andre's door, not leaving until he promised to put a ring on my finger...

Nope. Not going there. Not even in my nightmares.

"Zia, I have to get back to my chores."

"Come and visit me soon, I am getting old."

"You're not even in your mid-fifties." I chuckle.

"I'm Italian. My veins are filled with nothing but red wine and gluten."

"Evidence of a life well lived, Zia."

"Ti amo, bambina."

As she hangs up the phone. I let out a long breath and sit in the silence for a moment, thinking about what my auntie and Cassi said.

Should I be putting myself out there more? I know Sam burned me, but at some point, I will need to move on.

Part of me wished I had never overheard Andre's conversation so I could let myself live out the fantasy of him for a little longer.

Time to move. I still have some cleaning to do.

By the time I shower, pull on some fresh cotton under-wear, and climb into bed, I'm exhausted from the lack of sleep the night before. I must've only managed two hours, tops, but given the expensive silk sheets and naked man beside me, it was the best two hours of sleep I've ever had.

"Stop it, Lila."

Why does Andre De Luca live rent free in my head?

My skin pebbles at the memory of his calloused hands

on my body, my back arching as I remember how well he filled me.

I've never felt anything like it.

I mean, I've had plenty of good sex, but Andre? Nothing compares, and I hate that he will now be the standard I hold every man that follows him.

"You get today, De Luca." I let my fingers trail over my bare stomach. "But from the moment I wake up tomorrow, you're permanently evicted from my brain."

Now he's got me talking to myself? What has happened to me...

My eyelids flutter closed as I imagine it's Andre touching me. My fingers graze the underside of my breasts just as he did, flicking my thumb over my aching nipples as I fully embrace the memory of Andre.

It doesn't take long before I'm slick between my thighs, and I'm panting as I start working my clit. It's nothing compared to how Andre's tongue felt as he explored my pussy but any form of release will do because I'm so worked up my eyes start to sting as my orgasm builds.

Soon, I'm thrusting a finger inside my dripping wet core, then another, and my hips are rolling as I ride my own hand.

"Fuck." My free hand moves to palm my breast.

His name is on my lips as I let the phantom heat of his body on mine bring me to the edge. The strong, powerful weight of him as he hovered over me, his hips frantically moving as he thrust his cock inside me. The way he groaned as he spilled into me—

My orgasm hits me, and I'm crying out as my body arches off the bed, a thin sheen of sweat covering my skin.

My thighs shake as wave after wave of glorious pleasure

hits me, and I think of nothing but Andre as I continue to work myself until I'm completely spent.

"Now we're done," I say aloud.

My phone rings, snapping me out of my post-orgasm bliss, and I groan.

The only people who ever call me are Cassi, my aunt, or my boss. Seeing as I've spoken to two out of three today means I can't ignore this call.

Cringing, hoping he can't somehow sense what I've just done in my voice, I reach for my phone.

An unknown number? I frown

Against my better judgment, I answer it in case it's my boss on someone else's phone.

"Hello?"

"Lila?"

Andre?

I let out a squeal, the phone slipping out of my hand.

How the fuck did he get my number?

Actually, scratch that. I don't want to know.

I hit the end call button, tossing my phone across my bed as if it's a ticking time bomb. I sit staring at it, my knees tucked into my chest, trying to decide what to do.

Should I go to the police?

Andre's clearly done some digging on me if he's managed to get my phone number.

Did Cassi cave and call the hotel, asking for Andre?

The screen lights up again with another incoming call.

I have to decide right now how I'm going to play this, otherwise I could risk not only myself but the people I love most.

Andre De Luca is a dangerous man in more ways than one, and I can't let myself get sucked into his charm.

The phone screen goes dark once more, and I let out the breath I didn't realize I was holding.

My heart is pounding in my chest.

I decided from minute one that I would not let anyone know what I overheard last night. That includes the police.

But am I making a mistake wanting to protect him while trying to keep safe too?

The screen lights up once more, but this time it's a text message. I lean over to pick up my phone and swipe it open to read the message.

> Andre - You have to speak to me
> eventually, baby.

I curse under my breath.

There's no way Andre didn't figure out that I overheard him on the phone and that's why I left without so much as a goodbye. Why else would he have gone to all this trouble to find my number?

He wants to make sure I stay silent. And I will. Including when it comes to talking to him.

So, I quickly click onto his contact and block the number before switching my phone off. That way, I'm not tempted to reply.

I only hope that my lack of response kills whatever game Andre is desperate to play, and he decides to let this go.

For both our sakes.

12

ANDRE

I wasn't planning on bringing anyone with me to
the Ritz-Carlton penthouse suite tonight. Let alone the two
women slowly undressing for me as I lie naked in bed.

They begged to come home with me after I bought us a
round of old fashioneds.

Their eyes are heavy-lidded as they eye-fuck me, their
skimpy dresses falling to the floor, revealing lingerie that
would normally have me foaming at the mouth.

I thought I could have a good time. Take my mind off
things. Off certain people. But instead, I feel nothing.

My dick's hard, but not for them. Not because of them.

I'm like this because my mind is on the last person I
fucked in this bed.

Fuck me.

All I wanted was a quiet drink away from my brother
and sister.

It wasn't until I was behind the wheel of my lambo and
heading away from Westchester and back toward the city
that I realized I wanted to go back to the bar where I met

Lila. To relive the conversation we shared in that booth, the way her body first reacted to my touch...

She was electric. Fiery. Everything I look for. Everything that Valentina was—

I watch them slowly remove their bras, their tits springing free.

"Stop."

I sit up.

The two girls glance at one another, confused expressions on their faces.

I tilt my chin toward the door. "You need to go."

"But—" the redhead starts.

"I said *leave*."

"I thought we were having fun." The blonde pouts, wrapping her arms around herself, pushing her tits up as if to entice me.

Little does she know, nothing she could do would make me change my mind. My thoughts have taken a dark turn.

"Fun's over, sweetheart."

They finally leave, and I call up for another bottle of whiskey that comes in less than a minute later.

Sitting on the couch, I look out at the vast city below.

I'm surrounded by so many people, and yet I've never felt more lonely.

Loneliness.

It's not something I've thought much about.

After what happened with Valentina, the grief took over, and I drowned in her absence.

For a long time, it was more of a stabbing pain in my chest. But now, as I sit alone drinking whiskey and staring out at the city, I feel hollow.

"Fuck, Lila. What have you done to me..."

She reignited something in me, and I need to shut it down.

The fact that I just kicked two attractive women out of my hotel room because I was thinking about her terrifies me.

I made a vow to love Valentina for the rest of my days, and I plan to keep that vow. Since I lost her, I haven't slept with a woman more than once, never wanting to get close.

But it seems that's not enough to keep Lila Morano out of my head.

It's been three weeks since we spent the night together, and I've spent every single moment thinking about her.

It's clear she blocked my number after I called, but I'm glad. She should avoid me at all costs. I'm not a good person, and I'm definitely not good enough for her.

She didn't go to the police or told anyone about what she overheard that night. That both puzzles and amazes me.

Yet, I need to ensure she'll keep her mouth shut, no matter the cost. So, if Lila won't answer my calls, I guess I'll have to get a little more creative...

Because my family is at stake here, and I will protect them no matter what.

MAX MASON LEANS BACK IN HIS CHAIR. "I WAS surprised when I saw this meeting in my calendar."

He's everything I pictured Lila's boss to be—middle-aged, wearing a some-what expensive suit which has been poorly tailored, and with graying hair that's thinning around the temples. A sure sign of a man who's unhappy and unfulfilled.

"What can I do for you, Mr. De Luca?"

I keep my face neutral, crossing an ankle over a knee as I glance around the spacious office.

It's varying shades of gray, with a few faux plants and a big window behind the desk looking out over central park.

"My company has been looking into taking over a packaging company such as Mason's International for some time. I've just been yet to find a fit."

"And what is it that your company does?"

"Imports and exports." I keep my expression almost bored.

Max narrows his eyes.

"I appreciate your interest in my company, but it's a family business. I couldn't sell even if I wanted to."

I was expecting this answer, so I uncross my legs and lean forward, glancing at the framed picture on Max's desk of three young kids—two girls and a boy. "Are they yours?"

Max nods.

"Cute kids." Not that I notice either way. I have little interest in them. In kids in general. The thought of someone using my kids as a way to get to me has my blood running cold.

I would never risk their lives because of my work.

"Thanks."

"Are you expecting them to grow up and take over this company after they graduate from college?"

"Uh... I guess?" Max stumbles.

"You don't seem so sure."

"It's what I did, and my father before that."

"What's your son into right now?" I never normally take such time over convincing someone to sell their company to me, but I need to make this a smooth transition. I can't risk spooking him.

"Soccer. He wants to play professionally. But he's eight, so who knows..."

"Supportive," I mutter.

Max narrows his eyes. "Excuse me?"

"If you asked him right now if he wanted to run a company that sold packaging supplies, what do you think he'd say?"

Max chuckles, glancing fondly at the picture on his desk. "He'd tell me to get lost."

"Look, Max," I start, placing my hands on the table. "If you let me buy your company, I would take over as CEO, but would allow you to stay on as a director. You'd receive a hefty bonus, better work-life balance, and less stress. It's a win-win for both of us. Use this money to set your kids up for the future. To give them the freedom to pursue their own dreams, rather than the one that's pushed on them."

Max is quiet for a moment, his eyes fixed on the picture of his children.

I know I'm in just from the way his eyes soften. It's a predictable move, playing right into his weakness, but it's how I've gotten to where I am today.

"Think about it, and get back to me by the end of the day." I get to my feet, re-buttoning my suit jacket.

"It's a big decision." There's a slightly panicked look in his eye.

"Perhaps." I offer him a smile, glancing at the picture once more. "But they should make it an easy one."

I walk out of the office.

I keep my head down, wanting to avoid running into Lila. I can't risk seeing her yet, not until I've sealed the deal. That way she has no choice but to work for me, and I can keep a closer eye on her.

A smile tugs at my lips as I take the elevator back down

to the foyer and head out into the bright New York morning.

I have a few meetings scheduled for later over the phone, but until then, I decide to take a walk down fifth avenue to stop by *Mille-Fuille* bakery to pick up some macarons for Rosa. It's her last week of school, and she's cramming for finals so I know a sweet treat will cheer her up.

I feel bad at times like this when she doesn't have a female role model to look up to or to help with the emotional side of things. Rosa is extremely smart, but she's hard on herself and wants to be the best. I should be grateful she's such a focused teenager, but it does mean a lot of meltdowns over grades and papers, and Marco and I aren't exactly the best at handling things.

Valentina on the other hand was like the big sister Rosa never had, and I curse the universe for not only taking her from me, but from Rosa too.

I wonder how Lila would get along with Rosa.

Fuck. Where did that come from?

To distract me, I shoot Rosa a text.

> Thinking of you today. Good luck with the final!

> Rosa: Thx A <3 only two more after this!!

> I'm proud of you no matter what. Mom and Dad are too x

She sends me through a string of emojis that has me smiling down at my phone. I'm such a softie when it comes to my little sister.

"Next!" the server calls—a young girl who doesn't look

much older than Rosa.

"What's the largest size box of macarons you sell?" I reach into my jacket pocket for my wallet.

"Our largest has twenty-five assorted flavors."

"Great, I'll take four of those," I reply, pulling out a few hundred-dollar bills and placing them on the counter, as well as tucking one into the sad looking tip jar. The girl's eyes widen but she nods, quickly getting to work boxing up the treats.

***

A FEW HOURS LATER, I SIT IN MY OFFICE BACK IN MY Westchester house, drinking a double espresso and trying to organize our shipments for the next quarter. It's a ball ache of a job, but I don't trust anyone else to do it, *especially* after the situation with Tommy Munro. Serves me right being too trusting, even with employees who have worked for my family for decades.

Turns out anyone can be a snake if you look close enough.

A knock at my door has me lifting my head. "Come in."

"Hey, bro." Marco steps inside, closing the door behind him.

"What's up?" I run my hands through my hair, leaning back in my plush leather seat.

Marco leans against the door, folding his arms across his chest. He's dressed as if he's just come from the gym, in a white T-shirt and black shorts, his dark hair hidden beneath a backwards baseball cap.

Marco pulls his phone out of his pocket and waves it, a smirk tugging at his lips. "Heard something interesting through the grapevine."

"Well?" I don't have the patience to tiptoe around whatever it is that Marco has heard. I've had a long day, and I'm counting down the minutes until I can take a sleeping pill with a double whiskey and fall into a dreamless oblivion. It is the only way to escape Lila in my dreams.

"I spoke to Kyle."

I frown.

"Our private investigator? Why?" Fuck, does he know about Lila? Did Kyle say something about her?

I'm already reaching for my phone as Marco crosses the room to take a seat opposite me.

"Because he's our go to guy when we need info?" Marco shakes his head. "Are you drunk or something?"

"No, I'm not fucking drunk. I'm just tired of all this bullshit."

"Well, it might cheer you up to know what I know."

"Marco, I swear—"

"It's about Lorenzo."

I immediately shut my mouth, my pulse slowing.

"What about him?"

"I asked Kyle to follow that guy, Sergio, that Tommy told us about. Seems he's easy to break." A mischievous twinkle shines in Marco's eye, and I shake my head.

"Did he find out anything useful?"

"According to Sergio, Lorenzo is planning on attacking us in three weeks."

"By us, he means *what* exactly? The company? The shipments? Me specifically?"

Marco shrugs. "Does it matter?" Marco crosses an ankle over a knee. "Because we're going to get to him first."

"And how do you propose we do that?"

"Make Sergio an offer he can't refuse and take Lorenzo down from the inside."

13

——

LILA

What the hell am I doing? Why do I keep doing this to myself?

It's been six weeks since I blocked Andre's number, and every day since, the dance is the same. At random times of the day, I find myself looking at his contact, finger hovering over *unblock*.

The fact that that night still haunts my dreams and that he is still the dominant thought throughout the day makes me a pathetic person, right?

Who the hell falls in love with a guy she was with for less than twelve hours?

Woah! Falls in love? There is no love here. At all. This is an obsession. A crush.

Dear lord, I'm ready to be committed. There is no way this is normal.

How can this man affect me so much after such a short time we spent together?

Granted, it was the best sex of my life, and while I was in his bed, he made me feel things I had never felt before. Not just sexually, although, man, those orgasms were out of this world. But he also made me feel cherished and cared for.

Except now, he broke me. I'm no longer a rational, functional adult.

I'm no better than I was at fourteen when I had a crush on a senior at my high school because he smiled at me once in the cafeteria. I was *obsessed* until the day he graduated and left for college.

Did I consider following him to Stanford? Yes, I did.

Thankfully, Cassi was there to get some much-needed sense into my thick head.

Fuck. Maybe I could do with Cassi right now as my thumb, once again, hovers over *unblock*.

"Get a fucking grip, Lila." I shut my phone off and put it down as I stand in front of my bathroom mirror. "You have bigger things to focus on."

Like the purple bruises under my eyes, the grayish tint on my skin, the lack of color in my cheeks.

Food poisoning sucks. Granted I've been off work the last few days, but I had hoped that after getting a full eight hours last night, rather than waking every hour to chuck up my guts, I'd look at least a *little* better.

I was wrong.

I sigh as I start swiping concealer under my eyes. "Never. I repeat, *never*, buy sushi from a seven eleven again. You hear me, Lila Morano?"

Holy crap. I'm talking to myself. I've gone crazy. The batshit kind.

Pulling out my last clean work dress from my closet, I finish getting ready for work in a hurry.

I want to get in early before my boss does, to try and make up for the fact that I've been off sick the past four days. Granted, I've still kept up with as much as I could from home, but in my mind, it's not enough. I worked hard for this promotion, I want to live up to the high standards I've set myself—food poisoning or not.

I will say, I was grateful for the distraction that being sick offered as it meant that I wasn't as focused on Andre as I could have been. I mean, I still thought about him a lot, in between the puking marathons, but I was more of a lovesick puppy rather than a psycho stalker.

I haven't dared google him again, too scared by what I might find. I want to keep the memory of him in the bar when he swept me off my feet as the one I think about, not the thought of him putting a gun to someone's head and pulling the trigger.

My stomach churns again at the thought, but I ignore it.

I don't have time to fix my makeup if I throw up again, so I force myself to think of neutral things, like what shoes I'm going to wear, to stop myself from spending the next hour hugging the toilet.

I swear, this is the longest bout of food poisoning I've ever experienced, but I think it's just the universe's way of trying to teach me a lesson. From now on, I will eat nothing but kale and chickpeas, and the occasional donut. And maybe pizza.

"Don't think about food," I groan, forcing a brush through my tangled mane. It really needs a wash but I haven't had the energy to do my full hair care routine, so I'm opting for the slick back bun, which I hope makes me look chic and put together rather than dirty and ill.

Throwing a light sweater into my bag, along with my laptop and heels, I slip on my trainers and head out the door, breathing in the crisp morning air as I start walking toward the subway.

It's barely seven in the morning, but the sun is up, and

the air is still chill enough that I pull my sweater out of my bag, knowing that in a few weeks it'll be too humid for anything other than shorts and a tank top.

I decide to give Cassi a call as I walk. Normally, we see each other multiple times a week, but with me being sick, we've barely caught up, and I miss her.

"Hey, stranger," I say as Cassi answers the phone. "I'm surprised you actually answered. It's too early for you to be up."

"Never went to bed."

I can't help but laugh. "You're crazy. Where are you now?"

"Walking down fifth. Fancy getting coffee before work?" Cassi works for a top marketing agency a few blocks over from my office, which makes it easy for us to grab a cocktail or two after a long day.

"Oh, I'd love to, but I need to head in early. Make up for all the time I've missed."

"You've still been sick?"

"For like four days, it's ridiculous. I don't want Max to regret giving me this promotion—"

"Lila, stop. You're allowed to be *sick*. You're not a robot. Give yourself a break already."

I let out a long breath, my shoulders sagging as I start heading down the steps to the station.

"You know I don't like taking time off."

"Well, I don't like you working yourself into the ground, so there is that too."

I roll my eyes.

"I'm fine, honestly. Why don't we grab dinner after work? I'll make a reservation at Alessandro's, my treat."

"Seeing as you're ditching me for work, you owe me," Cassi mutters.

"How dare I go to my grown up job because my bills refuse to pay themselves." I laugh.

"We wouldn't be in this problem if you got yourself a sugar daddy. Oh, wait, you could've had one, you just chose self-respect instead."

"You're the worst." I chuckle.

"You love me, really," Cassi says. "See you tonight, Lils."

Even though it's barely seven in the morning, the subway car is packed, and with the heat radiating from all the bodies around me, I'm already sweating and feeling nauseous as I enter the office building twenty minutes later.

I discreetly dab my upper lip with a tissue as I cross the foyer, trying to slow my breathing so the redness in my cheeks will die down.

Max doesn't normally arrive until eight, so I'm hoping to get a head start on emails before then.

I hope he doesn't mention my sick days, but there's nothing I can do apart from being honest. I've been with the company for three years, and these are the first sick days I've taken, so I'm hoping they'll be brushed over.

As I wait for the elevator to take me up to the fifteenth floor, I decide to check my email. The email at the top of my inbox is from my boss, and the subject reads: *urgent.*

My heart stops as I click it open and scan the contents.

Meeting in my office at eight.

This can't be good...

I'M A NERVOUS WRECK AS I WATCH THE CLOCK, PACING around my office as each second ticks by.

This is it. Everything I've worked so hard for over the

past three years is about to be ripped away from me. I'm going to lose my apartment, my insurance, my 401k.

"Oh god, I'm going to have to move back in with Auntie." I let my head fall into my hands. That thought alone has my stomach twisting.

A soft knock comes from my open door, and I look up to see Max's assistant, Ally, hovering.

"He's ready for you." She smiles, but it doesn't reach her eyes.

This has got to be a sign, right? A bad sign.

"Great," I choke out, running my hands down my dress. "I'll be right there."

Ally offers an encouraging smile before disappearing from sight.

I quickly change out of my trainers, sliding into my black heels, and head down the corridor toward Max's office.

My heart is pounding in my ears as I mentally rehearse answers to any possible questions he might throw at me.

"You've got this," I whisper, bracing myself as I push open the door to Max's office.

Only, it's not Max sitting behind the large desk.

It's Andre.

14

———

ANDRE

'WHAT THE FUCK?"

I can't stop the smile that spreads across my face.

"I'd watch your language if I were you." I couldn't care less, if I'm honest, and my amusement is clear in my voice, but I'm still her boss, and I have a part to play here.

"Are you stalking me or something?" She looks around the office. "You can't be in here."

"Actually, I can." I set my hands over what is now my desk.

"What the fuck are you talking about?"

"Now now, Miss Morano, is that any way to speak to your boss?"

Her pouty lips part in shock as she glances at the desk, empty of all personal details, and realization dawns on her face.

She takes a step back toward the door.

"Andre..." she whispers.

I bite back the groan wanting to rip out from me at the sound of my name on her lips, my cock already hardening as I take in her form-fitting black dress and her more natural make up. She's beautiful, and my memories haven't been giving her justice.

"Lila." I lean back in the chair.

She is shaking her head. "No. You can't. This is... You can't be here."

"I own the company." I shrug.

Lila blinks.

I point to one of the black leather chairs opposite mine. "Why don't you take a seat, and we can talk?"

Lila frowns, but she walks over to stand behind the chair before me to the right.

"You bought the company because I wouldn't return your calls?"

I can't help but chuckle.

"Don't flatter yourself, Lila. I purchased the company because it was a good investment. The fact that you're here is an added bonus."

"What do you want from me?" Lila whispers, moving to sink into the chair.

Her shoulders slump, and up close I notice the dark circles beneath her eyes.

Has she not been sleeping too? Have I kept her up at night, plaguing her dreams as she has mine?

"Confirmation that you're not planning on doing anything stupid."

"You mean anything *else*? I already slept with you, so it's a bit late for that."

"You overheard me on the phone that night." I wait for her to deny it.

From the way her cheeks pale even more, I have my suspicion confirmed, and I grind my teeth together.

"I want to make sure that conversation is going to stay private."

"For god's sake. It's been weeks...No! Never mind!" She takes a deep breath. "Is that a threat?"

"Think of it more of a recommendation," I tell her, looking down at my laptop and pulling up my email.

"Andre—"

I glance up from the screen and almost melt at the sight of her ocean blue eyes.

Fuck, I'd forgotten how stunning she is. I know I need to be around her to ensure her silence, but this is going to be so much harder than I thought. Especially when my dick is throbbing in my pants, practically screaming at me to bend her over this very desk and show her who's her boss.

"You can go now." I try to sound bored. I can't let her know how much she affects me. Not when she could use it against me.

Lila opens her mouth as if to say something else, her eyes searching my face for an answer I refuse to give her.

At my silence, she gets up and stalks out slamming the door behind her, and I can't say my eyes aren't glued to her luscious ass the entire time.

Turning back to my laptop, I close my email and open up my security app which shows a live feed of all the cameras I had installed the moment Max signed on the dotted line.

I flick through them, looking quickly at the main reception area, the break room, my office, and finally Lila's office. I sit back in my chair, watching as she walks in and kicks off her heels. I smile as she rubs her hands over her face and starts pacing the room.

I love that my being here has such an effect on her.

"I'm in your head, Lila Morano."

And you're in mine.

As if to confirm that thought, my dick rubs against the zipper of my pants, and I bite back a groan as I watch Lila.

The smell of her perfume still lingers in the air around me, transporting me back to the booth at the bar, my tongue licking her neck as I teased her nipple through her dress.

"Fuck, Lila."

I let myself give into the temptation of her. Just because I have a no-sleeping-with-a-woman-more-than-once rule, doesn't mean I can't jerk off to her.

Before I have a chance to talk myself out of it, I reach down and undo my pants, reaching into my boxers and pulling my aching cock free.

It seems no amount of self-pleasuring satisfies the need to be buried inside Lila. Simply watching her perch on the edge of her desk, her legs crossed over one another causing her dress to rise up and expose her thighs, has me gripping my cock and pumping *hard*.

"Fuck." I press a few buttons on my laptop and zoom in.

I allow myself to remember what it was like to trail my fingers along the soft skin of her inner thigh, feeling the wetness pool between her legs as I slowly ran my tongue up her center.

I move my thumb over the tip of my cock, cursing at the bead of precum already forming.

With Lila, it's like I'm nothing more than a horny teenager, quick off the mark as I let my eyes fall to her chest on the screen.

Her dress is form fitting and barely contains her full tits, which beg to break free of the material.

What I wouldn't do to storm in there and rip it right off her before wrapping those delicious thighs around my waist and fucking her so hard she's screaming my name for the entire building to hear.

Because everyone needs to learn who Lila Morano belongs to.

I tighten my grip on my cock, hissing as I start increasing my pace.

She is mine.

Even if I can't have her in the way she deserves, the thought of someone else touching her, being inside her, has my blood heating with rage.

I want to mark her. Have her spread on the desk before me like a fucking dessert as I spill onto those luscious tits. To know that she walks around this office with the evidence of my claiming beneath her dress.

"Lila…" I pump my cock faster, my grip almost painful as my release starts to build at the base of my spine.

As if she can hear me call her name, she leans back on her hands, arching her back as she rolls her neck as if to release some built-up tension.

There are plenty of better ways I could help with that issue. I itch to barge into her office and get on my knees for her. Have her throw her legs over my shoulders as I sink my tongue inside her pussy, licking her until she's begging for release.

The phantom taste of her on my tongue has me working myself to the point of climax.

I reach for the box of tissues on my desk, knowing that there's no stopping it now, not when I'm thinking of nothing but Lila's glistening sex as she comes on my tongue.

My balls tighten as I flick my wrist, rubbing the slick head of my cock.

My hips buck as I spill into the tissue, a strangled noise escaping my lips as I watch Lila lift her arms above her head and stretch.

My eyes flutter closed for a moment as I pump every

last drop of cum from my cock before sagging back in my chair, panting as I come down from the high.

Footsteps sound down the hall, and I glance down at the sodden tissue in my left hand, my still hard cock in my right.

I hastily clean myself up and am just tucking myself back into my pants when my office door opens, and my new assistant walks in.

"Mr. De Luca, I have the file you asked for—"

"Don't you know how to fucking *knock?*" I slam the hand that had moments before been wrapped around my cock onto the desk.

Ally, I think that's her name, jumps, her cheeks reddening as she looks at me with wide eyes, clutching the gray folder to her chest.

"I-I'm so s-sorry—"

I shake my head, holding up a finger to silence her.

"You're fired."

"Please—"

"If you are incompetent enough to not even knock on my office door, then you're not fit to work for me."

"It'll never happen again." Ally's voice shakes.

"You're right, it won't. Because you're *fired*. Now get the hell out of my office."

Tears well in Ally's eyes, and a pang of regret hits me at acting so abruptly, but I stay silent as I watch her drop the file on my desk with a shaking hand before exiting my office.

"Fuck." I run my hands through my hair.

This whole business with Lila has got me so worked up. I need to get my shit together before I do something way worse than jacking off behind my desk and exploding at my assistant.

I reach into the top drawer of my desk and pull out a

small gold pendant on a long chain—a heart made with rose quartz.

It glimmers in the light shining through the window, and my heart aches as I turn the heart over between my thumb and forefinger.

"What am I going to do with you?"

15

LILA

THIS CAN'T BE HAPPENING.

There's no way in hell Andre De Luca is my boss.

And yet... There he was, mouthwateringly handsome in his suit, with his dark hair perfectly styled and that smirk on his lips.

Those lips...

I press my fingers to my own as I close the door to my office behind me.

Those soft, dangerous lips made my body feel things I've never experienced.

My breath catches as I picture him sitting behind that desk, all power and control.

It seems he has the same effect on me regardless of whether I'm standing before him in an office or a bedroom, and that's a problem.

He's here.

There's no way he happened to buy the company I work for. That's too much of a coincidence.

He wanted to ensure my silence by keeping a closer eye on me.

I'm not sure whether I should be flattered he's gone to so much trouble, or terrified about how quickly he's uncovered my life with nothing to go on but my first name.

Though if he's got contacts that can bury a body, what's to say he can't dig deeper into my world and use Cassi or my aunt to ensure my silence?

I have to keep them out of this as best I can and play along with whatever game Andre is playing. No matter what, I will ensure that those I love most in this world are protected from Andre De Luca.

I wish I could say the same for myself.

I'M A NERVOUS WRECK ALL DAY, CHOOSING NOT TO leave my office even for lunch, in fear of running into Andre. I read through the email the entire company received this morning about the new management, and find out that Max, my previous boss, has been made financial director.

I'm glad Andre didn't outright fire the poor man, he has three young kids and a wife at home to worry about.

But I worry about my colleagues picking up on any hint of a vibe between Andre and me.

The way his eyes heated as I strolled into his office this morning gave him away, and I know my own chest flushed and my pulse quickened in response.

I've worked too hard for rumors to spread around the office that I'm sleeping my way to the top. It's even more of a reason to stay the hell away from Andre De Luca. Which is hard, considering we now work together.

Surprisingly, Andre doesn't stop by my office all day. I receive no emails from him either. It's like he's not here.

And I'm stupidly a little disappointed.

When five o'clock rolls around, I quickly pack up my things, slip on my trainers, and head out the door, keeping my head down until I get to the elevator. Once inside, I finally release the breath I feel like I've been holding all damn day.

When I check my phone, there's a message from Cassi telling me she's outside the building. I cringe, knowing there's no way I'm going to be able to keep Andre's new business venture a secret. It'll come out eventually. I just need to make sure that's the only one of his business ventures she's aware of...

"Hey, Cass." I wave to my friend as I hurry down the steps outside my building.

Cassi looks particularly bright-eyed in jeans and a fuchsia pink blouse, her blonde hair swept back in a high ponytail.

"You look better than I do, and I got a full eight hours."

"Swap the sleeping for fucking, and you're golden, my friend." She laughs. "Keeps us looking young and fresh."

"Is that so." I laugh, linking my arm through hers.

"Hell, yeah. So, how was your day?"

"Urgh, can we leave the work talk until we get to the restaurant?"

"That bad huh?" Cassi laughs.

"Let's just say, I need a martini in my hand when I tell you about it."

"Ooh, now I'm *intrigued*." Cassi taps her fingers together like an evil genius.

When we get to Alessandro's, I head straight to the tiny bathroom at the back of the restaurant, feeling a little light-headed after the walk.

I would put it down to not having eaten much all day

due to avoiding Andre, but seeing as I've eaten hardly anything in the last *week*, I know I really need to stock up on the calories tonight before I even think about touching a martini.

"What'd I miss?' I slip into the chair opposite Cassi.

"Ordered us some water and a round of dirty martinis." She waggles her eyebrows.

I force a smile, a slight sheen of sweat starting to form on my brow.

Glancing around the tiny restaurant, I feel a sense of home.

It reminds me a lot of my Aunt Maria's apartment—covered in old photographs and magazine clippings of recipes tacked to the walls. There are only about ten tables in the entire restaurant, each with a red and white checked table cloth and a single tealight candle. The lighting is dim, and the servers barely speak English, but it has that Italian charm that never fails to make me smile.

"Ciao, Lila. Ciao, Cassandra." Antonio, the owner, places our drinks on the small table. "Where you been, huh? It has been weeks!"

"We are unmarried women, Antonio." Cassi sighs, shaking her head. "We actually have to *work*."

I grin. "Otherwise, of course, we would be here every day."

"Breakfast, lunch, *and* dinner." Cassi flashes a wink.

Antonio shakes his head at us, his hands on his hips.

"I bring you extra garlic bread. You girls, too skinny!"

"I'll take that as a compliment." Cassi tosses her long ponytail over her shoulder, smiling like a Cheshire cat.

Once Antonio has scuttled away, distracted by the other regulars, Cassi picks out the olive from her martini and pops it into her mouth.

"If I tell you something." I pause, taking a deep breath. "You have to promise not to freak out in the middle of this restaurant, ok?"

"Ok?" Cassi frowns, chewing her olive.

I run my hands over the frayed table cloth, keeping my eyes downcast.

"My mystery one-night stand guy from that night with Dirk? Turns out he's...my new boss."

There's a choking sound, followed by a fit of coughing.

I look up to find Cassi red in the face and bug-eyed as she reaches for her water and downs the entire glass in one go. I wait patiently for her to calm down, trying to read her reaction.

"What...The fuck?" She slaps her chest, coughing some more as tears stream down her face.

"I wish I was joking."

"I repeat, what the fuck?"

So, I dive into the story. Starting with the email I received this morning, thinking it was about my sick leave, only to find Andre sitting behind Max's desk, informing me that he has bought the company.

I, of course, leave out the way I instantly melted at the sight of him.

"Thankfully, I managed to avoid him all day." After finishing the story, I cave and take a sip of my martini—the alcohol burning my throat and making my stomach churn.

I grimace, placing the drink back on the table.

Cassi hasn't spoken a single word, so I glance at my friend who's shaking her head.

"Lila, this is not good..."

"I know, I slept with the fucking boss! But if he's anything like Max, we'll mainly communicate through email, and we'll see each other once or twice a week in meetings, where there will be other people around. I think I made it out to be this huge thing—"

"That's because it *is* huge. He bought the company where you work, Lila."

"Not ideal." I shrug.

"I don't think you understand. It's clear he went out of his way to find out where you worked, and now has done the ultimate power move. I don't like this guy, it's making me feel uneasy. This behavior is borderline obsessive."

"He won't hurt me." I find myself needing to defend Andre's character, despite us literally having a conversation earlier about me keeping his very dark secrets.

"You shouldn't trust him. Maybe you should talk to Max, switch departments or something."

I shake my head.

"I've worked too hard to get to where I am, Cass. I'm not going to let Andre ruin that for me."

"It might be too late for that, babe."

I force the conversation away from Andre until our food arrives.

Antonio wasn't kidding when he said he would bring us some extra garlic bread, placing a plate beside both Cassi and me, along with two huge bowls of carbonara.

Usually, the sight of the creamy pasta would have my mouth watering, but instead, I swallow down the bile that rises in my throat.

Cassi tucks in, slurping the spaghetti lady-and-the-tramp style. Even the sight of her eating has my stomach rolling.

I get to my feet, placing a hand over my mouth, bolting through the restaurant, praying that I can make it to the bathroom in time and thanking all that is holy for the *vacant* sign on the bathroom door.

I barely lock it behind me before I'm hurling my guts up once more over the toilet, my body covered in sweat, and my eyes streaming.

"Urgh."

I flush the toilet, closing the lid.

A knock sounds at the door.

"It's occupied!" I croak, my throat sore.

"It's me. Cassi."

I move to unlock the door before sitting down on the closed lid of the toilet, wiping my mouth with some tissue.

"You ok?" Cassi locks the door and leans against it. Her brows are furrowed as she takes me in.

"I know, I'm a hot mess." I sigh, wiping my forehead on the back of my hand.

"How long have you been like this?"

"Four or five days? Honestly, I've lost count." I sigh.

"That's a little too long for a stomach bug."

"I think it might just be the flu," I mumble, leaning back against the cold tile on the wall and closing my eyes.

Cassi steps toward me before placing a hand on my clammy forehead.

"Hmm... No fever."

She's silent for a moment, and I open my eyes. She's looking at me as if she's seen a ghost.

"What?" I sit up.

"I don't want to make a bad situation worse, but...could you be pregnant?"

I stare at Cassi, my brain just whine noise.

"Uh... Of course not, why would you suggest—" Wait a minute. "What's the date today?"

"It's the twenty-fifth."

My heart thumps as I count on my fingers, working out when exactly I last got my period. I knew it had been a while, but maybe I was only one or two days late.

I count again. I'm nearly three week late. "Holy shit."

I look up at my friend with wide eyes. "I think I might be."

Cassi's throat bobs, and I can tell she's trying to keep her face neutral so as not to freak me out any more.

"Ok... Well, there's no point in panicking until you've taken a test to confirm it. I could run out and get one right now?"

"No, I-I can't take one..." My chest hurts. I can't breathe. This bathroom is too small. I need to get out of here. I need some air. Now.

"Lils, you're going to have to take one, honey. I know it's scary—"

Oh, god. I'm going to pass out. "It's fucking *terrifying!*"

A knock sounds on the door, and I jump, my heart threatening to come out of my throat.

"It's occupied, dumbass!" Cassi yells. "Give us a minute!"

I shake my head. This cannot be happening. This *cannot* be happening...

"I've only been with one guy since Sam," I whisper. "There would be no denying who's the father."

"Oh shit."

"I thought today was bad enough when I found out Andre is now my boss. But add in potentially carrying his child? Fuck, Cassi, that's just too much to deal with. What am I going to do?" My voice cracks as I look up at her wide-eyed before burying my face in my hands.

Cassi places a comforting hand on my shoulder, squeezing gently.

"One step at a time, babe. First off, we need to stop by the drugstore and buy a test before we start throwing around the word *daddy*."

16

ANDRE

I LET LILA AVOID ME FOR TODAY. THE SHOCK OF finding out I bought the company will wear off, and then we can have an adult conversation.

But for right now, I will keep a close eye on her through the camera in her office.

When she starts packing up her things, I shoot a text to Jerry, my man who was at the club where we first met. I want tabs on Lila at all times, not just for her own protection, but for mine too.

He's stationed outside the office building in case she goes anywhere.

I wasn't surprised when she chose to sit behind her desk working until the clock struck five.

She's strong-willed, I'll give her that.

I refuse to face the drive back to Westchester in rush hour, so I message Marco and Rosa to let them know I'm staying in our penthouse.

When I stroll out of the elevator a few hours later, I find my brother sitting on the couch with a scotch in one hand and a cigar in the other.

"Put that shit out. Go to the roof if you want to smoke."

Marco grins, taking a long drag of his cigar. "The roof is where we go to kill people, Andre, not kick back with a cigar."

"You're the one who started bringing business back here, not me. You only have yourself to blame." I sigh, shrugging out of my suit jacket and tossing it over the back of the couch. "Pour me one of those, would you?"

Marco balances his cigar between his lips as he carries his own half empty glass to the bar.

I sink down onto the plush leather couch. "I'm surprised you're in the city."

"Rosa is having a bunch of her friends over to celebrate the end of finals."

"Ah." I grin. "I'm glad she's having fun."

"Me too." Marco hands me my drink before taking a seat on the couch opposite.

I grind my teeth as he kicks back and puts his shoes on the glass coffee table.

"I had a meeting with Sergio today."

"How the fuck did you manage that?" I down my drink in one gulp, hissing as the alcohol burns my throat.

"It doesn't take much when you threaten a guy's wife and kids." Marco shrugs.

"Fuck's sake, Marco." I rub my brow with my thumb and forefinger. "What did you learn?"

Marco drops his feet back onto the floor and leans forward, resting his forearms on his thighs.

"Lorenzo is planning on sending you a message."

"How?" Marco takes a deep breath, and I instantly sit up straight. "*How?*"

"Through Rosa."

"*Fuck!*" I get to my feet and throw my empty glass

against the wall where it shatters into a thousand crystal pieces. "You knew this, and you left her alone at the fucking house? I'm going to fucking kill you once this is handled, Marco." I storm around the couch, grabbing my jacket and heading for the elevator.

"She's not alone."

"No, she's got however many of her friends with her who are now all in danger because of *us*."

"Xander is there."

Xander is one of our personal bodyguards, and the only one I trust to look after Rosa when we're in the city.

"Get him to bring her here, *now*. Pull her from school immediately. I don't want her out of my fucking sight, you hear me?"

"Andre, listen." Marco gets to his feet.

The urge to grab my brother by his collar and slam him into the wall for being so fucking reckless about our sister's safety is making my hands shake.

Marco keeps his distance, probably feeling the rage emanating from me.

"If we pull Rosa from school, Lorenzo will know someone went behind his back and leaked the information to us. We can't afford for Sergio to get killed, not when we're this close."

"I'm not risking Rosa. It's not worth it. We'll find some other way—"

"No, we won't." Marco shakes his head, his dark hair falling into his eyes.

"Fuck," I exhale, running my hands through my hair. "What do you suggest?"

"We double Rosa's security for the time being. She barely has a month left at school, and after she's done, we'll keep her under close observation at the country house."

"She's not going to like it."

"Of course, she's not. She's fifteen." Marco chuckles. "She wants to spend all day going to the mall or wherever the fuck it is teenage girls do."

"We need to act now, Marco. We only have one shot with Lorenzo, so the sooner he's dealt with, the better."

"I agree. But it'll take meticulous planning if we want to ensure we're successful."

"Oh, we will be, little brother. Once I set my mind on something, I don't stop until the job is done. Whatever the cost."

Next morning, we drive back to Westchester.

I need to have this conversation with Rosa in person.

She's not going to like the extra security, but I don't fucking care.

When we arrive at the house, Rosa's in the kitchen with Xander, who's sipping an espresso as Rosa chats his ear off. It's a comical scene to witness, a shaved-headed, tattooed giant of a man listening to my teenage sister talk about Taylor Swift.

At the sound of our footsteps, Xander gets to his feet, relief on his face.

"Hey, Xander. Mind giving us some privacy?" I go to the coffee machine and pour a cup.

Xander nods and leaves the kitchen.

"Don't talk his ear off, Rosa. He's working."

She scoffs, pouring herself some juice.

"It's weird when they just stand in the corner of the room watching me eat."

"It's what they're paid to do."

"Well, I enjoy chatting with them."

"Not sure Xander would say the same," Marco mutters, appearing at my side.

I hand the coffee pot to him and turn to face my sister.

The smile on her face drops as she looks at me.

"What is it now? I swear, the girls and I tidied up the media room after we watched the movie."

"I'm sure you did." I sip my coffee.

"Then why does your face look like that?"

"He always looks like that sis." Marco chuckles, and I elbow him in the ribs.

He winks at me, moving to sit beside Rosa at the table, pulling her half-eaten plate of French toast toward him and tucking in.

"We need to talk. And you're not going to like what I'm about to say."

Rosa sets down her juice and folds her arms over her chest. She's wearing pink-and-white-striped pajamas, her dark hair piled high on her head. She still looks so young, but when she gives me that look, our mother's fierceness shines in her eyes. "Hit me."

I look at Marco, and he dips his chin.

"Xander will be accompanying you to and from school for the rest of the semester."

Rosa blinks.

"No sleepovers at friend's houses, or going to the mall. You will go to school in the morning and come straight home. You will stay at the house on weekends, or I will personally drive you into the city with me to stay at the penthouse where you will not leave my sight. Are we clear?"

Rosa looks to Marco. "This is a joke, right?"

Marco shakes his head.

"This is no joke, Rosa." I set down my coffee. "This is serious."

"Why are you putting me on house arrest?"

"That's a need to know issue."

"Bullshit."

"You'll do as I say, or I *will* bring you to the city. Your choice. This is *not* a negotiation."

"So, I have to choose between a full-time babysitter or being locked up for the rest of my life?"

"Teenagers." Marco scoffs.

"Fuck you," Rosa spits at him before getting to her feet. "Fuck both of you—"

"*Enough!*"

Rosa freezes as my tone, and this time, I take the lid off my rage.

"*Sit. The fuck. Down.*"

She does.

"This is serious, and you need to fucking do as you're told for once in your fucking life. Do you think this is a joke to me? That I am doing this for shits and giggles?

"N-no, but—"

"But nothing. This is what it'll be like, so deal with it, or I'll deal for you. Have I made myself clear?"

Rosa is silent for a moment, looking down at her lap. "Is someone after me?"

Marco glances at me, but I shake my head.

I don't want to freak her out more than I have to.

"They're after me. But I'm not taking any chances."

"Trust me, sis, Andre wanted to pull you out of school entirely."

"What?" Rosa exclaims, looking at me with daggers in her eyes.

"Like I said, your choice."

She huffs. "I can look after myself, Andre."

"No, you fucking can't. You're fifteen. You either accept this new situation, or I pull you out of school, and you can have a tutor."

Rosa's nostrils flare, but she doesn't fight me, just storms out of the kitchen and slams the door behind her.

"That went well." Marco chuckles, shaking his head. "I feel bad for Xander now."

"Better him babysit her than us," I mutter.

"You think you were a little too hard on her? She's not a kid anymore."

"Exactly. Besides, how much harder would it be if Lorenzo got his hands on her, huh?"

As I wait for Rosa to cool down, I go into my office to set up some new foundations for Mason's International.

It's clear Max was in over his head when it came to some of the more basic everyday runnings of the company. It's mindless work, but one I would rather do myself.

Marco comes knocking at around eight, bringing me a plate of food and a drink. "Thought you might be hungry."

"Thanks." I look up from my screen. "Being a maid suits you."

"Fuck you very much." Marco sets the plate of what looks like orange chicken down on the coffee table by the couch and takes a seat. "You doing ok?"

I frown. "Why would you ask me that?"

"You've been acting...different these past few weeks. Is it just this shit with Lorenzo, or is it something else? You can tell me, you know, I'm your brother."

"How could I forget?" I close down my laptop, getting to my feet.

My body hurts. My eyes fly to the clock on my desk.

I've been sitting in my office chair for the best part of ten hours, barely moving. I stretch out my arms and back before moving to the couch and tucking into my food, ravenous.

Marco sits forward. "I'm worried about you."

I roll my eyes as I chew on the delicious sticky chicken.

"I'm fine. Just a little preoccupied with setting up this new company."

"You know we have people who can do that for you, right? Saves you going to all this trouble."

I shake my head. "No, I need to make sure this is set up exactly how I need it. I can't risk there being any loose ends that could tie us back to the drug ring."

"Shit with Tommy's really got you looking over your shoulder." Marco shakes his head. "I'd like to think what happened to him sent a message, reminding our men where their loyalties should lie."

"Regardless, I don't want to waste time fixing someone else's mistakes later down the road. I'm doing it myself, and that's that."

"Fair enough." Marco leans back against the cream couch, the picture of ease in his white shirt and jeans.

Marco watches me as I eat, but I ignore him. He's one of the only people who can see through my mask, but this is my business. Besides, I need his focus on Lorenzo and our plan on taking him down.

That and I'm terrified talking about Lila out loud with him will make the feelings I have for her so much more real. Right now I can pretend the whole thing is in my head, like some wondrous fever dream.

But truth is, she's sunk her nails in deep, and I can't risk getting close to her.

Not when Lorenzo Rossi is planning on taking out everyone I care about.

17

———

LILA

"Not pregnant. Not pregnant," I chant to myself as I get ready, as if the words will somehow become my reality.

After dinner with Cassi, we stopped by the drugstore and bought a test, but I can't bring myself to take it, because once my fear is confirmed, I will have to tell Andre.

Then what? He pays me off, not wanting anything to do with the kid, or me? He doesn't scream white picket fence, and there's no way I can do this alone.

I'll wait a few more days. There is still time for my period to come, right?

I'm exhausted. I've barely slept in weeks, and this constant nausea is not helping.

I slap on more makeup than I would normally wear to work, but at this point, whatever makes me feel like a normal human is worth the extra time in the bathroom.

I pull out my favorite blue dress, which compliments my eyes, and slip on my converse, grabbing some nude heels to throw into my bag as I head out the door.

Cassi's working an event downtown, so I don't catch her at our usual coffee spot on the way to the office.

I pick up a cappuccino to go and walk the last two blocks from the subway station, enjoying the sun on my face.

Maybe a little extra vitamin D will help me feel better.

"Think it's the vitamin D that got you into this in the first place," I mutter as I ascend the steps up to my office.

I've barely sat down at my desk when I get a notification for a new email.

FROM: ANDRE@MASONINTERNATIONAL.COM
    To: lila@masoninternational.com

SUBJECT: URGENT

MY OFFICE. NOW.

I GROAN BEFORE GETTING TO MY FEET, GRABBING A notebook and pen on my way out.

My heart rate spikes as I head down the corridor to Andre's office, pausing to knock once.

"Come in." His voice is rough. It sends an instant shiver down my spine and has an uncomfortable heat building between my thighs as I open the door to him perched on the edge of his desk.

Fuck, he really knows how to wear a suit. His sleeves rolled up to his elbows, just enough buttons undone that I catch a glimpse of his dark chest hair.

I itch to run my hands over his skin, to feel the heat beneath my fingers as I explore him with my mouth—

"You know you can't subject every email as urgent." I clear my throat and turn around, closing the door.

"Everything's urgent when it comes to you, sweetheart."

"You can't call me that. I'd have to report you to HR." I glance over my shoulder.

"Have you reported our night together to HR? Because I'm sure they'd love to know how I fucked you with my tongue, before taking you from behind, spilling onto that plump ass of yours."

A choked sound escapes me as I turn around fully.

A smirk tugs on Andre's lips as his eyes roam over my body.

"You look amazing in that dress." His eyes flick to mine.

My cheeks heat, and I have to look away.

"Thank you," I clear my throat again. "So, no assistant today? Ally wasn't at her desk."

"Ally had to leave the company. A personal situation arose."

"Oh. Sorry to hear that. She'll be hard to replace."

"I've already found a replacement." He smiles at me, and I narrow my eyes. "You."

"Me?" I squeak.

Oh, *hell* no. Working this closely with Andre every damn day would be torture. It's bad enough there's a corridor separating us.

"Thanks, but I'm sure there are other people more suitable—"

"This isn't up for negotiation." Andre folds his arms across his chest, making the muscles in his forearms flex.

My mouth actually waters, and I have to bite the inside of my cheek to stop myself from making some inappropriate sexual noise. I swear my hormones are out of control—

I shut the thought down. There's a perfect explanation for that, but not one I want to address right now. *Especially,* when Andre is barely six feet away from me.

"Do you really think this is the best idea, given our... *history?* What if people pick up on something?"

"Are you planning on fucking me in the office, Lila?" He is so matter-of-factly. "Or what about the break room?"

"No." But I can feel my nipples harden at the thought of him bending me over that desk. I shift in place, too aware of the ache between my thighs.

"In that case, there's no chance of anyone walking in on us being *inappropriate.* So, what's the issue?"

"I don't want people to think I've slept my way to the top."

Andre stands, running his hands down his shirt as he strides over to me.

I hold my breath, watching his every move as if it's in slow motion.

He doesn't get too close, but I could still reach out and run my hands down his chest if I really wanted to.

"If you hear anything of the sort, come to me, and I'll take care of the situation."

"What, by firing them?"

"Yes." Andre frowns.

I notice the flecks of gold in his brown eyes, and I want to lose myself in the intensity of them forever.

"No." I shake my head, looking away. "Andre, this is my job. You can't mess with me like this. I've worked too hard."

"I'd like to remind you, Miss Morano, that *I* am the owner of this company." He takes another step forward so that my breasts almost brush against him.

I look up at him, and the hunger in his eyes has me wanting to sink in his arms and let him worship my body like he did the other night.

"So, if I want to fire someone for so much as looking at you the wrong way, I can. Besides, by being my assistant, you're getting a significant raise and a promotion. I've already emailed you over the new contract."

'Do I have a choice?" My nipples ache so much I bite back a whimper, desperate for Andre's touch. For his strong arms to wrap around my body. For him to tell me all will be ok.

But it's not. Because I can't tell Andre my suspicions. I'm in this alone, which means I'll need all the money I can get.

"No. You either accept, or you leave."

"I don't think you'd let me leave, *Andre*."

"We can test this theory, *Lila*. Decline my offer, walk away." The corner of his mouth twitches, and I know he's bluffing.

If he went to the effort of buying the company I work for, there's no telling what this man is capable of when it comes to me.

"Can I take the day to think about it? Look over the contract? Just to make sure I'm not being underpaid for my new role."

"I can assure you, the compensation is generous."

He holds my chin and runs his thumb over my bottom lip.

I gasp, my lips parting as his eyes flick to them as if he might kiss me.

"We're going to have fun, you and I."

Andre wasn't kidding when he said the compensation was generous. My eyes practically bug out of their sockets when I see my new salary.

I know it's not because the job is worth that kind of money, he's trying to buy my silence.

But when I think of the pregnancy test that is waiting for me when I get home, I know I have no choice but to accept. Now is not the time to be looking for a new job.

I print off the contract and read through it a few times before signing on the dotted line. Reluctantly, I head over to Andre's office at the end of the day to drop it off, but when there's no answer after I knock three times, I peek my head around the door and realize it's empty.

My disappointment that I won't get to witness his signature smirk as I drop the signed contract onto his desk surprises me.

I guess there's always tomorrow...

Stopping by the grocery store on the way home to pick up some chips and salsa as it's the only thing that makes me not want to hurl my guts up, I send Cassi a text to let her know I'm going to take the test.

She immediately offers to come over, which I appreciate.

I'm not sure I want to be alone when I find out the news that could literally change my life forever.

While I wait for Cassi, I busy myself with laundry and cleaning, hoping the mindless tasks will help keep me occupied. But Andre still plagues my thoughts as I think about what to do if the test comes back positive.

He'll find out eventually, especially if I'm now his new assistant.

The doorbell rings, and I sigh as I buzz Cassi up.

She'll talk me out of this downward spiral I can feel myself falling into.

As I glance around my tiny apartment, I try to picture where I'd put a crib or a changing table. Hell, I don't even have drawers, just a clothes rail with some storage containers underneath.

My eyes sting, and my heart wants to crawl out of my chest as I open the door and let out a strangled sob.

"Woah! Why the water works?" Cassi steps inside, closing the door behind her.

"Where the hell am I meant to put a baby?"

Cassi blinks. "You're pregnant? You took the test?"

"Not yet." I wipe my nose on my sleeve. "But look around, Cass. *I* can barely fit in this apartment."

"Lila." Cassi places her hands on my shoulders. "There's no point in getting worked up until you take the test. Let's see if we actually have something to worry about first. Come on." She takes my hand, leading me into my tiny bathroom.

"Where's the test?"

I point under the sink.

"I couldn't bear to look at it. Not when I knew I was going to..." My throat grows thick.

Cassi nods. "How was it today?"

"He made me his fucking assistant and gave me a stupidly high salary."

"What a dick."

My temper flares at the amusement in her eyes. "This is not *funny*."

"He likes you."

"You were literally just saying the other night that his behavior is creepy and giving off stalker vibes."

"I did." Cassi puts her hands on her hips. "I'm on a loss about this guy."

"Well, you're going to have to figure it out if he turns out to be my baby daddy."

Cassi rolls her eyes, bending down to pick up the box and pull out the test.

"Pee on the damn stick, Lila."

Two minutes feels like a lifetime as I sit on the closed lid of the toilet, Cassi leaning against the sink, the stick beside her.

"My life could literally change forever, Cass."

"This could be a blessing." Cassi offers me a warm smile.

"How? Please tell me how being a single mother is going to be a blessing?"

"You've always wanted kids."

I sigh, putting my head in my hands.

"Yes, but I imagined myself married, with a cute little house in the suburbs. Not some tiny studio apartment that I can barely afford. Plus, can you *imagine* what my auntie'll say? She'll kill me."

"If it's positive, are you going to tell Andre?"

I lift my head from my hands and look at her.

"I... I honestly don't know." I don't know him, except for the kind of information you'd put on a police report.

"He's the father. He has a right to know."

"But then I'm tied to him forever." I run my hands through my hair.

This is all happening too fast. Andre was only meant to be a night of mind-blowing sex to kickstart me back into the dating world after Sam tore my heart to shreds.

Instead, he might have ruined my career and impregnated me with the heir to his mafia empire.

"What does it say, Cass?" I place my hand over my racing heart.

Cassi takes a deep breath and reaches for the test.

"Fuck, Lila. It's positive."

18

———

ANDRE

"Lila, please come in here." I can almost hear her huff, and I smirk.

She knocks on my office door before letting herself inside. "Yes, Mr. De Luca?"

I want to hear her calling me Andre. Screaming my name as I thrust inside her. But this gives me ideas too, and my cock twitches in my pants.

"I'm getting hot. Can you please do something about it?" Yes, the double entendre is very much intentional.

Having an assistant is so much more fun than I thought it would be. But maybe that's because it's Lila Morano who's fetching me coffee and adjusting my air conditioning.

"You can't do this yourself?" she mutters under her breath as she picks up the remote control from my desk.

"I could. But I'd much rather you do it."

Lila glares at me over her shoulder, her long, dark hair hanging loose today. She's wearing a pair of dark burgundy slacks and a cream silk blouse that makes her breasts look incredible.

It's part of the reason I've come up with the most ridiculous tasks for her to complete today, just so I can have an excuse to look at her.

"Some would think you just want me around." she presses a few more buttons, causing the air conditioning to rumble to life.

"They'd be correct." I lean back in my chair, my eyes firmly glued to her ass.

"I can feel you staring, you know?"

"Just admiring the view." I chuckle.

Lila tosses the remote onto the couch and turns, crossing her arms.

My eyes flick to her breasts, and she must catch me looking as her cheeks flush along with her chest.

I clear my throat, ignoring the ache in my cock as she stands there, a scowl on her face.

Fuck, she's breathtaking.

"Anything else you'd like me to do?"

I lift an eyebrow. I lower my voice as I let my eyes devour her body. "I can think of many things."

"W-we have to keep things professional. You're my *boss*." The near breathlessness in her voice has me even harder.

Something else flashes behind her ocean blue eyes.

Sadness? Longing? I can't put my finger on it.

"I'm well aware of that." I lean forward to rest my forearms on the desk, not wanting her to notice the evidence of my arousal. "Have any of the tasks I've asked of you made you feel uncomfortable?"

Lila looks down, her shoulders sagging a little.

I ball my hands into fists, fighting the urge to go to her. To take her chin and lift her eyes to mine, to work out what's been eating away at her. Because something has. There's been an almost pained look in her eyes every time she looks at me, as if it hurts to be in my presence.

The very thought makes my chest ache.

"Lila, I want this arrangement to work for both of us," I say in a more serious tone.

She lets out a breath, looking up at me under her dark lashes.

"Is there anything else you need?" Her voice is void of any emotion.

I tense at the tone, irritated that she's not willing to let down her guard.

"You can go." I mirror her tone.

She nods, averting her gaze, before exiting my office.

Since she is now my assistant, I moved her into the office directly opposite my own. When both our doors are open, I can look directly at her.

But today, Lila keeps her door firmly closed.

If she wants to shut me out, I'll let her.

For now.

<hr>

"I need you to stay late and finish that report for me."

Lila looks up from her desk, frowning. "What report?"

"The one I asked to be sent over by the end of today," I lie, leaning against the door to her office.

"You never told me about any report."

I shake my head, crossing my arms over my chest, faking annoyance.

"It's not my problem if you failed to listen to my instructions."

Lila scowls, shaking her head.

"Is that going to be a problem?"

"I have plans." Irritation flashes across her face.

I didn't know three words had the power to send such a strong surge of rage through my blood.

It's Friday, which means it's likely Lila will be going home and getting ready for a date. She'll sidle up to him in a booth, let him put his hand on her thigh, letting it roam higher until his finger brushes her soaked panties—

"Cancel them," I growl.

"It's a fucking Friday night, Andre." She gets to her feet. "Can't this wait until Monday?"

"I've given you a very substantial pay rise, Miss Morano. I suggest you start working accordingly." I turn my back on Lila, strolling into my office.

I leave the door open so that when I take a seat behind my desk I have a clear view of her, and fuck does the anger in her eyes make my blood heat. I love that fire, and I wish she would let me get close enough to see how much it would burn.

My cock is straining against my zipper, and I want nothing more than to storm back into Lila's office and bend her over that desk.

The images flash behind my eyes—the fantasies I crave to act out with her.

I shift in my chair as I watch Lila toss her wave of dark hair over a shoulder, imagining twisting it around my fingers as I bend her over the desk.

I'd pull hard enough that she cries out, arching her back and pushing her ass against my rock hard cock, giving me no choice but to push her dress up around her hips and sink myself so deep inside her tight pussy.

It would be hard, brutal, the perfect combination of pleasure and pain. To remind us both who's really in charge.

Because right now, as I watch her work, it takes everything I have not to march into her office and drop to my knees before her, throwing her legs over my shoulders so I could devour her pussy with my tongue.

Lila must feel my gaze as she lifts her eyes, scowling at me as she continues to tap furiously on her keyboard.

I look away, not wanting her to notice the arousal in my eyes, but that doesn't stop me from palming my erection through my trousers, biting back a groan as I ache to pull it free and stroke myself to completion under the desk.

I force myself to work through my inbox and to look over the budget for the current quarter.

Max's old system needs updating, and I would normally palm off such lesser work to my employees, but I need something to distract me from Lila.

She turns me feral, and I know no amount of self-pleasure later will satisfy the need to be inside her.

"Is there a reason you're being so hard on me?"

My head snaps up to find Lila in the doorway, her arms crossed over her chest, pushing her breasts up.

She's wearing the same scowl on her face, but her cheeks have a pinkish tinge to them, as if she's been fighting her arousal for the last few hours too.

The thought sends me to my feet and crossing the room in a few strides.

"I don't recall you complaining about me being hard on you before..." I don't bother being subtle as I glance at those delicious breasts.

Lila's breath hitches, and I let my tongue wet my lower lip as I take her in. "Tell me, Miss Morano, do you ever think about that night in the penthouse suite of the Carlton-Ritz?"

"Andre..." Lila's eyes seem to glaze over, and I smirk.

"Late at night, when you're alone in bed, do you think about how I sank my cock so deep inside you that you screamed with pleasure?"

A strangled noise escapes Lila, and my hardening cock instantly goes rock-hard in response.

"Do you touch yourself as you remember how I devoured that delicious pussy of yours with my tongue?"

Lila's pupils dilate as her chest heaves, and I let my hand rub my hard length through my pants, letting the memories of our night together heat my blood.

I know I shouldn't be testing us like this, but fuck, I *need* her like I need air.

"This is harassment," she whispers, her cheeks glowing red as she looks down at the bulge in my pants.

I squeeze my cock harder and let a deep, guttural groan escape.

Lila's lips part, and I know she's imagining us fucking, and it smashes what small amount of self-control I had left.

"Not if you want it," I growl.

I reach out and run my fingers down her neck, watching as the skin instantly pebbles beneath my touch.

She stiffens, but a soft sigh escapes her lips.

"Tell me to stop, and I will."

19

———

ANDRE

She is about to walk away from this. From me.

But then she stands on her tiptoes, holding my biceps to balance herself before leaning in.

The scent of orange blossom and vanilla hits me as her tongue darts out and traces my lower lips.

My hands fly to Lila's hips, and I sink my fingers into her soft flesh as I fight the urge to spill into my pants.

"Lila." I ache to pull her flush against me, devour that pretty little mouth, but I wait, letting her set the pace.

I crave this, and I don't want to scare her off, no matter how badly I want to fucking rip those clothes off and take her right here.

"Was there something else you needed from me?" Amusement lines her voice as her lips move to my jaw.

"I need you to sit on the desk, now." I release my hold on her.

After her eyes flick once more to my very obvious arousal, she struts over to the desk and perches on the edge.

I watch her over my shoulder, my body so tense with need that I can barely think straight.

"Take off your clothes." I lock the door and pull down the blinds. It's almost nine, so we're likely to be the only ones left in the office, but I don't want to risk being caught fucking my assistant.

Though I'd be pleased that Lila would be marked as off-limits to any fucker who dared look her way.

Her clothes rustle, and I wait to turn around until no sound comes.

"Have you taken all your clothes off, Lila?"

"I thought you might want me to keep the shoes on."

Her voice sends a shudder down my spine.

I glance over my shoulder and let out a groan at the sight of her leaning back on her hands, her long, dark hair cascading around her shoulders as she pushes her swollen breasts out.

She's practically begging for me to worship them, but I look lower and almost fall to my knees as she slowly uncrosses her bare legs and exposes her glistening pussy to me.

"Lila..."

"I need you."

I'm pulling at my shirt as I cross the room to her, hating the desperation in her voice.

"I'm right here, baby." I fall to my knees before her and run my tongue along her slit.

She moans, throwing her legs over my shoulders, and I move my hands to grip her plush ass as I take her clit between my lips and suck.

Lila cries out, one of her hands sinking into my hair and pulling tightly.

Fuck, I love the slight pain.

I pull her tighter against me, wanting her to scream my name as she comes.

"Fuck," I hiss as I run my tongue along the length of her, my eyes rolling at the sweet taste.

"Oh, god, Andre." She grinds against my face.

I flick my tongue over her clit, and her thighs shake.

She's even more responsive to my touch than before, and I fucking love it.

I've barely gotten started, and she's already drenched, her body quivering.

"Someone's close already." I take a finger to her entrance, teasing it.

"Please, Andre." Her hips buck as I push my finger inside her so slowly her legs start shaking.

I desperately need to free my cock from my pants, the throbbing ache unbearable as it strains against my zipper.

But not yet. First, I need Lila to come on my tongue. I want to taste her for days.

"Do you want more, Lila?" I press a soft kiss to her clit.

Her body is writhing under my touch, and I chuckle, knowing that she hates how soft and slow I'm taking it.

"Such a greedy little thing."

"Oh, god, *please*." She tugs at my hair, trying to force my mouth onto her pussy, but I don't let her.

"I've missed this." I push my finger inside her.

She moans, her hips rolling, and I let her have another finger.

Taking her clit between my lips, I curl my fingers to brush her G spot, and it's Lila's undoing.

She cries out, her thighs tightening around my shoulders as I continue to suck her clit and thrusting my fingers.

I groan against her soft flesh, feeling my cock leaking as it aches to be released, but I know Lila won't last much longer.

The sounds she's making as she grinds against my face

are so erotic that I wish the office wasn't empty so they could hear what I do to her.

"I'm coming—"

My balls tighten at the words, and I increase my pace, fucking her faster with my fingers as I work her clit.

I look up to find her palming one of her breasts, her eyes rolling as she chases her release.

If I wasn't already on my knees, the sight of Lila right now would have them buckling beneath me.

She's so beautiful, and a selfish part of me wants to take her on this desk every damn day.

"Come for me, Lila." I stroke my fingers once more along her inner walls.

As if she was waiting for my permission, she goes crashing over the edge, crying out as she clenches around my fingers, her thighs shaking as she rides out her orgasm.

I don't stop licking her pussy until her body stills, her breath coming in heavy pants. I slowly pull out my fingers and take them into my mouth, moaning at the sweet taste of her.

"Andre," she sighs.

I press a soft kiss to each of her inner thighs, and one more to her clit, making her shudder. I smile at the sight of her, glistening and swollen before me, before getting to my feet.

Lila's eyes are glazed over, and as I shrug out of my shirt, she makes no attempt to hide the way her eyes roam over my chest before settling on my cock.

"Turn around."

Lila hops down off the desk, her breasts bouncing with the movement, before bending over until her upper body is flush with the desk and her ass is on full display.

I knead the soft flesh, reveling in the softness of her skin. "Are you ready for me, Lila?"

She moans, and I chuckle as I dip my fingers between her thighs, hissing as the wetness already pooled there.

"I love how responsive you are, sweetheart." I reach for my belt. undoing my pants.

My cock springs free, the tip already glistening with my arousal, and I take it in my hand and run it along the seam of her ass. "Can you feel how turned on I am?"

"Mmm..." Lila squirms against the desk.

I dip my cock lower, running it through her slick folds, desperate to sink myself inside her.

But not yet. I want to make her beg for my cock.

"I've thought about fucking you every moment since I took you in that hotel room." I tease her entrance with the tip of my cock.

She shudders, pushing herself back against me, desperate to take an inch. But I pull back.

"Your pussy was heaven, baby. So tight and wet."

"Andre." Her pleading is so delicious.

I smile, moving my cock up to rub against her swollen clit.

"Tell me you've thought about me fucking you against this desk, Lila."

She tenses, her clit still sensitive, so I make sure to be gentle.

"I've thought about it all day," she whispers.

"I've been rock-hard for you all day, sweetheart." I continue rubbing the head of my cock against her clit.

"You should've said something," she murmurs. "I could've taken care of it for you."

An image of Lila kneeling under my desk, sucking me

off as I work, flashes through my mind, and my restraint snaps.

I line myself up with her entrance and thrust my hips, burying myself to the hilt in one quick movement.

She cries out, her pussy clenching around my cock so tightly that my eyes roll.

"Oh, baby, I'm always hard when you're around," I grit out, pulling out and thrusting back into her so hard that she slams against the desk.

"Fuck," she groans.

"Maybe I'll add that to your contract," I growl. "You're required to suck me off at least once a day. Would you want that Lila?"

"Yes!" she moans as I fuck her harder, her ass bouncing against my cock.

"I knew I could fuck that scowl off your face. You just needed to come, baby."

"I think I just needed you to remind me how good your cock feels." She pushes against me, meeting me stroke for stroke, our pace quickly becoming sloppy as my spine starts to tingle with my release.

"Fuck, Lila. I'm close," I grunt.

Lila pushes herself up so I can reach around and take her breasts in my hands, running my thumbs over her hard nipples.

"Next time I want to finish on these perfect tits. But right now, I want my cum dripping down your thighs for the rest of the night."

"Andre..."

I keep my left hand wrapped around her body and move my right hand to between her thighs so I can rub her clit.

Lila groans, falling forward to brace herself against the desk as she starts grinding against my hand.

I have to grit my teeth to stop myself from coming. I want us to fall over the edge together and from the way her pussy is clenching around my cock, I know she's close.

I increase my pace, pulling out almost all the way before slamming my cock so fucking deep inside her that I see stars.

"S-so close—" Lila barely gets the words out before I thrust once more into her and send her orgasm crashing over her.

My cock instantly spills at the feeling of her clenching around it, and I continue moving inside her as she takes every last drop I have until we're both gasping for air.

I collapse against her, pressing soft kisses to her shoulder. My eyes close for a moment as I try to catch my breath.

Feeling Lila's soft skin beneath my fingertips has me wanting to tighten my hold on her, to keep her against me for as long as possible...

"You should go." I pull my cock free, dropping my hands from around her waist.

"Wait, what?" Lila pushes herself up, turning to face me.

I glance down at her naked body, the evidence of my release trickling down her thighs, and my chest tightens. I reach down to pull my pants back up, tucking my already hardening cock back inside and re-buckling my belt.

I clear my throat, looking away from Lila.

Fuck, I shouldn't have caved so easily. Because now I know that we can have this, and it'll only make it harder to resist.

She's too pure, too good for someone like me.

I can't give her what she deserves. Not when my heart will never fully heal after Valentina.

"Forget the report and head home." I turn my back on Lila to grab my shirt.

She says nothing as she moves to pick up her clothes and get dressed.

I can't look at her face, not wanting to see the hurt in her eyes after I fucked her and then tossed her aside like she's nothing to me.

Lila leaves without a word, and the sound of the door closing behind her has me flinching harder than if she slammed it.

She should be mad at me. But maybe I broke her.

The taste of her is still on my tongue, my fingertips tingling with the phantom feel of her skin.

Something in me snaps, and I crash my fist into the wall, tearing a hole in the drywall. My blood seems to boil.

I know I can't have Lila, not when I made a promise to love Valentina until my last breath. I cannot betray her like that, and yet... Lila Morano has sunk her claws so deep into me that I can't leave her alone.

I bought the fucking company she works for just to stay close to her.

Of course, I needed to ensure her silence, but if anything, the thought of seeing her every day was the main motivator.

I shouldn't be this obsessed, and yet, she's all I think about. All I *dream* about.

"What have you done to me, Lila?"

I only hope that she has the good sense to stay as far away from me as possible, before one of us ends up truly getting hurt.

20

LILA

I'M DELICIOUSLY SORE BETWEEN MY LEGS AS I WALK into the office on Monday morning. The fact that I can still feel the evidence of having Andre inside me three days later has me clenching my thighs together as I take a seat at my new desk.

I glance across the hall.

Andre is sitting behind his desk, muttering into the phone.

My cheeks heat as I remember how he bent me over that desk and fucked me like his life depended on it. How beautifully he ate me up. How much I wanted to fall to my knees and taste him.

When he mentioned adding that clause to my contract, my mouth actually watered.

How screwed up am I that I would willingly do it just to be able to enjoy that look on his face when I give him the ultimate pleasure?

This is so wrong. All of it. For so many reasons.

And I know we shouldn't have done it. The way he made me leave so abruptly afterwards proves that.

It hurt like hell to see him act so cold so quickly after fucking me, but I'm glad one of us still has the ability to keep their distance. There are already enough complications between us, what with him now being my boss and the fact that I'm pregnant with his child.

That knowledge has my heart thumping in my chest.

There's only so long I can hide this pregnancy before I start to show. And then what am I supposed to do? If I lie and say it was someone else's, Andre might be pissed as hell, especially if what happened Friday happens again. But if I tell him he's the father...

I bury my head in my hands and let out a groan.

"I need a coffee."

My head snaps up at the sound of Andre's voice.

He's leaning against the doorway, his arms folded over his chest. He's wearing his usual black suit and white shirt, unbuttoned to expose a little of his tanned chest.

My breath hitches as I take in his looming presence, but when my eyes find his, I'm a little hurt to find no warmth in them.

"Did you hear what I said?" His tone is flat.

"You want coffee," I repeat, getting to my feet.

Andre's eyes flick down to my dress, and I catch his nostrils flaring.

I chose the dress on purpose, hoping to put the ball back in my court, especially considering how easily he discarded me on Friday. I like to have control, and this dress gives me exactly that.

It's bright red and hugs every curve perhaps a little too tightly. Given how swollen my breasts are, they're practically spilling out of the dress. Add to the fact there's a zip that runs from between my breasts to the hem, meaning it could come apart in one swift motion, I know exactly the sort of thoughts running through Andre's mind.

I try to hide my smirk as I walk around my desk, knowing full well that my heels make my ass look incredible.

Two can play at that game.

As I approach the door, Andre steps to the side, his eyes narrowed on my face.

I raise my eyebrows in question as I pause beside him, letting the bergamot and sandalwood scent of him wash over me. I bite back a moan as I look up into his dark eyes, wanting nothing more than to sink to my knees before him.

"Black, no sugar?" I bite my lower lip.

Andre's throat bobs, but he sinks his hands into his pockets, shifting slightly on his feet.

"Yes," he grits out, and I know he's as turned on as I am.

Too bad. He doesn't get to be the only one to feel tossed aside.

"I'll be right back." I walk past Andre, making sure to swish my hips as I walk away.

His stare burns into my skin as I head down the corridor, and I can't fight the smile as I turn the corner.

I take my time in the breakroom, making his coffee, wanting him to squirm a little longer. I catch a few of my coworkers eyeing my outfit, but I keep my head down, not wanting to give myself away.

The last thing I want is for people to think I'm sleeping my way to the top.

Coffee in hand, I knock softly on Andre's door.

"Come in," he grunts.

I bite the inside of my cheek as I push open the door and gasp at the sight of a huge hole in the wall.

"What happened?" My mask falls as I take in the beaten-up drywall.

"No idea."

I look to Andre who's watching me with interest. His face is like stone, no hint of emotion in his dark eyes.

"This wasn't you?" I straight up ask as I walk over to the desk, still clutching Andre's coffee in my hands.

He leans back in his chair, resting his chin on his left fist as he slowly spreads his thighs. I glance at his hands and notice the knuckles of his right hand are a little bruised.

Interesting.

"I have complete control over myself, Miss Morano."

Liar.

This time, I don't bother hiding the smirk as I bend down to place the coffee cup on his desk, giving him a perfect view of my breasts.

"We'll see," I whisper, letting my tongue wet my lower lip before straightening.

His eyes flash with need, but he remains perfectly still.

"If you need anything else, and I mean *anything*, you just let me know," I add before turning and walking out of the office, not bothering to close the door behind me.

I'm breathless by the time I sit back down at my desk, and I can only seem to focus on the throbbing heat between my thighs.

Who knew pregnancy made you this horny?

I rub my hands up and down my thighs, almost whimpering with the need to take them higher.

Not yet. I want him to be the one to do it, to beg to taste me as I come. And in order to do that I need to play the game a little longer.

ANDRE HAS CALLED ME INTO HIS OFFICE FOUR TIMES today, and three of those were to fetch something from a cabinet. The other was to make him another coffee.

Asshole.

But I did everything he asked with a smile, and made sure to bend over as much as possible, giving him perfect views of my ass and tits throughout the day.

By the fourth time, I caught him screwing his eyes shut as if trying to collect himself.

I knew he would be sporting a hard on all day, and such a thought had me moaning under my breath as I worked, on the verge of running to the storage closet to take care of myself.

I glance at my clock. Almost six. Everyone in the office left at five, but in my new contract I'm not allowed to leave until Andre does or he specifically dismisses me for the day. So, I find myself yawning, wanting nothing more than to stop by my favorite ramen place on the way home to pick up dinner and snuggle under my comforter and watch *Friends*.

Looking across the corridor into Andre's office, I find him with his back to me, his phone propped against his ear. He's been on the phone for almost an hour, and it doesn't seem like he's hanging up any time soon.

"Screw it," I mutter, getting to my feet to head to the break room.

I never normally drink coffee so late, and I know I should probably be limiting my intake with the pregnancy, but it's either caffeine or falling asleep at my desk.

I turn on the Nespresso machine and hunt through the cupboards in search of a clean mug. There's just enough oat milk left in the fridge for a small cappuccino, so I empty the carton into the milk frother and switch it on. As I drop in an espresso pod and click the machine into action, heavy footsteps approach.

There is only the two of us in the office, so I don't need to turn to know who it will be.

A war rages inside me as desire to have him take me again battles the need to come out on top this time and maybe deny him, and me, of the pleasure I know is waiting if I let myself go.

He is wrong for me. A mafia boss. *My* boss. My baby's father.

He has no idea I'm carrying his child. And I have no idea how to tell him. Or even if I should.

Would he even want this baby?

The steps are so close now.

If I close my eyes, I can almost smell him.

With my eyes closed, all our shared moments play non-stop for my delight. Or maybe to torture me.

The footsteps stop behind me.

I brace my hands on the counter top, my chest heaving as I wait to hear his voice.

21

———

LILA

"A bit late for coffee, don't you think?" Andre's voice is like melted chocolate.

My eyes flutter closed as a delicious shiver runs down my spine.

"My boss likes to keep me working late." I reach for my espresso.

"Maybe it's because you're not efficient enough with your work." A jab. To try to rile me.

I shrug. "I think it's so he can get me alone in the office."

I reach for the milk frother.

His strong hand is around my wrist in an instant, halting my movements.

My breath catches as his hard body presses up against me, his erection digging into my ass.

"Why would he want to do that?" Andre's heated breath in my ear leaves me soaked.

My skin is on fire, and it takes everything in me not to moan at the feel of him pressed against me.

"I think he's obsessed with me." I push my ass out so it rubs against his cock.

Andre hisses, his other hand moving to grip my hip.

I chuckle, knowing he's moments away from losing control.

"Is that so?" he growls.

"Uh huh." I wiggle my hips a little. "I can't even make a coffee without him trying to fuck me."

Andre releases my wrist and snatches the milk frother out of my hand, slamming it down onto the counter, making me jump. He places both of his hands on my waist and spins me around to face him, his eyes wild as he stares down at me.

"What game are you trying to play, Lila?"

I keep my eyes locked with his as I reach out and graze my hand over his hard cock.

"Isn't it obvious?" I shrug. "I'm playing your game."

"Don't mess with me, princess," he rasps, his eyes flashing with need as I stroke him once more. "You'll lose every time."

"I'm ok with that."

He moves so fast I only have time to gasp before his mouth crashes against mine.

I instantly part my lips, giving him full access to my mouth, and I melt at the feeling of his tongue tangling with mine.

Andre doesn't waste any time before he wraps his hands around the back of my thighs and lifts me onto the counter, spreading my legs.

"This dress is very inappropriate for the workplace." He reaches for the zipper.

I hold my breath as he slowly starts to pull it down, my swollen, aching breasts springing free.

"Fuck, Lila. You're not wearing a bra?"

"The dress's too tight for a bra." I shrug, a smile pulling at my lips as I glance down at my heavy breasts.

The hormones have made them insanely sensitive, and just the feel of the dress against my nipples has had me wet and aching all day. I nearly stormed into Andre's office at lunchtime and begged him to fuck me against the wall just to ease the ache.

"Please tell me you're at least wearing panties." There's a pained look in his eyes as he takes in my breasts.

"There's an easy way to find out." I take hold of his wrist and pull downwards.

I can't hide the smirk as Andre pulls the zip down fully and my dress falls open, revealing my very naked pussy.

"Have I won yet?" I lick my lips.

Andre takes hold of my thighs and forces them even further apart, his eyes locked on my glistening sex.

I squirm under his gaze, the cold granite of the counter feeling so good against my hot skin.

"Fuck me, Andre."

Andre looks up at me, and I moan at the look on his face.

There's nothing but feral need in his eyes as he reaches for his belt.

When his cock is free, I'm practically panting with need, my pussy clenching around nothing as he strokes himself.

"Baby, you're the one who's begging to be fucked. Not me." He smirks.

I respond by wrapping my ankles around his waist and pulling him closer.

He chuckles, the sound making my skin pebble as he lines himself up with my entrance.

"Tell me I've won, and you can have my cock."

I scowl, but my hips buck as he teases my entrance.

Fuck, I need him so badly I could scream. I can't get enough, and despite being sore for a few days from how hard he took me on Friday, I still want more.

"Come on, Lila." He pumps himself once more.

I watch in awe as the tip of his cock becomes slick with his arousal.

My mouth waters, and I know I'm entirely at his mercy.

"You won," I moan as my head falls back against the cabinet, and Andre sinks himself inside me.

He doesn't waste any time, getting into a hard and fast rhythm that has us both moaning and groaning.

I lift my hips up and meet each of his thrusts, the angle so perfect that he grazes my inner walls with his cock.

My eyes roll as he pounds into me, and I can't help but reach between our bodies to rub my clit.

"Fucking hell, Lila."

I arch my back, pushing my breasts up, and he answers my silent plea by taking my right nipple between his teeth.

I gasp at the pain, but then he wraps his lips around the sensitive bud and sucks.

"More," I moan, arching into his touch.

Andre moves to my other breast, as his fingers sink into my hips, pulling me harder against him as he fucks me.

I'm already close, my clit throbbing as I work it harder.

I wrap my other hand around Andre's neck and hold him against me, craving the heat and weight of his body against mine.

I love the rough sex, especially with how out of control my hormones have been. But part of me also wants to feel cherished.

I know I shouldn't, but knowing that I have his baby growing inside me has me wanting so much more than a quick fuck in the break room. I need the connection, but I know that if Andre were to find out, he might not hang around.

It means it will hurt even more when the sex is over, and he walks away again. So, for right now, I'm going to make the most of being close to him, in whatever way he'll let me.

"Andre," I murmur in his ear as my orgasm starts to build.

I tighten my ankles around his waist, my thighs shaking as my release threatens to take me over the edge.

"I've got you, baby," he whispers against my skin, grazing his teeth over the sensitive flesh between my neck and shoulder.

I arch against him, crying out with pleasure as I come.

Andre wraps an arm around my waist and slams into me, his heavy pants filling my ears and making me shiver.

My orgasm barely finishes before another one builds, and I furiously rub my clit, desperate to come again.

"Another one already?" Andre murmurs against my shoulder, his breath tickling my skin and making me moan.

"Yes," I practically growl as the frustration grows.

I dig my heels into Andre's ass, wanting him to move inside me faster, harder.

He doesn't hold back, his cock slamming into me so hard a flash of pain hits me before transforming into the most glorious pleasure.

I know he's close as his teeth sink into my skin, his pants turning to grunts.

The sounds are music to my ears, and to know my body makes him feel this way is addictive.

He moves his hand up to cup my face, tilting my chin up to look him in the eyes.

"Come with me," he demands, his dark eyes filled with

such hunger my thighs start to shake with release. "Now, Lila."

A strangled sound escapes me as I come once more, my pussy clenching so hard around Andre's cock that he instantly spills inside me as his expression turns to one of pure ecstasy.

I can't stop the smile that tugs at my lips as his eyes close as he comes down from the high.

I take his face in my hands and press a soft kiss to his lips.

So many words threaten to spill out of my mouth as I look at Andre, the post-orgasm bliss making me want to confess all the feelings I've been ignoring. But thankfully, his phone rings, and he's immediately pulling himself free from me and reaching into his pants pocket.

"Fuck." He glances at the screen. "I have to go."

I open my mouth to reply, but Andre's already tucking himself back into his pants and heading for the door, leaving me naked on the granite countertop as if I'm nothing more than a discarded toy whose owner has outgrown.

He was right, he won again. But that is not the problem. The problem is that I'm starting to think there is no way I'll ever get out of this little game unharmed.

I never expected to be in this position again, but Andre has more power than I ever anticipated. And willingly or not, I will be the one crushed when all is said and done. Because as much as I tried to avoid it, my heart became somehow involved.

Now I just need to decide how much of it I'm willing to risk.

22

———

ANDRE

"WHAT THE FUCK DO YOU MEAN, ROSA IS MISSING?" I stalk outside the office to my car.

Marco sounds desperate. "She hasn't come home from school."

"Where the hell is Xander?" I reach into my pocket for the keys to my Mercedes. "He's meant to be with her."

"He dropped her off at school, and then I sent him on a few errands regarding Sergio."

I tighten my grip on my phone, fighting the urge to launch it across the street.

"Why the *fuck* would you do that?"

"She had gone inside the fucking building, Andre. There's no way in hell Lorenzo would storm in there and take her. She was safe."

"Clearly, she fucking wasn't!"

I ignore the concerned looks of bystanders as I unlock my car and climb into the driver's seat, pressing the ignition and letting the engine roar to life. "He is meant to be watching her *at all times*. Find someone else to do your dirty work. We have plenty of lackeys desperate to kiss your ass if it means getting in our good books."

"I trusted Xander the most with this—"

"*Enough*, Marco. If something has happened to Rosa, it's on you, not Xander." I let out a long breath. "So, what do we know?"

"Xander called when she didn't show up at six, wondering if volleyball practice ran over, but the coach said she never showed. Apparently, you called up this morning and said she would be missing practice today."

"I did *what*?" My fists clench around the wheel as I pull away from the curb.

"That's what I thought..."

The screen on my dashboard flashes with an incoming call from Xander.

"Stay on the line, Marco."

I push the button to answer the call, narrowly dodging a yellow cab. "Yes?"

"I've tracked Rosa's phone to the Westchester mall, sir. I'm on my way ther—"

"No, I'll deal with this. Meet us back at the house."

"Yes, sir." Xander hangs up.

I click back through to Marco and grind my teeth as I realize what my sister has done.

"She's at the fucking *mall*."

"Of course, she is." Marco chuckles.

"There is nothing remotely funny about this Marco." I slam my hands down on the steering wheel.

"This was always going to happen, Andre. She's fifteen, for Christ's sake, she wants to go out."

"For once, can you not play devil's advocate here, Marco. Especially not when our fucking sister's life is on the line!"

My brother lets out a sigh.

"Fine. Do you want me to go collect her?"

"No, I'm already on route. I'll meet you back at the house." I disconnect the call.

My hands are shaking the entire drive out of the city toward the Westchester Mall.

I send Rosa a text telling her to meet me outside in thirty minutes. The message comes back as read, but she doesn't bother to reply.

Fine. If she wants to be like that, so be it.

I load up the tracking app on my dashboard so I can make sure she doesn't wander off anywhere else. I try to ignore the feeling of dread that Lorenzo might have planted her phone at the mall to distract us.

"She's safe," I repeat to myself the entire drive out of the city.

The mall is packed with students looking to blow off some steam after classes.

I drive across the entire parking lot and park outside the entrance, scanning the sea of navy and white uniforms for Rosa. I spot her almost instantly, sitting on a bench with her friends, slushy in one hand and an armful of bags in the other.

When she spots the car, she rolls her eyes and gets to her feet, waving goodbye to her friends.

I grind my teeth together, my eyes never leaving her as she takes her time walking over to the car. I lean over and open the passenger door and she slides in, tossing her purchases onto the back seat.

"Shut the door." My voice shakes with rage.

She sighs, slamming the door shut and leaning back in the plush leather seat, taking a long slurp of her slushy.

I wait to speak until we're back onto the highway, heading out of the main city.

"Would you like me to remind you of the conditions of our deal?" I keep my eyes forward on the road.

"I went to the mall. Jeez, Andre—"

"You did not just *go to the mall*," I snap. "I gave you clear rules and boundaries to keep you safe, Rosa, and you broke those rules."

"It was Haley's birthday, we wanted to get food—"

"I don't give a shit why you did it." My jaw hurts from clenching it so hard, but I do my best to keep a lid on my anger.

I don't want to scare my sister into obeying me. I'm not my father. But she needs to understand the severity of her actions.

"It won't happen again," she mutters, sipping her slushy.

"You're damn right it won't because I'm pulling you out of school."

"WHAT?" Rosa turns in her seat.

Her glare on me almost physically burns, but I keep my eyes forward. "There's literally only two weeks left! Come *on*, Andre, I have varsity games and homecoming—"

"Not anymore. And don't even think about summer camp."

"Are you trying to ruin my life? I didn't skip school to do drugs or get wasted. I went to the *mall*. Scratch that, I didn't even skip my classes, I skipped one volleyball practice!"

"I don't care what you skipped or where you went. You broke the rules, and I warned you this would be the consequence."

"Fuck you," Rosa spits. "You're an asshole. You can't treat me like a child, I'm fifteen."

"You want me to treat you like an adult?" I yell at her. "Try fucking acting like one."

"You should trust me," she yells, her voice thick with tears.

"And you should trust me! Yet, you purposefully disobey." I blow out a breath.

"Look. I do trust you, Rosa." I run a hand through my hair. "It's everyone else I don't trust."

ROSA IS QUIET FOR THE REST OF THE DRIVE BACK TO the house. I'm glad because I'm too caught up in my own thoughts to have the energy to argue with her. All I can think about is what Lorenzo could have done if he got his hands on her...

"Go to your room," I order her as I park the car in the garage.

She doesn't even bother getting her bags from the backseat, choosing to storm past the row of supercars and disappearing through the door that leads to the kitchen.

I sit in silence for a moment, letting my body calm down. It was already on edge after fucking Lila in the breakroom, and now this...

"Fuck." I lean back, closing my eyes for a moment.

Every muscle in my body is tense, and I instantly think of Lila. How in this moment I want nothing more than to have her straddling my lap, bouncing up and down on my cock. The feeling of spilling inside her would definitely take the edge off.

I curse myself.

How can I give Rosa a hard time for breaking the rules when I did the same today? I knew Lila was trying to taunt me, to get me to break. And it fucking worked.

That *dress*. My cock had been rock solid all day, and I snapped.

My fingers itch to touch her again, to drive straight to her apartment in the city and storm through the door and pin her against the wall, the door, the bed.

"I'm losing my goddamn mind."

I force myself to get out of the car before I make another stupid decision.

The kitchen is empty, with no sign of Marco either. He's likely in his own study on the other side of the house.

I have no interest in talking to him either, so I head up the stairs toward my office.

It grates on my nerves when Marco doesn't side with me when it comes to matters regarding our sister. I hate always being the bad guy, but he's young and still has a lot to learn.

I never signed up to play the guardian role, it's not something I was interested in. Even with Valentina, I was hesitant to bring children into our world, knowing that they'd likely have a target on their head from the moment they took their first breath.

How could I do that to an innocent child? It would make me just as much a monster.

The moment I close the door to my office, I pour myself a scotch and take a seat behind my desk, switching on my computer and opening up my security app.

I quickly check all the cameras in the house, noting Rosa pacing around her room on the phone.

She looks pissed, but I'd rather have her mad at me and alive, than dead.

Marco's in the main living room, also with a scotch in hand as he works from his laptop.

I move on to the penthouse apartment in the city, and to the cameras at Mason's International. Everything is as it should be.

I'm about to switch over to my emails when I notice a new folder named *Lila* in the app.

23

ANDRE

I HOLD MY BREATH AS I CLICK ON THE FOLDER NAMED *Lila* and find four new camera feeds.

"Quick work," I mutter, impressed by my security guy's swiftness.

I asked him last night if he would be able to install a few cameras in Lila's apartment so I could keep an eye on her at all times. I was expecting the job to take at least forty-eight hours, but there she is, lying in her bed, eating a bowl of ramen.

I click through all four cameras, getting the full layout of her small apartment. If you can even call it that. It's more of a large room with a bathroom.

I maximize the feed that shows her bed and lean back in my chair, taking a sip of my scotch.

Fuck, she's beautiful. She's wearing an oversized T-shirt, her toned legs stretched out in front of her, and her hair loose around her shoulders. She's watching something on her laptop, a smile tugging at her lips as she eats.

Part of me aches to be beside her, enjoying her company. Laughing at a show together as we eat in bed.

I haven't had that in so long, and didn't realize it was something I was missing.

Until Lila.

I quickly shut off the camera, not letting the thought develop. I have more important things to think about, like what the hell I'm going to do with my sister.

Knowing I have access to Lila at the touch of a button has me on edge, but I choose to reward myself with a glimpse of her after I've worked for a few hours.

I'm trying to put through the paperwork to change the name of Mason's International. It's my fucking company, it should have my name on the door. But it's not an easy task. It requires changing everything from our logo, domain names and email addresses, down to our stationery. The board will want to hold off, considering it's such an expense, but I'm willing to put the money down for it.

I have a call with Kyle, my private investigator. I need him to look into some of Rosa's friends, to ensure they're not being bribed for information by Lorenzo. They're teenagers and easily tricked, and I'm not willing to compromise Rosa's safety.

If she knew I was vetting her friends, she would lose her mind, but it's for her own good.

Around nine, a knock sounds at my door, and I let out a sigh, expecting it to be Marco, but it's not.

Rosa's head peeks in. "Have you got a minute?"

I get to my feet and signal for her to take a seat on the leather couch.

She shuffles inside, wearing sweats and her varsity jumper, her hair piled on top of her head. She's wiped off her makeup and her eyes are red rimmed, as if she's been crying. The sight of her like this has my anger flickering out as I perch on the arm of the sofa.

"I don't enjoy doing this to you. I hope you know that, Rosa."

She nods, tucking her legs up underneath her. She doesn't look at me, but I know she's taking in everything I'm saying.

"We're doing our best to handle this situation as quickly as we can, but we can't afford to make any rash decisions or any wrong moves."

She nods again, wiping her cheeks on her sleeve.

"This isn't forever, I promise." I move to sit beside her.

I reach for her hand and she takes it. I squeeze three times, and she finally looks at me.

"Why do you get caught up in all this, Andre?" she whispers.

"Trust me, it's not by choice." I lean back, folding an ankle over my knee.

"Is it just about money?"

I shake my head.

"Then what is it about?"

I let out a long breath and look at my sister.

"It's about justice, Rosa."

"Is it worth potentially dying over?"

"Yes."

"Is it worth *me* potentially dying over?"

My chest aches as I look into my sister's eyes.

"Nothing is worth that, Rosa. Don't think for one second I would ever risk your life, or Marco's. You're my family, my *everything*, and I will do whatever it takes to keep you safe."

Rosa is quiet for a moment before she gets to her feet.

"You're not going to try and convince me to let you go back to school?" I tease, trying to lighten her mood.

"You're more stubborn than I am. I don't like fighting

fights I'm already primed to lose." She forces a smile.

"Try and get some sleep." I get to my feet, walking her to the door. "We can talk more tomorrow." I press a kiss to her hair.

She nods and walks away, her shoulders hunched.

I try to ignore the growing feeling of guilt as I shut the door and turn the key in the lock. It's for her own good, I keep reminding myself.

I decide to pour myself another scotch and open up Lila's cameras once more before I head to bed myself.

It's almost ten, and when I click to the camera over her bed, I smile to find her asleep, the covers pulled up high around her neck, her dark hair fanned out over her pillow.

I settle back in my chair and watch her for a moment, letting the scotch warm my throat as I slowly sip it.

Just when I'm about to close down the app and head to bed, she tosses her head from side to side, her hair tangling around her face.

I sit up a little straighter.

Her eyes fly open, as if she can sense me watching her, and she runs her hands over her face.

"Can you not sleep, sweetheart?" I whisper, a smile tugging on my lips.

I've seen that look on her face before. It's the very look she gives me when I deny her pleasure.

I lean forward, my blood heating as I watch her squirm beneath the covers.

Her eyes are screwed shut, as if she's trying to fight the arousal that's coursing through her body.

"Come on, baby. Let's have some fun." I lick my lips.

She throws the covers off, and I'm more than delighted to find the oversized T-shirt has been removed, revealing her very naked body to me.

I let out a groan at the sight of her, my cock instantly hardening in my pants as I take in her full breasts, the luscious curve of her ass and thighs.

"Spread those legs for me, Lila." I palm my erection through my trousers.

She rubs her thighs together, her hands out to the sides, as if she's not wanting to give into her urges.

But I know it's me she's thinking of right now, me that's got her so worked up. I know I'm just as much under her skin as she is mine. Why else would she wear that fucking dress today if not to get me to fuck her. Her breasts were practically springing free from the material, and to realize she had not worn panties all day...

The thought has me reaching for my zipper, desperate to release my cock.

I shudder as I take my throbbing length in my hand and begin stroking it, the tip already glistening.

Lila is still writhing on the bed, but her hands have moved to her stomach.

"Come on, baby. Show me how you touch yourself." I run my thumb over the bead of arousal.

Her back arches off the bed, and her thighs fall open.

My hips buck at the sight of her pussy, and when her hand moves to start rubbing her clit, I have to bite back a groan.

Her movements are hurried, as if she's already close to climaxing.

"Someone's very worked up." I chuckle, pumping myself harder.

She wastes no time pumping two fingers inside herself as her other hand tweaks her nipples.

My mouth waters, wanting to suck on those tits until

she's crying out my name. My spine already tingles, and my balls tighten as I watch her ride her hand.

Fuck. I wish I was inside her right now. To know she's still not fully satisfied leaves me feeling unsettled. I want to fuck her until she's limp with pleasure.

I *need* to feel her coming around my cock.

"Lila," I groan as I lift my hips, tightening my grip on my cock.

She kneads her breasts once more before moving to rub her clit, her other hand still fingering her glistening pussy. There's such agony on her face as she chases her release, as if she knows this won't satisfy her.

Only I will.

My cock feels as if it's about to burst, but I want to come with her.

I know Lila's close by the way her chest is rising and falling rapidly, her breasts bouncing as she rides her hand.

She's quickening her pace as she rubs her clit, her eyebrows pulled together as her mouth falls open.

"That's it, sweetheart."

As if she can hear me, her legs start shaking, and her back arches even further off the bed. "Come for me, Lila," I moan, working my cock so hard it's almost painful.

Her back bows off the bed, nothing but pure ecstasy on her face as she comes.

I grunt as my cock spills all over my hand, but I continue stroking it, getting every last drop out as I watch Lila ride out her orgasm.

She's so fucking beautiful, and I collapse against my chair, panting as I watch her slowly slide her fingers out of her pussy.

"You've made a mess of me, Lila Morano." I look down at my lap. "And you have no idea."

24

LILA

I tap my foot against the linoleum floor as I wait for my name to be called. The waiting room at the OBGYN's office is filled with pregnant women with huge bellies, looking exhausted and swollen. But many of them have their partners at their sides, rubbing their hands on their bumps and looking blissfully happy.

My chest aches as I glance at the empty seat beside me.

I sit on my hands to stop myself from picking at my nails. I've been a wreck all morning, but thankfully, Andre has been pretty busy with meetings.

I honestly thought when he bought this company, it would be more of a vanity project, and he'd only show up for a day or two. But it's clear I was wrong.

He's always the first one in and the last one out, which means I have to be the same now I'm his assistant.

It also means I have to clear all appointments with him first, and there was no way in hell I was telling him about my ultrasound.

He thinks I'm at the dentist, and I will continue using that excuse until my belly pops.

Although I'm surprised he hasn't put two and two together. Perhaps he just thinks I'm just naturally super horny because he's continued fucking me after hours for the last two weeks, against every possible surface in the office.

It's now Friday, and I'm starting to wince when I walk from how hard he's taking me. But I can't get enough.

Even when I get home, I'm having to pleasure myself in order to fall asleep because all I can think about is sex with Andre.

He's still leaving almost immediately after we finish, but I'm glad. It's tricking my mind into thinking this is only a physical relationship, because facing the reality of him not wanting anything more is too hard.

Then again, being alone waiting for an appointment with the obstetrician, about to see my baby for the first time, is a pretty harsh reality.

I never imagined that when I got pregnant, I would be doing this alone.

I keep my eyes down, not wanting to look at all the happy couples. Cassi did offer to come with me, but I didn't want her to get in trouble at work. She's coming over later with pizza so I can share all my news with someone at least.

There's no way I'm ready to tell Aunt Maria yet. Not until I figure out what the hell I'm going to do about Andre.

If I don't tell him, I'll have to leave before he figures it out. There's no other way. We've been fucking enough, and oral contraceptives don't always work. He'd put two and two together, and I can't stand the idea that he might force me to get rid of this baby.

"Lila Morano?"

I glance up and find Dr. Waite smiling at me.

He must be in his late fifties, with graying hair and kind eyes.

I get to my feet, my legs shaking as I wipe my sweaty palms on my dress.

"Yes, that's me." I cross the waiting room.

I follow Dr. Waite down a corridor until we get to his office.

"I'm going to need you to remove your underwear and take a seat on the chair for me, ok?" he says.

"Uh, ok."

He smiles at me, pulling a curtain around the chair to give me some privacy.

I kick off my flats and reach beneath my dress to remove my underwear. I opted for something more flowy rather than the skin tight number I wore the other day. Though I don't think it would make much difference what I wore right now. From the heated looks Andre gives me when I'm near, I know I could be wearing a garbage bag and he'd still bend me over his desk and fuck me.

My cheeks redden. I shouldn't be having such thoughts in the OB's office.

I slide onto the chair, the blue paper rustling beneath me, and pull the modesty cover over my lower half.

"All done," I say.

Dr. Waite pulls back the curtain and takes a seat on the rolling stool.

"Ok. So, today we're going to do a trans-vaginal ultra-sound," he explains. "Because you expect you're only around eight weeks along, correct?"

"Yes."

My ears are ringing as I watch him pick up a long probe and cover it with a condom and some gel.

I'm gripping the edges of the chair so tightly my knuckles are turning white.

"No need to be nervous. This won't hurt a bit. Please,

place your ankles together and let your knees fall open for me."

I lean back, looking up at the ceiling as I open my legs. I wince as I feel the ultrasound wand be inserted.

"You're doing great."

I nod, my eyes pricking with tears. Not from the pain, but from the fact that I have no one beside me to hold my hand.

"Ok, let's see what's going on," Dr. Waite mutters as he turns on the monitor beside us.

I watch, hardly daring to breathe as a black and white image appears on the screen.

He continues to move the wand around, not saying anything as he watches the monitor.

"Is everything ok?" My heart is starting to pound in my chest. "There is a baby, right?"

He chuckles.

"Yes, there's a baby. Look." He turns the monitor toward me, pointing to a tiny blob on the screen. "Right there."

My breath catches.

"That's...my baby?" I whisper.

"It sure is." He smiles. "I'm just going to do a few measurements to determine your due date, and then we can listen for the heartbeat."

My eyes glass over as I watch the screen, in complete awe of the tiny blob.

How can that little bean turn into a fully-formed human in only a matter of months? It's both incredible and terrifying at the same time.

"Ok, here's the heartbeat." Dr. Wait presses a few buttons on the keyboard, and suddenly I hear a soft thumping noise.

"Oh, my god." I cover my mouth as I listen.

"A very special moment." He smiles at me. "I'm just going to print off a picture for you, and then we'll finish up.

By the time I'm getting dressed, my cheeks are damp with tears.

"I'd like to see you again in four weeks for another scan." He hands me the ultrasound picture.

"Thank you so much." I sniffle, smiling, my vision blurry from crying.

"You're most welcome."

I wipe my eyes as I walk back toward the waiting room, clutching the picture to my chest the entire time.

After I book another appointment, I head outside and call Cassi.

"How did it go?"

"I heard the heartbeat." My voice cracks.

"Woah! That's amazing!"

"It is," I sob, looking at the picture again. It barely resembles a baby, but I can make out the head and an arm. "It's so real now."

"I can't wait to see the picture."

"I'm so glad I have you, Cassi."

"You'll always have me, Lils," she says. "I have to go back to work, but I'll see you in a few hours, okay?"

I hang up the phone and start the walk back to the office. I have no idea how I'm meant to act normal for the rest of the day, but I can't suddenly call in sick. It would only make Andre more suspicious.

Andre.

I heard our child's heartbeat today, and he has no idea it even exists.

A wave of guilt floods me, and I almost cave and call him.

But I realize it's because I crave what I witnessed in the

waiting room today. A partner, someone to hold my hand through this life-changing process.

I know I have Cassi, and eventually my aunt will come around, but they won't be sitting up with me at all hours of the night as I feed the baby or help pick out a pre-school or teach it to walk.

I'll be doing this alone.

And I need to start reminding myself of that.

As I start the twenty-minute walk back to the office, I keep one hand on my abdomen, lost in thoughts about my childhood.

When my mother was in this position, she had no idea that the very life she was growing would be the one to take hers.

I did that. I took her life.

What if the same thing happens to me?

The thought of leaving this child without a mother has my heart cracking open.

Who would take care of it?

Maria already took me in, and I always felt as if she resented me for it. I know my dad blamed me for the fact that mom died. It haunted him to be around me, and eventually he bailed.

I have no reason to believe that Andre wouldn't do the same.

There is an actual life growing inside me, and yet I've never felt more alone.

25

———

ANDRE

Lila's lying.

She's been acting strange all morning, barely looking at me. As if my presence is causing her physical pain.

"I'm off to my dentist appointment." She appears in the doorway to my office. "I'll be back at two."

I nod, watching her with narrowed eyes.

She doesn't look me in the eye, and her body is angled away from me. It's the exact opposite of how she's been for the past few weeks. She's been nothing but a tease, constantly getting me so riled up that we end up fucking on my desk, or hers, or on the floor of the breakroom like animals. We can't get enough of each other's bodies, but that's been as far as it goes.

The moment we finish, I walk away, and so does she.

I don't want to give her any inclination that I think about her beyond sex. It complicates things too much.

So, the fact that she seems almost ashamed right now has me on alert.

Is she meeting someone for lunch? Is that why she's seeming so off?

Anger flares, and I fight the urge to demand she stay here, regardless of an appointment.

"I'll have my phone on me if anything urgent comes up," she adds before disappearing from sight.

I wait for Lila's soft footsteps to disappear down the hall until I get to my feet.

I won't accept her lying to me, even if it's nothing important. I want to know what she gets up to at every minute of the day, so I grab my phone and keys and stalk out of the office.

By the time I'm descending the steps outside the building, she's already crossing the street.

I keep a safe distance from her, not wanting to give myself away.

How am I meant to explain the fact that I'm following her without spooking her? She's still under the impression that all I want from her is sex, and I intend to keep it that way.

She heads down East 73rd street. We walk for about six blocks before she turns right and stops outside an obstetricians office.

I stop dead in my tracks as I watch her walk inside.

My blood runs cold. There is no way this is what it looks like because if it is...

Lila's pregnant.

I know from the very first time we met that she hadn't even dated anyone in the year since her last breakup, let alone slept with anyone. And I've had eyes on her ever since we hooked up that night almost two months ago.

I know I'm right. Why else would she go to an OB clinic? There's no question.

As there is no question the baby is mine.

I fight the urge to storm in after her and demand to know what the fuck she's playing at. How could she keep something like this from me?

I see nothing but red.

I claw at my hair, a pained sound escaping my lips as I pace up and down the street opposite the OB's office.

This can't be happening.

This can't be happening.

I can't be a father.

I can't risk having something else that can be taken from me.

Valentina flashes in my mind, and I almost sink to my knees in the middle of the street as the deepest agony pierces my heart.

This was *never* supposed to happen.

My body is shaking with rage as I wait across the street for Lila to come back outside. Half an hour later, she appears, her cheeks tear stained, clutching a picture to her chest.

I swallow back the bile that's risen in my throat as I watch her gaze at the photo I *know* is of our baby.

I'm torn between storming over there and demanding answers, or letting her walk away.

Has she not told me because she's scared I'll tell her to get rid of it? Or does she plan on walking away and raising this child alone? Is the thought of being tied to me for the next eighteen years so terrible?

Fuck, my mind is racing.

It's clear that neither myself nor Lila are in the right frame of mind to discuss this right now, but that doesn't stop me from wanting answers.

Thankfully, I'm familiar with the doctor who owns this

practice, so I wait until Lila is around the corner before crossing the road and storming inside.

"Is Dr. Waite with a patient right now?" I lean on the reception counter.

The receptionist's eyes widen as she takes in the fury in my eyes, but she shakes her head.

"Wonderful."

"Sir, wait!" She gets to her feet, but I'm already storming down the corridor and throwing open the door to Richard's office.

It crashes against the wall, and Richard jumps up from behind his desk, fear flashing across his face as he looks at me.

"I suggest you start talking about Lila Morano."

"Andre—"

"Is she pregnant? How far along?"

It's all I need to know if the baby is mine. But I can see that Richard isn't going to give up the information easily.

"Please, take a seat." He gestures to the uncomfortable-looking plastic chair before him.

"I don't plan on staying."

"Andre." He clasps his hands together. "I'm afraid I can't share patient information with you. It's against the rules."

"I think you'll find that you can, given what I can share if you refuse my demand." I step toward him. "If you need reminding of the illegal procedures that take place here after hours..."

"Andre—"

"The money's under the table, correct? To fuel your gambling addiction? I'm sure your wife would be very interested to learn where her kids' college funds have disappeared too..."

"You wouldn't," he breathes, his face paling.

"Oh, I would." I let a feral smile tug at my lips. "So, I suggest you start talking."

"She came in for an ultrasound. Baby is healthy, strong heartbeat—"

"How far along?"

"Eight weeks."

Fuck.

The breath seems to leave my lungs as my fear is confirmed.

"That's all I needed." I turn my back on Dr. Waite. "And don't even think about mentioning this little conversation to Lila. Trust me, I'll know." I storm out of the office.

Once I'm outside, even the fresh air does little to satisfy the ache in my lungs.

Lila is pregnant with my child. And she kept it from me.

I can't face her at the office. I'll say something I'm bound to regret, and she's clearly in a fragile place right now.

Not that I'm much better. Fuck.

How long has she known? And I haven't been gentle with her in our after-hour "sessions".

Does that even matter? What am I supposed to do?

I never wanted children because they are targets for my enemies, but I was never in this position before.

That is my baby Lila is carrying. *Mine.*

I was already wrapped around her sexy finger, obsessed with her, but knowing she is pregnant with my child?

Fuck me, I'll be feral if someone even looks at her funny.

But more than that, I'm pissed that she kept this from me.

Why?

I'm going around in circles in my head, no answers just more and more questions.

So, no matter how badly I want to punish her for lying to me, how badly I need these answers, I pull my phone out of my pocket and call Marco.

He answers after the first ring.

"How do you fancy a little old-fashioned shootout?"

I SEND AN OUT-OF-OFFICE EMAIL TO LILA AS I MAKE the walk to my penthouse apartment on the Upper West Side. I was hoping the walk would help clear my head, but it only gives me more time to dwell on the fact that Lila is carrying my child.

I furiously check my inbox the entire way to see if Lila has dared to ask me where I've gone, but she stays quiet.

That only angers me more.

Marco is already waiting for me in my office when I get to the penthouse, tucking a gun into the inside pocket of his jacket as I walk in.

"You look pissed, what did Rosa do now?" He's wearing dark slacks and a matching shirt, his dark hair neatly styled.

"Rosa did nothing, and I don't want to talk about it." I head to the safe under my desk. After unlocking it, I pull out a gun and a spare magazine, along with a six-inch knife. I tuck the knife into my jacket along with the spare magazine, and keep the gun in the waistband of my pants.

"You sure?"

"I'm sure," I grunt, storming over to my liquor cabinet and taking a shot of scotch straight from the bottle.

"So, what's the plan here?"

"We head over to *The Vault* and have a good time."

"And by good time, you don't mean liquor and pussy." Marco chuckles, reaching for the bottle in my hand and taking a swig.

"No, little brother, I do not."

26

ANDRE

I give Jerry a call as we head down into the garage. "Meet us there in fifteen minutes, and bring Dez and Sloan with you."

"Yes, boss."

That's why I like Jerry. He's loyal as fuck and never questions my motives. He just does as he's told and doesn't leave a trail.

"It's a little early to be heading over there, don't you think?" Marco and I walk over to the blacked-out Hummer.

"This needs to be done, now." I grab the key from the lock box and unlock the car.

As I'm about to slide into the driver's seat, Marco puts his hand on the car door and slams it shut.

"What the hell?"

"I wasn't going to ask, but I'm worried you're going to do something stupid."

"Stick to your original plan, Marco, and don't ask," I growl, knocking his hand from the door.

Marco ignores me, refusing to move out of my way.

"Has this got anything to do with a chick named Lila?"

"How the *fuck* do you know about Lila?"

Marco drops his hand from the door and folds his arms across his chest, shaking his head.

"Fuck's sake, Andre. You're getting this worked up over some chick? I've not seen you like this since Val—"

I whirl on Marco, grabbing him by the collar and slamming him against the car.

"I suggest if you value your life, you keep her name from your lips, you hear me?" I lift him away from the car and slam him back against it.

He heaves as the breath leaves his lungs, but there's challenge in my brother's eyes.

"Now, I'm not going to ask you again. How do you know about Lila?"

I step close to Marco until our noses are practically touching, but there's no fear in his eyes.

We're evenly matched, but that doesn't stop me from putting him in his place when he needs reminding of who's in charge.

"I saw the emails to Kyle when I was having him look into Sergio."

"You went through my emails?"

"I used your computer at the penthouse the other week when I contacted Kyle. I didn't realize they were part of a chain."

"And you didn't realize you were emailing him from my account?" I tighten my grip on Marco, fighting the urge to beat the shit out of him for invading my privacy like that.

Marco scoffs. "I was more concerned with the information on Sergio rather than what address was being used, Andre."

"There was no need for you to go back through those messages."

"I thought you were hiding something from me, and it's clear you have been. You've been acting weird, like you're a grenade about to explode at any second."

"I am not required to share everything with you." I push him against the car before releasing my grip.

I take a step back, running my hands through my hair.

"You are when it causes you to make potentially idiotic decisions. You're sending us into a shootout with Lorenzo because you're throwing a tantrum. Let me guess, she didn't call you back?"

My gun is out in an instant, and I click the safety off.

Marco only grins at me, holding his hands up in mock surrender.

"You're like a dog marking his fucking territory. It's *pathetic*," Marco spits out.

"You don't know anything about it, and I suggest this is the last time you bring it up unless you want me to put a bullet in your skull."

"Fucking hell, Andre. I'll drop it." Genuine concern flashes in his eyes. "But seriously, you need to get control over this situation, quick, before you do something stupid."

It's too late for that.

"Get in the car." I pocket my gun.

Marco is silent on the ride over to the club.

My mind feels even more chaotic as I navigate the busy New York streets.

The fact that Marco could so easily access information about Lila... The more people who know about her means the more risk to her life.

I know I would never break under interrogation by Lorenzo if he ever managed to get his hands on me, but Marco or Kyle or even Dr. Waite?

I can't risk any more people knowing, *especially* now that she's pregnant.

I want to trust my brother. I really do. And under normal circumstances, I wouldn't question him. But something about Lila and this baby makes me not see straight.

I'm hoping I can clear my head by taking out a few of Lorenzo's men, reminding him that we're not to be messed with.

We park a few streets over from *The Vault*.

Jerry, Dez, and Sloan are already waiting for us, and they climb into the back of the Hummer as we discuss the plan.

Jerry looks at me. "I don't think the place opens until ten."

"I'm well aware." My jaw is sore from clenching it. "But I know he has his men in there at all hours of the day. The place is a front for money laundering, so it's likely they'll be down in the basement."

Sloan nods. "We taking out all of them, boss?"

Marco's grinning like a Cheshire cat. "I think we should leave at least one, don't you?"

I glance sidelong at him.

"It only takes one man to send a message. I say we carve the words into his chest."

Dez chuckles, loading his gun. "This is why I like working for your guys. There's much more...creative freedom."

"We aim to please." Marco smirks, loading his own gun.

"Cover your tracks, and leave the messaging to me, got it?" I'm anxious to blow the lid on the rage that's been simmering inside me all day.

Three voices come at once. "Got it."

There's something about it being broad daylight that

sends a thrill rushing through me. Lorenzo wouldn't expect us now. It's not our style to be so obvious, but he's given me no choice. He's already threatening to take out my sister. If he catches wind of the fact there's a woman walking around New York carrying my heir? All hell will break loose.

"Check the exit," I hiss under my breath at Jerry.

He nods, keeping his gun close as he heads around the side of the club.

There's no one in sight, the place appearing deserted, but I know better.

Jerry makes quick work of the lock with nothing but brute force and a crowbar he pulled out the back of his pants. He quickly waves us over, and we hurry inside, making sure to keep our footsteps light and our guns locked and loaded.

"Basement's this way." Jerry tilts his head left. He's worked the rounds of most of the clubs in New York, which is why he's worth every penny I pay him. The information he offers is specific, but invaluable, especially for situations such as this.

I follow close behind him as we head past the bathrooms and down a flight of stairs.

Jerry glances over his shoulder at me and nods.

Muffled voices come from a bit ahead, and I hold up three fingers to Marco, Dez, and Sloan.

My finger itches to squeeze the trigger, and the adrenaline coursing through my body is clearing my mind. This is *exactly* what I needed.

Three.

Two.

One.

Jerry kicks down the door, and I'm already pulling the trigger at the two men sitting around the table in the center of the dimly lit room. Stacks of dollar bills surround them, and soon enough blood is turning the green notes red as their heads hit the table with a heavy *thump*, their mouths open in silent screams.

Marco charges past me toward a guy cowering in the corner, fumbling with a handgun.

"We'll use him!" I order Marco as I turn and find Dez and Sloan taking on the final two guys.

I duck as they stupidly try to fire at Dez, but are too panicked to aim correctly.

With two shots, they're both slumped against the wall.

I whirl toward the man Marco has pinned to the floor, his foot to the guy's throat.

I pull out my knife and stalk toward him, a smile tugging at my lips as I take in the fear in his eyes. He's gagging against the pressure on his throat, his hands scrabbling at Marco's leg, but my brother doesn't budge.

"I was hoping you could deliver a message to Lorenzo Rossi." I crouch down beside him and slice open his shirt with my blade.

He tries to kick out at me, but I move to pin his legs between my own, tracing the tip of my knife along his torso.

"And I want to ensure the message doesn't get lost in any way." I apply more pressure to my blade.

A thin sheen of sweat is coating the man's tanned skin.

"This might hurt just a little. Or maybe a lot," I add before I get to work writing my warning in blood.

27

———

LILA

"I still haven't told Andre about the baby," I mutter under my breath to Cassi as we walk back to my office after our lunch break.

"*Lila!*"

"I know," I groan, running my hands through my hair. "He's going to be so mad."

"He'll be even worse when he realizes how long you've kept this from him."

I shoot her a glare, but she shrugs.

"You should do it today. Get it over with."

"I don't know... He's been pretty quiet today. I've barely seen him all morning. He's been in a meeting with the head of the sales department since nine, so I doubt he'll want me barreling into his office declaring the that I'm having his child."

"Maybe don't do it like *that*," Cassi mutters. "Maybe it's better if you look at this in terms of the financial gain."

"What do you mean?" I glance over my shoulder to ensure no one from the office is nearby. My ice coffee is dripping down my hand, and I quickly wipe it on my dress.

"I know your insurance covered your appointment with the OB the other day, but soon enough, you'll start to dip into your own pocket for stuff. Like potentially, a bigger apartment? A deposit for a pre-school? These are all things that Andre needs to help you with."

"I don't want his money." I shake my head.

"Why?"

"Because..." *I don't trust where it's come from.* "I don't want to rely on him in case he decides to bolt."

"He might not."

"No, he could be like my dad who stuck around for the first decade but then decided to throw in the towel. I'd rather him walk away now rather than break the heart of the child I'm carrying."

Cassi sighs, rubbing my arm reassuringly.

"Well, at least we can count on this kid having a fun aunt who will take it to get its first tattoo at fourteen."

"Cassi!" I laugh.

"Tell him. Lils. He deserves to know," she says in a more serious tone.

I nod and she squeezes my arm.

"Let me know how it goes."

I hurry back into the office, nervous and on edge as I head across the main floor.

I glance down, not having realized that my hand was rubbing at my lower abdomen.

My cheeks heat as I look around, searching for Andre.

It's almost one in the afternoon, so I assume he would have finished his meeting by now and headed out for lunch. But as I walk down our little private corridor, I glance into his office and find him sitting behind his desk with his head in his hands.

My chest tightens as I watch him so lost in his own thoughts.

Without thinking, I push open his door and walk over to his desk.

He doesn't look up as I place my coffee on the desk and move to stand beside his chair.

"Andre," I whisper, placing my hand on his shoulder.

His entire body tenses under my touch, but he makes no move to push me away.

"Look at me."

His heavy sigh fills the silence, but he turns in his chair, and I step between his legs, my arms wrapping around his neck and holding his head to my body.

His hands find my waist, and he presses a soft kiss to my stomach as I gently run my hands through his silken hair.

A deep ache fills me as I look down at Andre resting against my stomach.

This is how I imagined him to react when I told him about the baby—pulling me into his arms and pressing soft kisses to my abdomen. But he keeps pushing me away the moment we get close, and I don't want this child to be the catalyst that tears us apart forever.

So, if I have to keep it a secret a little longer purely for my selfish desires, then so be it.

I gently run my fingers along Andre's broad shoulders, then his arms, before I clasp his wrists and remove his hands from around my waist.

"Lila," Andre groans, finally lifting his eyes to meet mine.

I sink to my knees at the sight of his pained expression, wanting nothing more than to lift the shadow that is veiling him. I say nothing as I reach for his belt, my blood thrumming in my ears as I pull his cock free.

Andre grips the arms of his chair so tightly his knuckles turn white, but he makes no move to stop me as I softly run my fingertips along his length.

I'm already desperate for him, wanting to climb into his lap and sink down onto his cock, but it seems like he needs this more. So, I'll be patient, no matter how badly I ache between my thighs.

I gently brush my thumb over the tip, and Andre lets out a pained hiss.

Biting the inside of my cheek to hide my smile, I continue stroking him so softly.

From the way he shifts in his seat and how the muscles in his forearms flex, I know he's getting worked up. But I won't give in. Not yet.

"So perfect," I murmur, tightening my grip and stroking him harder.

Andre's hips buck, and I stroke him again. "I can't wait to taste you Andre."

"Fuck, Lila," Andre groans.

I glance up, and his head has fallen back against his chair, his eyes screwed shut. I marvel at the strong lines of his jaw, his cheekbones, the way his throat bobs as I work his cock harder.

A soft whimper escapes my lips as I lean forward and brush my tongue along the slick head of his cock. My eyes flutter closed at the taste of him, and I lose hold of my restraint.

I wrap my lips around him and take him so deep my eyes sting, but the deep guttural growl that comes from Andre makes me want more.

I want him to lose all control, and to release all the pent up tension in his body.

I take the base of his cock in my hand, squeezing hard as I suck.

Andre's fingers find my hair, and I moan as he fists the strands, the sharp pain making me gasp around his cock.

I let him lead, pushing my head down so I can take more of him.

Whatever he wants from me, he can take.

I swirl my tongue around the head, moaning at the salty taste as my other hand squeezes his strong thigh.

The pure strength that radiates from his body makes my pussy clench, desperate for him to fill me.

The mere thought of Andre pulling me off of him and bending my over this desk so he can finish inside me has me increasing my pace.

My movements become sloppy as I suck and lick his thick shaft while simultaneously pumping him with my hand.

Andre tugs at my hair, his breathing becoming ragged, and I know he's close from the way the tip of his cock leaks.

"Take me deeper, Lila," Andre moans, and I oblige.

I relax my throat and let him brush the back of it.

Andre's body jerks, and his restraint seems to snap.

Keeping his hand in my hair, he starts pumping himself into my mouth, groaning every time he brushes the back of my throat.

I move both of my hands to his thighs to steady myself, my eyes watering as he thrusts his hips harder, faster.

Whatever you need, Andre.

"Going to...come," Andre groans.

I sink my nails into his thighs, matching his pace as he fucks my mouth, my clit throbbing so painfully that I'm desperate to reach between my thighs to chase my own release. But Andre is so close, and I want this to only be about his pleasure.

I hollow my cheeks, suctioning my mouth around him as he thrusts, and it seems to tip Andre over the edge.

With one last hard thrust, he spills down my throat, his body shuddering as he empties himself.

I continue bobbing my head up and down, greedily sucking him until I swallow every last drop, moaning at the taste of his release on my tongue.

"Mmm..." I pull my mouth off his cock and marvel at the way it glistens. "I'm so ready for you Andre." I get to my feet, moving to lift the hem of my dress.

But Andre doesn't look at me. Instead, he hastily tucks himself back into his trousers and clears his throat.

"I have a meeting now. You should probably get back to work." He turns his chair around so that he's facing away from me.

I blink, dropping the material off my dress so that it fans around my thighs once more. I wait to see if perhaps this is him trying to tease me, to get me to beg for him to fuck me which seems to be something he enjoys. But when Andre logs onto his computer and opens up his video call, I realize there is no game to be played here.

Or rather, not one I can win.

28

———

LILA

I'm racked with shame for the entire rest of the day.

How is it that I keep throwing myself at this man when he is making it more and more clear that he is only interested in sex? What did I expect to happen? Suck his cock and then he'd offer to take me on a date where I would then reveal the fact that I'm pregnant?

If Andre was looking for something serious, he would've made a move by now. And yet, I keep taking his sexual advances as a sign that he might feel something for me, rather than seeing them for what they are. A bit of fun, a way to release some pent up sexual tension.

Maybe Cassi is right. If he's using me for my body, maybe I should use him for his money...

I stay out of Andre's way for the rest of the day, not bothering to stick around past five even though he's still in his office. I should be putting myself and my baby first, and that means going home and watching TV while eating pizza.

When I get home, I can't help but smile at the sight of

my sonogram photo that I pinned to the fridge. I press a kiss to my fingertip and gently touch the tiny bean-shaped blob on the photo.

"I can't wait to meet you," I whisper, letting myself feel excited for a moment.

Of course this is not how I planned things would go, but it feels somewhat healing to know I get to mother this child when my own mother was never given that chance. "You are so loved."

While my pizza is in the oven, I take a quick shower and pull on an oversized T-shirt, forgoing any underwear because it's too hot.

Bypassing the wine that I would normally choose to accompany my dinner, I settle for a soda and plate up my dinner, silently vowing to grab a green smoothie on the way to work tomorrow to make up for my lack of nutrients tonight.

Just as *Friends* is loading on the TV, a knock sounds at the door.

"Seriously?" I get to my feet. "Can I ever get a moment's peace?"

Throwing open the door, I let out a surprised gasp as I find Andre leaning against the doorframe, his arms folded across his chest and a deep scowl on his face.

"A-Andre?" I glance past him into the hallway. "What are you doing here? Wait. How do you know where I live?"

"You're pregnant," he growls.

My blood runs cold as I look into his eyes.

"You...know?" I whisper.

He nods, his eyes filled with contempt. "I suggest you let me inside."

My body obeys him, and I step to the side.

He turns his back to me as he closes the door, and I suddenly feel unsafe.

I press myself against the kitchen counter, glancing around for a knife or a pair of scissors—

"I wouldn't if I were you," Andre says under his breath.

I freeze, my breath catching in my throat as he turns to face me.

"What do you want?" My voice shakes.

"I want to know why you didn't *fucking tell me!*" he yells.

I flinch, my hands instinctively moving to my abdomen.

Andre clocks the movement, and his eyes narrow. "I had a right to know, Lila."

My knees are threatening to buckle beneath me.

I can't bring myself to look at Andre, to see the anger in his eyes.

"Start talking."

I shake my head, my hair falling in front of my face as tears start to run down my cheeks.

"*Lila!*"

I cover my mouth with my hand to muffle the sob that escapes my lips.

"Please," I manage to whisper. "D-don't make me get rid of it. I want nothing from you. I'm begging you, Andre—" My voice cracks, and my entire body is overcome with sadness as I look toward the fridge, at the sonogram photo pinned there.

"Is that why you didn't tell me?"

I nod, my vision blurring with tears as I look at the photo of my baby. *Our* baby.

"I wanted you to have a choice." My voice breaks.

I bow my head, hiding my face as Andre moves to stand before me.

I want nothing more than for the floor to open up and swallow me whole, to stop me from having to see such hatred in his eyes.

"Look at me, Lila."

"I can't," I whisper.

"Please." His fingers find my chin and force my gaze to his. "You lied to me. I don't take that lightly."

I frown. "I never lied."

"You didn't tell me the truth," Andre snarls, his eyes flashing.

"I was terrified you would be angry, and I was right—"

"I'm pissed, but not because of the pregnancy. Fuck, Lila." He sighs, letting go of my chin to run his hands through his hair.

His white shirt is wrinkled, the sleeves rolled up to his elbows. Images of what we did mere hours ago run through my mind, how I ran my fingers along those shoulders, those thighs, how I submitted myself to his pleasure.

"I don't want anything from you," I repeat, feeling foolish.

"I don't think that's true."

"You're free to leave, Andre." I fold my arms across my chest. "I release you from any obligations."

"I think we both know I'm anything but free when it comes to you."

"What are you talking about?" I search his face for answers.

But his features are set and cold as he regards me.

"Even if you weren't pregnant with my child, I would not be able to stay away from you, Lila."

"You can fuck any woman you want, and you'll forget all about me."

"Oh, I definitely could." His voice, low and guttural, cuts through me.

He takes a step toward me, then another, until his body is almost flush with mine.

He places his hands on the counter on either side of my body, trapping me within his arms as his eyes search mine. "But the truth is, I don't want to."

"Well, I can't just let you keep using me for my body. It hurts too much, Andre."

"Is that what you think?"

"How could I not?" I cry. "Every time we've had sex over the last few weeks, you can't leave quick enough once it's over. It's another reason why I put off telling you about the baby, because I knew you wouldn't want anything to do with it. With me."

Andre bows his head as he lets out a long breath.

I wrap my arms around my body, hating how vulnerable I feel.

"I leave because I care too much." He looks up at me under his dark lashes. "It terrifies me, Lila, how much I care for you...and this baby,"

I'm speechless. There is no way this is happening, right?

"I was scared of getting close, that you would push me away."

"Why? All I ever wanted was to get you as close as I could." My throat thickens with tears. "But I want you to have a choice. To not be tied to me because of a child you never wanted."

Andre says nothing but moves his hands to my waist and lifts me onto the counter.

"I've made my choice." He runs his hands up my thighs. "But I want to make one thing very clear, Lila."

His fingers trail up the inside of my thighs.

My breath catches as his fingers graze my pussy, brushing my clit so softly that I whimper with pleasure.

"You will never lie to me again. Do you understand?"

I nod.

"I need to hear you say it."

"I understand," I gasp, my head falling back as he dips one finger inside me.

"I'm very angry with you, Lila," he growls, adding another finger.

I clench my teeth as he slowly starts pumping his fingers inside me while his thumb works my clit.

"I know," I whimper.

"How do you think I should punish you...hm? To make sure you don't make the same mistake again?"

I squirm against the counter as my orgasm builds.

My breath is coming in heavy pants, and the anger in Andre's eyes is only turning me on more.

If this is his way of punishing me for keeping this baby a secret, I'm more than happy to endure it.

He quickens his pace, working my clit so perfectly that my thighs start to shake.

"I'm coming," I choke, grinding my hips to take his fingers even deeper.

"No, you're not." He pulls his fingers free.

I cry out at the loss of his touch, the ache between my thighs painful as my pussy clenches around nothing.

"Andre," I whimper.

His hands move to lift my shirt over my head, leaving me naked on the counter.

His eyes roam over my body before settling on my stomach. A look of devastation crosses his features as he takes me in.

"I'm so sorry." I move to cover myself with my hands. "I never meant to hurt you."

"Don't." He takes hold of my wrists, pinning them to my sides.

"There's a sonogram picture if you want to see it." I want to break this wall that's gone up between us. "It's on the fridge."

Andre's head snaps to the side, looking toward the picture, and I know the minute he sees it because his eyes widen.

"I know it's only a blob right now, but it has a strong heartbeat."

"Lila..." he breathes, turning to face me once more.

I open my mouth to offer more, but his lips crash against mine, devouring me with such need that I cling to him.

His tongue traces my lower lip, and I part my own, groaning as his tongue entangles with mine.

But then it's over.

29

LILA

ANDRE PULLS AWAY FROM ME LEAVING MY LIPS burning with the phantom touch of his.

I deserve this. I hurt him.

But then he bends down and runs his tongue along my center.

I gasp, my hands going to his hair as he finishes what he started.

It does not take long for my pleasure to build, especially when Andre starts pumping his tongue in and out of my pussy before moving to suck my clit.

"Oh god," I moan as my thighs start to shake.

Andre's fingers grip my hips tightly, and I watch him greedily devour my pussy, the sight of his tongue lapping at my clit making me cry out with pleasure.

"You can come this time, Lila," Andre murmurs before kissing my swollen bundle of nerves.

I rock against him, desperate for more, and he seems to read my body language as he sinks two fingers inside me, curling them to brush my sensitive walls as he wraps his lips around my clit.

My entire body convulses as my orgasm hits me, warmth pooling between my thighs as Andre continues to suck my clit as I ride out my pleasure.

My skin is covered in goosebumps and my limbs shake as I come down from the high.

"Come here," Andre murmurs as he gets to his feet and wraps my legs around his waist, lifting me off the counter.

I bury my face in his neck as he carries me across to my bed, savoring the closeness he's offering me.

He settles me against the pillows, pressing a soft kiss to my lips before pulling away and undressing.

I take in every muscle, every ridge of his body, the way his skin softly glows under the orange light coming in through the window.

He looks down at me. "So beautiful."

I smile shyly as I part my legs, silently inviting him to join me.

He smirks, climbing onto the bed and hovering above me.

"You're in my bed," I breathe, as I look up at Andre.

He tilts his head to the side, his dark hair falling into his eyes, a frown forming between his eyebrows. "Do you not want me in your bed?"

I take in his powerful form above me, running my hands around his broad shoulders and down his muscled back. "I want you everywhere."

He leans down and presses a soft kiss to my neck, just below my ear.

My back arches off the bed, my breasts pressing against his bare chest, and I squirm with the need for friction.

"Your wish is my command." He chuckles as he settles himself between my thighs.

I groan as his cock teases my entrance, but it soon turns

to a gasp of pleasure as he slowly thrusts into me, filling me so deliciously that my eyes roll.

"I don't think I'll ever get used to this." He pulls out and gently thrusts back in, taking his time with each movement.

I wrap my legs around his waist, clinging to his body, wanting to get as close as possible to him.

"Me neither," I whisper, burying my head in the crook of his neck, breathing in the scent of him. "It's never been like this for me before."

Andre says nothing, but presses another kiss to my jaw, and then my mouth.

The tenderness in his actions speaks louder than any words he could say, and as he sinks himself inside me, I let myself become consumed by the feeling of wholeness he gives me.

There is nothing hurried about the way he fucks me, as if he wants to savor every moan, every thrust of his cock inside me.

I close my eyes, grinding against him, letting my release build so slowly it has me whimpering with need.

Andre continues to litter my skin with kisses, exploring my neck and chest, before exploring my breasts.

"Are they tender?" He runs his thumb along the underside of my right breast.

"Yes," I moan.

"I'll be gentle, sweetheart, I promise," he murmurs before taking my nipple in his mouth and running his tongue along the swollen nub.

I arch into his touch, and he softly kneads my other breast.

"So responsive." His breath tickles my nipple.

"It's the hormones." My body's on fire as Andre continues to slowly thrust into my pussy. "I'm so...*horny*."

"I've noticed." He laughs again. "But I'm not complaining."

"Me neither." I take Andre's face in my hands and bring his lips to mine.

I instantly part my own, letting his tongue explore my mouth. I can still taste myself on his lips, and a fresh wave of warmth spreads between my thighs.

"Fuck, Lila. You're so fucking wet," Andre groans, burying his face in my hair.

"I'm sorry—"

"Don't ever be sorry," Andre growls, taking my chin in his hand, forcing me to look at him. "Your pussy feels like heaven around my cock, and the fact that I'm the one who makes you this wet... Fuck, I just want to be buried inside you always."

I let out a whimper as my pussy clenches.

Andre screws his eyes shut for a moment, groaning at the sensation.

"There's nothing I love more than fucking you hard, Lila, but *this*..." He pulls out of me so slowly.

I cry out at the emptiness.

"Fuck, this feels *incredible*," he moans as he grinds his hips, thrusting himself back inside me inch by inch until he's buried to the hilt.

"More," I gasp.

Andre chuckles but obliges.

He takes me slowly, over and over until my thighs are slick with wetness.

I glance down as Andre pulls himself out and gasp at the sight of his glistening cock.

"That's all you, baby."

My tongue darts out to lick my lips.

"I'll happily fuck that mouth of yours once I'm done with your pussy. Do you want that, Lila?"

"Yes," I moan, gripping Andre's hips as he pumps himself inside me.

"I want to have my come dripping down your thighs, your chin, your tits. You're *mine*, do you understand?"

"Yes. God, yes," I moan again.

"Good girl." Andre slams his cock inside me.

I cry out, clinging to him as he quickens his pace, taking me harder.

Our heavy pants fill the air as we get closer to the edge, our lips crashing together to muffle our moans.

"Come with me," I gasp against Andre's lips.

He moves to grip my hips, tilting me at an angle that sends him even deeper inside me.

I'm overcome with pleasure as he pounds into me, his cock grazing my inner walls, and I know he's close from the way his movements have become sloppier.

"Look at me, Andre," I whisper, taking his face in my hands.

"Lila," he breathes, his dark eyes meeting mine.

I cry out as my pussy clenches around his cock, causing Andre to shudder as he's hit with his own release.

I watch in awe as he spills inside me. I want to take this as confirmation that he's willing to stick by me through this.

After we've cleaned up, I lie wrapped in Andre's arms, the warmth of his body enveloping me as I let my eyes close.

"I apologize if I frightened you earlier." Andre runs his hands over my hair. "I can be jealous and obsessive, *especially* when it comes to you. The thought of any man trying to get near you while you're carrying my child... It made me see red, Lila."

"No, you? Seeing red?" I tease, rolling over so I can look at him.

He rolls his eyes, his arms wrapping tighter around my waist.

"I've been hurt before." His eyes cloud over. "I'm not sure I'm willing to put myself in the position where I can be hurt again."

"We've all been hurt. Life sucks sometimes." I kiss his chest. "But not trusting, not fully opening yourself up, means you're missing out on the best parts of living. I mean, I never met my mom because she died giving birth to me, and my dad was an alcoholic who abandoned me when I was twelve. I tend to go for guys who end up hurting me, I think because of that. But if I didn't believe there was more to life just out of fear of getting hurt, then what's the point?"

Andre traces circles on my skin as he looks at me.

"I wish I could promise that I won't hurt you, Lila." A frown forms between his eyebrows. "But my life is...complicated and dangerous. But I will promise that I will do everything in my power to protect you and this baby."

I can't stop the smile that spreads across my face as his words.

"Thank you," I whisper against his chest, feeling safe as I fall asleep in his arms.

The last thought that crosses my mind is whether they were nothing but empty words.

30

ANDRE

I hold Lila until she falls asleep, drinking in the soft sounds of her breathing, the warmth of her body tucked against mine.

She's pregnant.

I let my hand stroke soft circles on her stomach, trying to calm my racing heart as I think of the child growing inside her.

She's so fragile, and I want to keep her by my side at all times.

If Lorenzo were to ever find out about this baby...

I force the thought from my mind. I've already lost so much, the thought of losing Lila too has my heart cracking open.

I have to ensure that this knowledge is kept quiet for as long as possible, no matter the cost.

I lie awake for hours, thoughts of Lorenzo finding Lila running through my mind on repeat until my skin is covered in sweat, and my heartbeat is pounding in my ears.

Lila remains asleep, but she tightens her arms around

my waist, snuggling further against me as if she can sense my distress.

I press a soft kiss to her head and wait for the sun to rise.

She'll be confused when she wakes to find I'm gone, but I don't want to wake her when she looks so peaceful.

I slowly pull myself free from Lila's arms and move to gather my clothes, deciding to leave her a note for when she wakes, explaining that I wanted to leave without being seen. It's only a precaution, but I hope she'll understand.

As I button my shirt, I walk over to the refrigerator and run my finger over the sonogram picture, praying that this isn't too good to be true.

Being the child of a mafia don ultimately means a target on your back, but I will do whatever it takes to ensure my family is safe, and that family includes Lila and this baby.

I press one last kiss to Lila's hair as I tuck my note beside her pillow before I leave. My Mercedes is parked outside, and I decide to head back to Westchester to check on Rosa as Marco is at the penthouse.

The streets are fairly quiet as I head across the city toward the freeway. The sky is clear, and I feel some of the cloud starting to lift around my mood as I think of Lila sleeping peacefully in her bed.

I know I will see her in a few hours at the office, but I already feel the ache from being apart.

I've spent the past five years avoiding such a feeling. After losing Valentina, I never thought I could be whole again, and I never wanted to replace her. But Lila has changed that, and for once, I'm not running from the life she could offer me.

I glance in my rearview mirror before signaling at the lights, frowning at the blacked-out Range Rover behind me.

The guy behind the wheel has a shaved head and is wearing dark sunglasses despite it not even being five a.m..

An uneasy feeling swirls in my gut, so I quickly change my turn signal and pull off at the next set of lights.

The Range Rover does the same.

I make a last second left turn down a small side street, barely wide enough to fit my Mercedes, let alone a huge Range Rover and yet—

"Fuck."

Everything around me seems to slow as I try to process what to do.

I reach over and open my glove box, sighing as I find a loaded handgun. I reach beneath my seat and find another.

I take a sharp right turn, pressing buttons on the central screen as I try to shake off whoever it is that is following me.

"Come on, pick up the fucking phone," I mutter, hastily making a right turn.

Marco hisses, "What the fuck, Andre—"

"Marco, I need you to do something for me." I keep my voice calm as the Range Rover gains a few feet on me.

"At five a.m.?" my brother groans.

"Yes, at five a.m.. It's urgent."

"You suck, I hope you know that."

"I couldn't give less fucks what you think right now, Marco." I glance again in my rearview mirror. "I'm being followed by a blacked-out Range Rover, looks like it could be one of Lorenzo's men."

"Shit!" Marco exclaims. "What do you want me to do? I can track your phone and try to intercept—"

"I need you to drive to 135 West 19th street and collect Lila. Bring her back to the Westchester house."

"You're not serious."

"Marco, I've never been more serious about anything in my life."

If this guy was waiting outside Lila's apartment for me, even if I manage to shake him off, there's no saying whether he might go back to her building and try to take her and my unborn child along with him.

I won't let that happen.

"Lorenzo might still have someone watching her place, so don't go through the front." I dodge a slower car. "There's a window in her bathroom you can get to via the fire escape. It's cracked open. Go through there."

"Why is this woman so important to you?"

"Just do as I ask, and I'll explain later. Please. Bring her back to the mansion. But take the long way, in case anyone follows you."

"Fine," Marco huffs. "I'm grabbing my keys now."

"Hurry. Oh, and Marco?" I take one last glance in my mirror before pressing the gas pedal to the floor and running the next three red lights to try and shake this guy.

"Yeah?"

"Lila's pregnant, so don't use any significant force, otherwise, I will kill you," I add before hanging up the phone and calling Delilah, my housekeeper at the Westchester house.

"Good morning, Mr. De Luca."

"Delilah, please ready one of the guest rooms immediately. I have a friend coming to stay with us for a while, and she'll need all the relevant toiletries and clothing stocked."

"Of course, sir."

"I will be at the house shortly before she arrives."

"Everything will be ready for your arrival. I'm assuming you would like to bring in some extra security?"

"Have Xander sort it." I smile as I realize the Range Rover is stuck behind a line of yellow cabs.

"Very well, we will expect you soon, Mr. De Luca."

"Thank you, Delilah."

She hangs up the phone, and I let out a breath.

I want to shake this guy off my tail, but I don't want to risk him turning around yet.

It won't take Marco long to get to Lila's place, but who knows what sort of fight she might put up.

I would do it myself, but Lila is strong-willed. She'll likely stand her ground and not take the threat on her life seriously. I can't risk anything happening to her, so if she has to hate me for a while in order for me to keep her safe, then so be it.

I reach over to the glove compartment and pull the gun free, not wanting to take any chances. This guy has been following me for a while through the city but has made no move to pull a weapon.

"What do you want?" I narrow my eyes as he overtakes the cabs and narrowly misses colliding with the oncoming traffic.

I take my foot off the gas enough for him to catch up until we get to the interstate.

I glance at the time.

Marco should be almost at Lila's apartment by now, and I want to shake this guy off before I get too close to the Westchester house where Rosa is.

"Fuck." I hate having my family scattered around like this. It leaves too many openings for Lorenzo to make a move on someone I care about. He's done it before, and he will do it again.

As I spot the turning for the interstate, I flatten my foot

on the gas pedal, driving up on the sidewalk to overtake the morning traffic.

Ignoring all stop signs and red lights, I speed through the city, determined to lose this guy before I reach the turning.

Just as I'm about to turn off onto the interstate, I swerve, disappearing down a connecting road.

I watch through my mirror as the Range Rover pulls onto the interstate where he'll likely get stuck in the morning rush traffic.

"Amateur." I turn around and program my GPS to take me the scenic route back to my family's mansion.

Xander walks beside me. "I've got two men watching the main exits to the house, and two more on their way. I've got Dez in the security room watching the cameras."

It took me almost two hours to get home, constantly watching my back in case Lorenzo's guy managed to track me again.

"Marco is on his way." Xander pulls out his phone, showing the tracker. "He should be here within the hour."

"Good." I run my hands through my hair. "And the room is all ready?"

"Yes."

"I need to add a few more...*touches*."

Xander nods.

He leaves me to head to the basement, while I make my way up the stairs.

Lila will be in the guest bedroom directly next to my room so I can keep a close eye on her. She's going to be furious with me when she realizes who it was that took her, but I don't care. I'd much rather her be mad at me and alive, than tortured to death by Lorenzo Rossi.

Delilah has done a good job with the room. It's light and spacious, with a huge double bed, a seating area with TV, and an ensuite bathroom with a jacuzzi tub.

I check all the drawers to find all the relevant toiletries she might need along with the wardrobe.

I choke back a laugh at finding an array of lacy underwear has been folded neatly in the top drawer.

"I don't think this will go down well." I run my finger along the tiny scraps of lace.

A knock sounds at the door.

"Come in." I shut the drawer and turn to find Xander waiting in the doorway with a set of restraints in his hands.

"Will these do?"

"Unfortunately, yes." I move to take them from him.

I'm hoping Lila will be cooperative, but I also don't want to risk her hurting herself if she gets too emotional. It won't be good for her or the baby, so if I have to tie her to the bed in order for her to listen to me, I will.

My phone dings in my pocket, and I quickly hand the restraints to Xander before pulling out my phone and seeing a message from Marco.

"They're here." I smile.

Lila is safe.

31

———

LILA

A HAND IS OVER MY MOUTH, WAKING ME FROM SLEEP.

My eyes fly open to find a man towering above me.

I try to scream, but there is no sound.

"I'm not going to hurt you." His voice is gruff as he removes his hand from my mouth. "If you do as I say."

My ears are ringing, my heart pounding so hard in my chest it hurts to breathe. I know I should fight, to try and escape, but my body is frozen.

I'm going to die. I'm going to die.

He moves to the end of the bed and tosses me my pajamas.

"Get dressed." He's wearing a black shirt and pants, his dark hair tousled as if from sleep.

He's making no attempt to hide his identity from me which makes me think he has no intention of keeping me alive.

I can't move. I glance down at the thin sheet covering my naked body.

Where is Andre?

I look to the empty space beside me, and a strangled sob escapes my lips.

He left.

"Andre's waiting for you," the man says, as if he can read my thoughts. "He sent me to collect you."

My life is complicated and dangerous.

This is exactly what he warned me about.

I knew from the start who he was, the sort of life he was caught up in, and I chose to ignore it. To look past it.

And look where it's gotten me.

"What do you want?" My voice shakes.

"Andre sent me to collect you. You're in danger, Lila, and I'm here to help."

Glancing around my apartment, he tucks his hands into his pockets, and that's when I notice the gun tucked into the belt of his pants.

Andre sent him?

"I don't believe you," I whisper.

"You don't need to believe me, sweetheart, you just need to do as I say."

I move to gather the sheet around my very naked body, my eyes locked on the gun.

Andre can't have sent him. They're just using him to get me to obey.

Is Andre hurt? Have they taken him too? Is that why he's not here?

I know I'm running out of time. All it would take is for this guy to pull out his gun and shoot me right here in my bed for it all to be over.

I keep my eyes on him as I slowly move to pick up my pajamas.

He watches me closely, his eyes narrowed as I pull my T-shirt over my head, careful not to expose myself.

I slide on my shorts and get to my feet, my knees shaking so bad it's a miracle I can even hold up my own weight.

I glance over to my kitchen counter where I notice my knife rack. I would have to be quick, but it wouldn't be impossible.

I touch my hand to my belly and whisper a silent prayer before I lunge.

The guy moves. "Fuck."

I throw myself at the counter, desperately scrabbling to pull the largest carving knife free.

His arms are around me in a second, pinning me against the counter as his hand goes to my mouth.

I sink my teeth into his skin and throw my elbow back into his stomach.

He grunts, but it's not enough for him to loosen his grip.

"Lila," he hisses. "I'm not going to hurt you—"

I get the knife free, and just as I'm about to reach back and sink it into his neck, his hand over my mouth is replaced with a damp cloth, and my world turns black.

My head is pounding, and I'm exhausted.

My eyes flutter open, and I'm surprised to find daylight streaming in through large windows. A soft cinnamon scent hits my nose as I turn my head to look out the window, silk sheets brushing against my cheek.

Was it all a dream?

But then I go to move and find my hands tied to the bed frame.

I yank against the chains, panic setting in as I realize I'm trapped.

It all comes flooding back to me.

"No." I pull over and over at the chains, wincing as they dig into my wrists.

I can barely take a full breath as I think of my baby.

Is this what Andre was trying to warn me about? How could I have been so stupid as to get sucked into his world, when I knew all along what he was? The sort of circles he ran in?

He has powerful enemies, and it seems they're using me to send a message.

Heavy footsteps approach the door, and I think I'll be sick.

I frantically try to pull my hands free from the restraints, thinking of nothing but Andre and the baby, praying that whatever they decide to do to me, I can endure long enough for him to find me.

The sound of the door unlocking makes my blood run cold. But when it swings open, my fear turns to rage.

Andre holds his hands up. "It's not what you think."

He's changed into a crisp black shirt and black pants, and the sight of the freshly laundered clothes makes me see red.

"It feels exactly like I fucking think. You kidnapped me? And from the looks of it, you even had time for a nice long shower while I was tied to a fucking bed!"

"Lila, please." He moves to stand at the foot of the bed, placing his hands in his pockets—the picture of ease. "I was being followed. I was worried—"

"I don't care. You had no right to send one of your drones into my bedroom to kidnap me in the middle of the damn night!"

"My brother."

"Excuse me?"

"The drone who took you is my younger brother, Marco. He's the only person I'd trust with you."

"I don't give a fuck if you sent your fucking housekeeper to get me. You still *kidnapped* me, Andre! And after everything you said last night when we made love..." My voice cracks, and I have to look away from him. "Why is it that I keep falling for your bullshit."

"Everything I said last night was true, Lila. *Believe* me." He moves around the side of the bed, crouching in front of me.

I turn my head, screwing my eyes shut as his gaze bores into me.

"I couldn't risk you bolting if I told you of the threat."

"I would've gone with you if you asked," I whisper. "You should've trusted me enough to tell me the truth. Not treat me like some fucking cornered animal."

"I'm sorry, sweetheart."

A strangled sob escapes my lips at his words, but I refuse to open my eyes and look at him while my hands are chained to the bed.

"Untie my hands, Andre." I try to keep my voice steady.

Rustling tells me Andre gets to his feet and starts working on untying the chains.

My wrists are screaming from where I tried to break free from the restraints.

"You're hurt." He reaches for my wrists, but I slide out of his grip, scrambling back on the bed.

"Don't fucking touch me."

Andre tosses the chains on the bed and holds his hands up.

"It was for your own good, Lila."

"I'm finding it hard to believe that your intentions here

were good. This is not how you treat the mother of your child!"

"That is exactly why I had to do this!" Andre's eyes narrow. "A car was waiting outside of your fucking apartment for me, Lila. Sure, I could have lost them, but then they would have come straight back to you, and trust me, it would've been a hell of a lot worse."

"Are you seriously trying to have a dick-measuring contest about who's the nicest kidnapper right now?" I scramble off the bed, putting it between us so I can't do anything stupid like strangle him.

Andre lets out a long breath, his jaw clenching as he looks at me.

"I'm trying to shield you from the reality of my life, Lila. You want to have my child, then these are the consequences."

"The *consequences*?" A hysterical laugh escapes me as I let his words sink in. "I never asked for any of this, Andre. Besides, I thought *we* were having this child, or have you decided to lie to me about that too?"

"Don't fucking talk to me about lying."

"I. Didn't. Lie."

"I'm not having this conversation with you while you're like this. When you've calmed down—"

"*Calmed down?*" Oh, hell no. "You've got some fucking *nerve.*"

I glance at the bedside table, reaching for the glass lamp and throwing it across the room at Andre.

He ducks, and the glass base smashes as it collides with the wall.

I don't stop. I pick up the vase of flowers on the dressers and launch them at Andre, too. Water flies everywhere, and the purple tulips lay scattered on the cream carpet among the broken glass.

Anything I can find, I throw, not caring about the mess I make in my wake.

Andre takes it, staying by the window, ducking every time something comes close to hitting him.

Breathless, I collapse on the end of the bed.

I hadn't noticed the tears fall, but my cheeks are damp, and my heart is pounding.

Andre moves toward the door. "You will stay in this room, Lila, until I can be sure you're not going to run."

I blink at him. "You're locking me in here…"

"This is for your own good. I will protect what is mine at all costs."

He walks out of the room, closing the door behind him.

"I didn't think that including kidnapping me!" I yell after him.

His only response is the sound of the key turning in the lock, trapping me inside his gilded cage.

"Please. Let me *out*!"

I bang on the door again and again until my fists are red and throbbing. My cheeks are wet with tears, throat raw from yelling for hours on end.

How could Andre do this?

I don't care that he insists he's protecting me. He *kidnapped* me and is holding me hostage, refusing to give me answers.

I'm so exhausted from crying and yelling that I eventually fall asleep, curled up on the floor. I wake to find a tray of food has been left for me, but I can't find it in me to eat.

It seems I become stuck in the cycle of yelling and crying myself into exhaustion, waking to a fresh plate of food, but that is all. Andre has not come to see me. No one has.

I am alone.

Days must passed, but I stay curled on the floor with my eyes screwed shut as I try to imagine myself back in my apartment. Before any of this happened. Before I even decided to go on that ridiculous blind date with Dirk the dick. When the only worries I had was which new latte to try from my favorite coffee shop.

My breath hitches as the key turns in the lock.

I scramble backwards and watch as the door opens.

"Andre?" I breathe, standing up, but I blink at the sight of a young girl.

"Here." She holds out a sandwich and a bottle of water. "I thought you might be hungry."

"Who are you?"

"I'm Rosa." She steps inside the room, closing the door behind her. "I'm Andre's sister."

"Sister?"

"Yes."

She has the same striking dark hair and eyes as Andre, and her skin is a soft golden brown. She's beautiful, though she can't be much more than sixteen.

I frown. "Did Andre send you?"

She shakes her head, looking sheepish. "He doesn't know that I know about you. I overheard him talking to Marco."

"Your other brother," I mutter. "The kidnapper."

"Technically, yes. But Marco is a good guy, really."

"I find that hard to believe."

I move back to the couch, running my hands over the pale lilac fabric. "You need to help me get out of here. You have to know that locking me up here is wrong, right?"

She shakes her head, looking awkward. "Andre's worried you're in danger. He's just trying to keep you safe."

"It's not up to him to do that!" I snap.

Rosa flinches, and I silently curse myself.

"I... I'm sorry. This isn't your fault. I'm just...scared."

Rosa nods and moves to come and sit beside me.

"I always question my brother's methods too. He took

me out of school and essentially put me on house arrest because of a threat against my life. I fought him, but ultimately, he is only doing it to keep me safe."

I frown at Rosa. "What about your mom and dad? What do they say?"

Rosa fiddles with a gold ring on her finger, not looking at me.

"They died in a car accident when I was five. So, Andre essentially raised me. Marco was older, he was sixteen, but he went off the rails for a while after the accident. Andre did the best he could, and eventually, got Marco back on the right path. I don't know what would've happened if it weren't for my brother."

"I had no idea..." I rest a hand on my flat stomach, thinking about my own parents.

"He's crazy protective." Rosa shrugs. "It drives me nuts sometimes, but I know he loves me and would do anything for me."

"I'm sure he would."

"He must feel very strongly about you if he's gone to all this trouble." Rosa glances at me.

I nod, keeping my mouth shut. There are so many questions I want to ask her, but I think I would rather the answers come from Andre himself.

"Trust him, Lila. That's all I can really offer. Anyway, I'll leave you alone now." She gets to her feet. "I could come back later if you like?"

"Sure." I offer her a small smile.

I watch Rosa leave and flinch at the sound of the key turning in the lock.

I spend a while staring at the door, thinking of all she told me.

Andre raised his two siblings, alone, and it's clear he

would do anything for those he cares about. While his methods are questionable, can I deny the fact that all he wanted was to keep me and this baby safe?

But how can I trust Andre when I barely even know him?

THE CREAK OF THE DOOR WAKES ME UP.

I'm tangled in the silk sheets on the bed.

After a few nights of sleeping on the floor, I gave in and crawled onto the bed after eating the food Rosa brought for me. I passed out almost immediately at the feeling of the silk caressing my bare legs.

"Lila?"

I sit up at the sound of Andre's voice.

He looks tired, his shirt sleeves rolled up and his hair tousled as if he's run his hands through it over and over.

I lick my lips at sight of him, my heartbeat quickening as he stalks toward me.

"Have you calmed down yet?" His eyes search my face.

I scoff, folding my arms over my chest. "Would you be calm if someone locked you in a shoebox?"

Andre glances around the room.

It's dark outside, but I left the curtains open and the one remaining lamp on to help me not feel so trapped.

A chuckle spills from Andre's lips, and I shoot him a glare.

"What?"

"It's hardly a shoebox, princess. And I'm not going to apologize for trying to keep you from being tortured to death."

My breath catches at his words.

"Lila," he sighs, moving toward the bed. "I don't mean to frighten you, but you need to know I'm doing this to keep you and the baby safe."

I nod, blinking back tears.

"Sweetheart." He comes around to my side of the bed.

I reach for him, my walls crumbling as reality hits me.

I'm terrified, not of Andre, but of him not being there to protect me. I should be grateful that it was only Marco who took me from my bed and not one of Andre's enemies who would use me to send a message.

"I will protect you, Lila."

I nod, biting my lower lip as I try to ignore the thoughts of what could've been.

Andre takes a step toward me and wraps his arms around my waist. "I promise."

I rest my forehead against his chest, closing my eyes and letting the bergamot and sandalwood scent of him calm my nerves.

"What can I do?" He runs his hands up and down my back.

"I'm so scared," I whisper against his shirt, my hands sinking into the soft fabric.

"I know, baby. But you don't need to be, I've got you."

He cups my chin and tilts my face so he can kiss me softly.

I melt into him, parting my lips so his tongue can explore my mouth.

He groans, tightening his arms around me as the kiss deepens. He tastes of whiskey

Heat instantly pools between my thighs as I realize he's here with me. He didn't leave. He was trying to protect me.

"I need you," I gasp against his mouth.

He smiles against my lips as he reaches for the hem of my T-shirt and lifts it over my head.

My nipples instantly harden, and he bends down to take each one into his mouth.

I moan, my eyes closing, hands running through his hair as he worships my breasts.

"Lie on the bed, Lila." He squeezes my hips once more.

I lie among the silk sheets in nothing but a pair of lace panties I found in a drawer.

The lust in his eyes has me moaning, and I have to reach for my breasts, kneading them to try and ease the ache in my body.

"Is this your way of apologizing?"

He peels of his pants as he growls, "I will never apologize for keeping you safe Lila."

I glance down and whimper at the sight of Andre kneeling before me.

My thighs part, exposing my glistening pussy, and his gaze turns molten as he takes me in.

"But I would be happy to remind you how much I care for you." He leans in and runs his tongue up my center.

My head falls back against the bed, my hands finding Andre's hair as he greedily licks at my clit.

His hands move to grip my waist, holding me in place as he moves to sink his tongue inside me, pumping it in and out so deliciously that I'm panting with need.

My thighs rest over his shoulders as he feasts on me, moving between sucking my clit and thrusting his tongue inside me until they shake with my budding release.

"More." I arch my back off the bed.

Andre chuckles against me, his breath tickling my clit and making me shudder. But he does as I ask, removing one hand from my waist and sinking two fingers inside me.

My hips buck as he curls them, brushing my inner walls, and I cry out.

He wraps his lips around my clit, sucking so hard that my legs shake uncontrollably. He pumps his fingers harder, faster, his movements desperate and hurried, and my body instantly responds.

I bow off the bed, screaming out his name as my orgasm hits me.

Warmth spreads between my thighs, and I'm gasping for air, clutching onto Andre as he continues to lick my pussy as I ride out my pleasure.

"Oh god," I whimper, collapsing onto the sheets.

"So fucking delicious," Andre growls, getting to his feet, making quick work of his clothes and taking his throbbing cock in his hand. "Now, get on your hands and knees, Lila."

I turn onto my stomach, pushing myself up into position, my pussy already clenching at the thought of his huge cock inside me.

"Beautiful." Andre's hands knead my ass.

I sigh at his touch, wiggling my hips back until his cock nudges my entrance.

"That's it, baby. Set the pace."

I do as he says, pushing back until his first inch is inside me. Moaning, I let myself adjust to his size before continuing.

"Oh, fuck, Lila," Andre groans as I take another inch. "Doing great, princess."

My eyes roll, already so full of him, but it's not enough.

"Andre," I groan.

"Do you want more, Lila?" His fingers dig into my hips.

"More."

He thrusts his hips, slamming his cock inside me all the way.

I cry out as he stretches me, but he gives me little time to adjust before he pulls out and thrusts into me again.

"Mmm..." I move to rest on my elbows to push my ass up higher so his cock can hit that sensitive spot inside me.

"Look at you," Andre groans, his hands kneading my ass. "Fuck, I'm in so deep."

"So fucking good!" I cry out as I match Andre's pace, bouncing back against his cock as he thrusts so deep inside me I see stars.

His grunts have me so wet and aching that I have to reach between my legs to work my clit.

Andre has to keep my hips lifted as my body threatens to collapse with pleasure.

"I can feel you're close, Lila," Andre groans as my pussy starts clenching around his cock. "Fuck, I'm going to come."

"Yes!" I rub my clit as I chase my release. "I want to feel you dripping down my thighs."

"Such a dirty girl." Andre chuckles.

My moans grow louder as my orgasm builds with each thrust, with each brush of my G spot.

"Lila."

My name on his lips is enough to send me over the edge.

I cry out as Andre slams into me once more before he comes.

His body collapses onto mine as my pussy milks every last drop from him.

He wraps his arms around me, holding us up as we ride out our pleasure, gasping for air, our bodies covered in sweat.

"Promise me one thing, Lila." He presses a kiss to my shoulder.

"Mmm..." I'm barely able to think straight.

"If I let you move around the house, you have to promise you won't leave it without my permission."

"I can leave this room?" I glance over my shoulder.

"If you promise me this." He runs his nose along my shoulder.

"Ok," I whisper.

33

———

ANDRE

How is this my life now?

Three months ago, only darkness surrounded me. I had to get up and put on a brave face for my siblings and my men, but all I really wanted to do was disappear, embrace oblivion.

Then, one of my darkest nights brought me the brightest light.

Life isn't perfect, not even close, but it is fucking worth it for once.

When I asked my brother to kidnap Lila, I knew I was buying a fight I would struggle to win.

Those days when she was hurting, mad at me, crushed me harder than I thought possible.

Last week was my breaking point. I couldn't bear stay away from her for a second longer. I rather her throw more furniture at me but have my eyes on her, than to go another minute without breathing the same air as her.

And now, as I stand in the doorway to the kitchen, life gets even better as I watch Lila and Rosa talk over breakfast together.

They're both in their pajamas, their legs tucked underneath them as they chat away.

The sight makes my chest swell. Not only does Rosa have a huge smile on her face but color has returned to Lila's cheeks, and she's eating well.

I hate that I had to do this to her, lock her up like a prisoner. But it was the only way to ensure her safety, and I will do anything I need to make sure she'll forgive me.

Clearing my throat, I walk into the kitchen.

Lila looks up at me, and her eyes turn molten.

I smirk, letting my eyes fall to her pouty lips.

Every night for the past week I've crawled into bed with her, taking her in every way I can until we both pass out from exhaustion. It's been heaven, but I have to keep reminding myself that the only reason Lila is even here is because of Lorenzo.

Who has gone silent over the past few days.

I had Dez and Sloan try to track the Range Rover that was following me, but they came up empty. There's also been nothing regarding the man we left with a message carved into his chest at *The Vault*.

It's unnerving.

Lorenzo will be planning something, but until that happens, Lila and Rosa will stay in this house where I can see them. Where I can keep them safe.

Rosa smiles. "Morning. There's fresh coffee."

I smile at my sister and stroll over to the coffee pot and pour myself a cup.

"What are you two talking about?" I lean against the counter.

"Lila was giving me some book recommendations." Rosa grins.

"Oh, yeah?" I look at Lila who offers me a shy smile.

"Like what?"

"Nothing you'd like." She glances at Rosa who bursts out laughing.

"They're all smutty romances, not your taste at all." Rosa giggles.

"They shouldn't be your taste either," I warn her. "You're fifteen."

"Lila says she was reading them at thirteen."

I glare at Lila, but she only laughs at my expression.

"You left me alone with her." Lila holds up her hands. "You can't blame me."

"She was also telling me all about her college days at NYU." Rosa laughs. "College sounds *fun*."

"You're not going to college. You can take online classes here."

Rosa rolls her eyes and nudges Lila with her elbow.

"See what I mean?"

"Ok, enough. I don't want to have to separate you two."

"Spoil sport," Lila mutters, taking a sip of her tea.

I catch the gleam in her eye, and my cock twitches in my pants. "Do you need reminding who's in charge here?"

Her tongue darts out to moisten her lower lip, and she dips her head.

My hands itch to touch Lila. Teach her a lesson. "Rosa, go to your room."

"Hey! What did I do?"

"We'll chat later." Lila places a comforting hand on my sister's shoulder.

I watch in silence as Rosa gets to her feet, taking her cup of coffee with her, and leaves the kitchen.

Lila watches her go. "I like your sister. She's more fun than you."

"Is that so?" I chuckle, moving around the table and

perching beside her.

She rests her chin on my thigh, gazing up at me with those ocean blue eyes.

I trace her lower lip with my thumb, letting myself get lost in her gaze for a moment. "I have a surprise for you."

She blinks, lifting her head. "Oh yeah?"

"It's to say thank you for putting up with...all of this."

Lila dips her chin.

"I know you meant well, Andre. Even if it took me a while to realize."

"Today is me making it up to you." I smile. "So, why don't you get dressed and meet me at the front door in twenty minutes."

IT'S THE PERFECT DAY TO WALK OVER TO THE SECLUDED park that backs onto my family's estate. The sky is clear and the sun casts a warm veil over Lila and I as we stroll hand in hand.

Her eyes take it all in. "Where are we going?"

"There's a clearing about twenty minutes away with a river and a waterfall." I look down at her.

She's wearing a white sundress, her hair loose around her shoulders, strands of red and gold glistening in the sunlight.

She's breathtaking. And she's all mine.

"That sounds wonderful." She sighs.

I glance over my shoulder to make sure the blacked-out Hummer is close by. Two of my security guys are inside, following at a distance.

Even though my family's estate is private and far from anything that poses a threat, I wouldn't put it past Lorenzo to have his men try to infiltrate the neighboring land. I'm nervous to take Lila outside of the house, but I want to meet her halfway.

She's done as she's told, even if somewhat reluctantly, and I want to offer her something in return.

We chat mostly about my family as we walk, with Lila asking lots of questions about Rosa in particular.

"My sister seems very taken with you."

"I like her. She's like...a breath of fresh air."

I laugh, wrapping my arm around her shoulders.

"Trust me, after you've spent fifteen years with her, you won't be saying that."

"Does she know?" Lila looks at me, then away into the horizon. "About us? About the baby?"

I suck in a breath.

"No. I mean, I think she's worked out that there's something between us, but she doesn't know about the baby. I want to keep that knowledge a secret, even from her, for as long as we can. The less people who know... Well, it will be safer if we keep it quiet."

Lila nods, glancing around the wooded area that we've ventured into.

I squeeze her shoulder. "It's not much further."

We walk for ten more minutes through the trees, enjoying the shade they provide from the beating sun.

Lila's skin has a soft flush from the heat, and I want nothing more than to press her up against a tree and explore every inch of that delicious skin with my tongue.

The engine of the Hummer cuts, the security will have to go one foot from here, but they're armed and ready should anything happen.

She looks at me wide-eyed. "I can hear water."

I squeeze her shoulder again and smile at the look of

wonder on her face.

Has it really been that terrible being locked up in the house?

I ignore the churning in my gut as Lila walks ahead, following the sounds of the river.

I thought perhaps she would enjoy some time away from work. I put in a last-minute annual leave request for her, and I've been working from my home office so no one at Mason's International suspects anything.

I don't want to risk Lorenzo looking there too, so I have Dez monitoring the security cameras along with the ones at Lila's apartment.

"Oh, Andre, it's beautiful." Lila sighs as we walk into the small clearing at the edge of the woods, the trees parting to reveal a waterfall that cascades over the rocks into the river.

The lush grass on the bank has been donned with a picnic blanket as well as a basket filled with food and a bottle of sparkling cider.

"I'm glad you like it." I walk up behind her, wrapping my arms around her waist.

It is amazing being here with her, being free to touch her, to just enjoy her without having to worry about who will walk in on us or having to restrain from just enjoying her company.

"The water looks inviting." Lila wiggles against me.

I hiss as she rubs against my hardening cock.

"Lila, we have an audience." I spin her around so she can see my guards behind us.

A sly smile creeps across her lips.

"You don't strike me as the shy type..."

She steps back and reaches for the ties of her sundress.

Lord help me.

34

ANDRE

Fucking hell how is *THIS* my life?

Knowing my men are watching has me wanting to both tear their eyes out and fuck her even more.

My mouth dries as my eyes follow her every movement.

Her sundress falls to the floor, exposing her full breasts and lace panties.

I choke at the sight of her. I think of my security watching, knowing that I'm the one to have her.

She bites her lower lip as she trails her fingers inside the waistband of her panties.

"Do you need some help with those?" My cock's already hardening at the thought of fucking her.

She shakes her head, her thick brown hair falling around her bare shoulders.

"Not with this, but I might need help with something else..." Her eyes trail down my body until she lands on my erection.

I watch her throat bob and her cheeks redden. It's all the confirmation I need to reach for my belt and start undoing my pants.

Lila watches eagerly as I shrug out of my clothes, my cock already leaking at the thought of being inside her.

"Take off your panties, Lila." I wrap my hand around my cock, pumping hard.

I groan as I watch her shimmy out of the scrap of material, her perfect breasts bouncing with the movement.

My mouth waters, wanting to wrap my lips around her sensitive nipples and suck until she's begging for me to fuck her.

"I think I might go for a swim." She smirks at me as she strolls over to the water's edge. I watch in awe as her hips sway, her body so lush and perfect that I can't stop myself from stroking my cock at the sight of her.

"Are you coming?" she asks over her shoulder.

"Fuck, yes," I growl.

She grins before sliding into the water.

"That's cold!" She laughs, wrapping her arms around her body.

"I can warm you up." I smirk, following her into the water. I hiss at the cold temperature, sliding all the way in so the water covers my shoulders. "Fuck, that's cold!"

"I told you." Lila laughs.

I watch her as she dips her head back to wet her hair, her puckered breasts popping out of the water.

"Come here."

She lifts her head back and grins at me.

I reach for her waist, pulling her flush against me and lifting her legs around my waist.

My cock is throbbing, desperate to be inside her, and I love how turned on she is by the thought of being watched.

"I need to be inside you," I groan against her shoulder.

"I'm all yours, Andre," she whispers.

I reach beneath the water to line my cock up with her

entrance, tightening my hold around her waist with my other hand to bring her down upon me.

We both gasp as I stretch her pussy, but she's instantly moving, grinding against me as I thrust up into her.

The water isn't deep, so her tits are on full display as I fuck her hard.

"Andre!" she cries out as she grinds on my cock.

I bury my face in her tits, sucking and licking her puckered nipples, groaning as she clenches around my shaft.

"Fuck, this is so hot," I groan as she cries out.

"Harder, Andre."

My smile is feral as I tighten my grip on her, slamming my cock all the way to the hilt, her swollen breasts bouncing in my face.

"Yes!" Lila cries, gripping onto my shoulders as she matches my pace. "Fuck, yes, I'm close!"

I fucking love how loud she's being right now. It's making my balls tighten and the base of my spine tingle.

"Let them see you come, Lila," I growl.

She looks down at me and grins, her eyelids heavy as she rocks her hips.

Her mouth parts, and her eyes flutter closed, and I know she's reaching the edge.

I quicken my pace, taking her nipple in my mouth and sucking hard.

"*Lila*," I groan as she comes around my cock, crying out.

My cock spills into her at the sound, and I'm holding onto her so tightly I know I'll leave bruises.

"I want to do that again." She chuckles breathlessly as she rests her forehead against mine.

"Let's get some food in you first, sweetheart."

"Can I ask you a question?" Lila says as she lies back on the picnic blanket, nibbling on a chocolate strawberry.

"Within reason, yes." I rest back on my elbows.

She's wearing nothing but my white shirt, leaving her tanned legs exposed.

I slipped my pants back on, letting my skin dry off under the heat of the sun streaming through the trees overhead.

"Have you had a serious girlfriend before?"

I let out a long breath. I knew this question would eventually come up, and Lila has a right to know about Valentina. But she doesn't need to know the full truth. "Yes."

"How long were you two together?"

"A year or so."

"What happened?" Lila sits up, reaching for her glass of cider.

I clench my hands into fists, trying to push down the pain that creeps in whenever Valentina enters my thoughts.

Lila must sense my hesitation as she reaches for my hand, running her thumb in soothing circles across my palm.

"We were...engaged." I clear my throat. "But she died."

"Oh, Andre." Lila presses her hand to her heart.

I look into her eyes, and they're glistening with tears.

I reach for her cheek, wanting to touch her, to know she's real.

"It was a long time ago."

"What was she like?"

"She was..." I take a deep breath. "Beautiful, kind, *sassy*."

Lila laughs, shaking her head. "I'm not surprised."

"She was the most perfect woman I'd ever met. And after...well, no one has ever come close to her until..."

"Until...?" Lila gazes up at me with those ocean blue eyes.

"Until you." My voice is tight.

I lean in to press my lips to hers, sighing as her tongue licks my lower lip.

"I'm honored," Lila whispers against my lips. She presses her palm to my chest. "Lie back."

I do as she says, my eyes widening as Lila climbs on top of me, reaching for the button on my pants. I rest my hands behind my head, enjoying watching her pull my cock free and start to pump it in slow strokes.

She looks up into the distance and a feral smile tugs at her lips.

"They're still there, baby."

"Oh, I know." She lets go of my cock to pull my shirt over her head.

"Such a dirty girl." I chuckle as she reaches for my cock and lines it up with her entrance. I groan as she slowly lowers herself down onto it, her tight walls clenching around me so perfectly.

She's already so wet, and my eyes flutter closed for a moment as I try to steady myself.

"You make me want to do very bad things." She smirks as she rocks herself against me.

"I could stay like this forever," I murmur, opening my eyes and watching her slowly start to grind her hips, her full breasts bouncing with the movement.

"I feel so full," she groans, her head falling back.

I reach up to knead one of her breasts, brushing my thumb over the sensitive bud as she rocks back and forth on my cock.

"And I love that we're being watched." She laughs.

"Does that turn you on, Lila?"

"Mmm..."

"Do you like the thought of people watching how well you ride my cock?"

"Oh god." She braces her hands on my chest.

She lifts herself off my cock before slamming back down, impaling herself on my shaft. I groan as I feel her clench around me, and she grins.

I move my hands to her hips, helping to lift her off before pulling her back down harder.

She cries out as she rocks against me before lifting herself off once more.

"Fuck, baby, look at you," I grit out as she quickens her pace.

My balls are already starting to tighten at the thought of spilling inside her, but she needs to come first.

I reach for her clit and start rubbing the sensitive bundle of nerves, watching her mouth fall open as she gasps with pleasure.

"Andre," she whimpers as her pussy clenches around me.

"I know, sweetheart."

Her breathing is coming in short pants, her movements sloppy as she rides me. I'm so fucking close, so I thrust my hips up, matching her stroke for stroke.

"Coming." I slam myself up into her pussy, the tip of my cock brushing her inner walls. Lila screams as I hit her G spot, her body convulsing as her orgasm hits her, and I instantly come with her, my cocking spilling over and over until I'm completely spent.

We stay out in the clearing for another hour or two but

when Lila starts yawning, I take her back to the house, to shower and take a nap.

I take the time to head to my office to check in on Dez and Sloan's reports, eager to know if there's been any sighting of Lorenzo. I'm surprised to find Marco waiting for me in my office when I enter, his expression grave as he looks at me.

"What is it?"

"I think it's best if I show you."

<hr>

"You have got to be fucking *KIDDING ME*!" I slam my fist into the wall as I take in the mutilated body of Sergio Mantini. "How did this happen?"

I turn to face Marco, Dez, and Sloan. "Speak!"

"All of our leads have been coming up short," Marco says. "There's been radio silence apart from the Range Rover incident."

"Nothing about the guy we left for him at *The Vault*?"

Dez shakes his head.

"For all we know, others might have cleaned up the mess, choosing not to tell Lorenzo."

"Fuck," I hiss, turning back around to look at Sergio. He's completely naked but every inch of his skin is covered in blood. He has multiple stab wounds to his chest that I know are in places which meant he bled out slowly. Likely while Lorenzo's men got the information out of him that they were looking for.

"I don't think he'll be staying quiet for much longer." I crouch down beside the body.

I dip my finger in the blood of one of the stab wounds

and find it still warm. It's not been here long. "He can't have gotten far."

Dez nods. "A few of his clubs are nearby."

"I don't think he would be that obvious," Marco counters. "He knows we know about those places."

"Unless he wants us to think that..." I mutter.

"You think he's double bluffing us?"

"It wouldn't be the first time." I get to my feet. "It's his style."

Sloan straightens up. "We'll get straight on it, boss." He slaps his friend on the shoulder. "Dez, let's swing by *Neon* to pick up Jerry. We'll have something to report to you within the hour, Andre."

I nod and wait for Dez and Sloane to exit the abandoned loft before turning to my brother.

My brother looks at me. "What could Sergio have offered him? Did he know about Lila or Rosa?"

I run my hands over my face, trying to calm the rage that's burning in my veins.

"I have no idea, but that's what we need to find out, Marco. Before it's one of their bodies bleeding out on the floor."

35

———

LILA

ANDRE LEADS ME INTO MY BEDROOM. "I'M NOT DUE another scan for a few weeks."

"I just wanted to make sure everything was alright, what with the stress over the last week." He places a reassuring hand on my back. "You can never be too careful."

"So overprotective." I smile at the thought of him wanting to take care of both me and the baby.

"Yes, and it will likely only get worse." He opens my bedroom door.

Dr. Waite is setting up a portable ultrasound machine by the bed, and he looks up when we enter.

"Ah, Lila, so lovely to see you again. How are you feeling?"

"I'm good, the nausea isn't as bad, and I'm managing to eat more again."

"That's very good to hear."

I notice the wary glance he gives to Andre, and that's when I realize they must already know each other. How else would Andre have found out about the baby if he didn't know who my doctor was? It's not like he cornered Cassi about it, otherwise I would have heard from her.

I push the information aside, determined to confront Andre about it later. But first, I want to check my baby.

"Why don't you get yourself ready, and we can get started."

I slip into the ensuite bathroom and slide out of my panties before heading back out into the bedroom and climbing onto the bed.

Dr. Waite offers me a modesty cover which I place over my legs.

Andre moves to perch beside me, holding my hand as Dr. Waite preps the ultrasound scope.

"Are you excited to hear the heartbeat?" I glance up at him.

He seems tense, but he offers me a nod as he watches Dr. Waite work.

I squeeze his hand to try and ease his nerves, but Andre keeps his eyes locked on the portable monitor as the ultrasound probe is inserted.

I hiss at the coldness of the jelly, and Andre tightens his grip on my hands.

"Let's see your baby, shall we?" Dr. Waite offers me a reassuring smile before he starts pressing buttons on the monitor.

I look away, wanting to watch Andre's reaction to seeing the baby for the first time. As the heartbeat sounds through the monitor, his eyes soften in awe as he looks at the screen.

My heart swells at the happiness in his eyes. But there's something else there too. Sadness? Worry?

Thinking about what Rosa told me, about Andre losing his parents and raising his two siblings, I know he worries.

This past week has shown me some of the realities of his life, and I know he wouldn't want to do anything to put himself or his child in danger. But he did such a wonderful job with Rosa, and I'm sure he will be the most amazing father.

"That's our baby." I turn to look at the screen.

"It sure is," Andre whispers, pressing a kiss to my hair.

After Dr. Waite leaves, Andre tells me he has some business to attend to with Marco.

I eat dinner down in the kitchen with Rosa, catching up on her day.

She's finished for the summer with school, despite having to do the last few weeks of the semester online, and now she's eagerly reading up on her sophomore reading list.

"You've got months until you go back," I remind her, tucking into my cob salad.

Rosa scoffs. "It's not like I've got anything else to do. I'm surprised I'm even allowed outside to play tennis!"

"Who do you play with?"

"Xander."

I burst out laughing as I look over to the kitchen island where Xander is sitting eating his own dinner. He's huge, over six feet and built like a brick shithouse, his thick arms covered in menacing tattoos.

"I let her win," he says gruffly.

"How gentlemanly of you." I chuckle.

"He's getting better." Rosa grins. "But I've still got so much time on my hands. My friends aren't allowed to come over, so I Facetime them, but most of them are off at summer camps." Her shoulders slump as she picks at her food, looking defeated.

"I'd be happy to play tennis with you tomorrow. And maybe we can have a picnic by the pool and download some of those romance books I was telling you about onto your phone."

"Thanks, Lila."

"Do you fancy watching a movie or something tonight? Andre is working, and I've got no plans, obviously."

"I think I might have an early night if that's ok." Rosa doesn't look at me. "I fancy a nice bubble bath and some Bridgerton."

"You know, I might join you with that. In my own bathroom, obviously." I laugh.

I also make a mental note to give Cassi a call. She's been blowing up my phone over the past week, wondering where I am when I didn't show up to meet her for coffee before work.

I've been as vague as I can, not wanting to catch myself in a web of lies that I can't unravel, but she deserves to know I'm ok. I don't want her to worry.

"See you for breakfast?" Rosa gets to her feet.

"Sounds good."

I finish my dinner and head upstairs to run myself a bath. There's an assortment of oils and salts lining the jacuzzi tub, and I add generous amounts of most of them to the water.

"This beats my crappy shower."

I turn on the TV built into the wall and load *Netflix*. I strip out of my clothes and slide into the warm water, moaning as I inhale the lavender and vanilla scent of the oils.

Part of me hopes that Andre will be back soon to join me in the bath, but I never know with him. He still keeps so much of his life secret, which I know is for my own protection, but it only makes me worry more.

I turn on *Friends* to try and distract myself, long enough for my eyelids to start feeling heavy.

Reluctantly, I climb out of the bath and pull on a more modest pair of pajamas. It's clear Andre is the one who stocked my wardrobe from the copious amounts of lace and silk, but seeing as he won't be around to enjoy them tonight, I slip into the cotton check trousers and oversized T-shirt.

I'm asleep before my head even hits the pillow.

RINGING FROM MY PHONE ROUSES ME FROM SLEEP.

My eyes are blurry as I blindly search for my phone on the nightstand, not even looking to see who's calling before I swipe the answer button.

"Hello?" I croak.

"Lila?"

I sit up at the hint of panic in Rosa's voice. Her voice sounds muffled, and there's music blaring in the background.

"Rosa?" I reach for the light. "Is everything ok?"

"Uh... N-no, not really." Her voice cracks.

I'm throwing off the covers, tucking my phone between my cheek and shoulder as I hastily dash into the dressing room in search of clothes.

"What's going on? Why do I get the impression you aren't in your room?"

"Because I'm not." Rosa's voice is thick with tears.

I let out a long breath.

"Rosa, where are you?"

"I'm at *Vision*."

"*What?* You're fifteen! How the hell did you get in?"

"You can get in anywhere if you flash enough cash, Lila."

"I can't believe this." I groan. "Are you alone?"

"I met up with Emilia, but she took off with some guy so I was going to head back home, but this guy's been harassing me. I've already fought him off once, but he's not getting the message. I'm hiding in the bathroom, but I know he's waiting outside."

I put my phone on speaker as Rosa talks, hastily pulling on a pair of leggings and a jumper as I try to think through what to do. "We should tell Andre."

"No! *Please* Lila, you can't tell Marco or Andre. They'll kill me if they find out I snuck out."

"How the hell did you get past Xander?" I press. "You know what, it doesn't matter. What matters is getting you the hell out of there."

I pinch the bridge of my nose between my thumb and forefinger, trying to think through a plan that doesn't result in Andre wanting to kill us both for disobeying him.

"Lila, you have to help me." Rosa's voice breaks. "You're the only person I can trust."

I'm touched by the comment, and I'm glad that she can feel comfortable enough around me.

"You're going to have to help me get out of the house, Rosa."

"Oh, my god, thank you, Lila. I owe you one."

"You owe me a million, but we'll get to that later. Now, I'm assuming you climbed out the window?"

Rosa instructs me to head to her bedroom, so I do as she says.

I tread lightly across the carpet, praying that Xander is a deep sleeper. He's been put in the room beside Rosa's, but as I pass it, I freeze at the sight of the open door.

36

LILA

That open door can only mean one thing. And it is not good news.

"Everything okay, Miss Morano?"

I jump at the sound of Xander's voice behind me, my heart pounding in my throat.

Fuck, I knew it.

I turn to find him wearing jeans and a black T-shirt that hugs his biceps, carrying a plate of leftovers from dinner.

"Uh, yes." I force a smile.

Xander's eyes narrow as he glances down at my attire, and I silently curse myself for not keeping my pajamas on at least until I was inside Rosa's room.

"Going somewhere?"

"Rosa messaged me, asking if I wanted to have a slumber party with her." I wave my phone. "This house gets a little...lonely when Andre and Marco are away." I ramble on, hoping Xander buys my reasoning for sneaking into Rosa's room.

"Sure." Xander's eyes are still narrowed. "If you need anything—"

"I'll make sure to call for you."

Xander hesitates a moment longer before disappearing inside his room.

I exhale, waiting a moment to ensure he's not coming back out before hurrying over to Rosa's room and sliding inside.

Turning on the light, I'm met with a sea of pale pink and lavender. It's the sort of bedroom I would have loved to have had as a teenager, with a huge four-poster bed with a white canopy, a vanity covered in makeup and perfume bottles, and a wall of bookshelves that have been color coordinated.

Unlocking my phone, I call Rosa back, making sure to keep my voice low in case Xander decides to come snooping. "Rosa?"

"I'm here."

"I bumped into Xander on the way to your room. Thankfully he seems oblivious to the fact that you're not here."

"Oh, thank god." She sighs. "I hope he doesn't get into trouble for this."

"We'll deal with that later. Right now we need to focus on getting me to *Vision* before Xander decides to do a midnight check-in."

Rosa informs me of a fake book on her shelf where she's hidden a stash of hundreds, in case of emergencies. I grab a handful, along with a bum bag that is hanging on the back of Rosa's door.

"Why do I need this?"

"To get into the club, and to keep anyone quiet if it comes to it."

"Great..." I mutter. "Ok, I've got the money. Now what?"

"Now you're going to have to climb out the window."

"Fuck."

"It's not that high. I climbed down the trellis that the climbing rose is attached to, and jumped the last ten feet."

My stomach churns as I realize how reckless this is.

I'm pregnant, I shouldn't be climbing out of windows where I could quite easily fall and land badly.

But I have to help Rosa. I can't leave her to fend for herself when she's surrounded by drunk men who won't stop until they've taken what they've come for.

"Ok, I'll call you back."

"Good luck."

I hang up the phone and tuck it into my bag before hurrying over to the large window. It's pitch black outside, which only adds to my nerves. If Andre were to ever find out I did something this stupid, he would lock me in my room until I gave birth to this baby.

But I can't think about that right now. The longer I hesitate, the longer Rosa is in danger.

So, I take a deep breath and pry open the window.

Without looking down, I climb onto the ledge and reach out for the wooden trellis structure to the right of the window.

My heartbeat is pounding in my ears as every possible scenario plays out in my head of how I could fall to my death.

"Come on, Lila." I mutter under my breath as I swing one leg over the ledge and blindly start to find my footing.

The thorns from the roses cut into my hands as I cling to the trellis, bringing my other leg over until my entire body is out, and I begin scaling down the wall.

I force myself not to look down, focusing on taking my time as I find my footing.

The trellis groans under my weight as I descend it, fighting the climbing rose the entire way.

My foot slips, causing my stomach to churn as I scramble to keep my hold on the trellis. "Shit! Come on, Lila. If Rosa could do it…"

I take another deep breath and move my foot lower, testing each ledge until I feel secure enough to move my hands.

When the window to the living room below becomes level with my feet, I glance down. The trellis has run out which means I have to jump the rest of the way just as Rosa told me.

"Here goes nothing." Lifting one foot off the trellis and turning my body so I'm facing the grounds, I push away from the wall, trying to hold in my scream as the ground comes barreling toward me.

I grunt as my feet hit the ground, and I go toppling over.

The grass beneath my hands is dewy to the touch but it softened the landing enough where I know I won't have any bruises to give me away—just a few cuts and splinters from the rose, but those will be easy enough to cover up.

I crouch down and hurry around the side of the house.

The kitchen light is still on, but as I peer into the window, it seems empty. Perhaps Xander left it on when he went to get himself some food.

Before I have a chance to test that theory, I hurry across the front lawn, keeping to the trees lining the long gravel drive to ensure the shadows keep me hidden.

I shoot Rosa a text letting her know I'm almost at the edge of the property. I don't want to risk anyone hearing me on the phone so I assure her I will call once I'm in an uber.

She sends me a pin to the club situated in White Plains, about a twenty-minute-drive away. If we manage to pull this off without anyone tipping off Andre, it'll be a miracle.

Once I reach the edge of the property, I call for an uber. Within two minutes, a silver Prius is pulling up, and I quickly hurry over to the passenger door, eager to get away from the house before the sight of the headlights draws Xander's attention.

The driver looks at me and nods. "Evening."

"Hey," I climb into the backseat.

"Heading to *Vision*?"

"Yes, please." I glance down at the map so I can keep Rosa updated on my arrival time.

The driver puts the car on drive. "Won't take us long to get there at this time."

"Great..."

He turns the radio up, and I tap my feet to the music, or maybe just a little bit too fast, as I watch our arrival time like my life depends on it.

Rosa assures me that she's still safe inside the club bathroom, but I know it wouldn't take much force for this guy to break down the door if he really wanted to.

"Come *on*," I whisper under my breath as we speed along the highway.

Our car swerves and I sway.

I look up, and the driver is frowning at the rearview mirror. "What is this fucker doing?"

I'm instantly on alert, twisting in my seat to look out the back window.

A blacked-out Range Rover is tailgating us despite it being clear for him to overtake.

I frown. "Maybe something is wrong. Can you pull over to let him pass?"

"I can try." The driver slows the car down, pulling over

a little, despite it being a two-lane highway.

The Range Rover swerves and moves to pull up along-side us. Almost glued to us.

My heart lurches in my chest as the two cars almost collide.

"What the fuck?" The uber driver swerves so as not to scrape alongside the car. "This fucker must be drunk or something."

Oh god. I don't want to die. "Pull over!"

The driver looks left and right, probably choosing his best option to escape this maniac.

He signs to move to the left lane. As he tries to slow down to let the other car overtake him, they swerve behind him and nick the back of our car, making it dance for a second.

I'm now holding on, one hand on each door, praying this madness will end, and this is nothing but a bad memory soon enough.

My driver gets the car stabilized, and tries moving back to the right lane, but the Range Rover swerves after us, almost hitting us again.

The driver is looking to the rearview mirror. "Fuck. What do I do?"

Suddenly, the Range Rover swerves to the left lane, and speeds up.

The uber driver's eyes cross with mine as something like relief crosses his eyes.

I start to smile before my eyes lower to the road, and I watch as the Range Rover swerves at the last second, right in front of us.

I open my mouth to scream, but my body is slammed against the seat in front of me as the uber smashes into the side of it.

37

ANDRE

"We're wasting time."

I pace the living room of the penthouse as Marco, Dez, and Sloan load up *The Vault*'s security footage on the TV.

Marco rolls his eyes. "We have to make sure we've covered all possible scenarios, Andre—"

"He knows we're watching him."

"Perhaps," Marco muses, pressing a few buttons on the remote. "But he's one to get sloppy when he thinks he's got the upper hand. He'll want us to get bored and move on to another location, and that's when he'll strike."

"You better be right, Marco."

My phone buzzes in my pocket, and one glance at the screen has my blood running cold. "I want this up and running by the time I finish this call."

Marco offers me a mock salute, and I shoot him a glare as I turn my back on him and swipe my phone screen.

"Rosa? It's one a.m.."

"Andre," Rosa sobs. "It's Lila. She's missing."

My stomach revolts and my eyes flutter closed as I try to digest Rosa's words.

"She snuck out to try and help me, a-and she's not here. She said twenty minutes, It's been an hour. Andre, *please*, you have to help—"

"Stop." I turn around to face Marco.

He glances up at me, and the look on my face has him straightening, signaling to Dez and Sloan to pay attention.

"Calm the fuck down, Rosa, and tell me everything."

I pull my phone away from my ear and put it on speaker, setting it down on the glass coffee table.

"I snuck out to meet Emilia at *Vision*."

Marco and I both curse, glancing at one another at the realization that our fifteen-year-old sister is at some shady club in White Plains. "But she left, and then some guy was harassing me—"

"*Fuck*," Marco hisses.

I hold up a hand to silence him. "How the hell did Xander let this happen?"

"It's not his fault, Andre. I climbed out the window."

"It is his fucking fault, he's meant to be watching you at all times!"

"Please, Andre. Don't blame Xander. This is all on me. I'm the one who put myself in this situation."

"What the hell does this have to do with Lila?"

"After this guy refused to leave me alone, I hid in the bathroom and called Lila," Rosa's voice is thick with tears. "She texted me and said she was in an uber and would be here in twenty minutes, but that was over an hour ago. So, I went outside to try and see if she was waiting for me, and the guy who had been harassing me comes over and tells me that Lorenzo thanks me for all my help."

I sink down into a leather armchair and run my shaking hands through my hair.

"He took her, Andre, and it's all my fault," Rosa cries.

"Send me your exact location, and we'll come and get you."

"I'm so sorry, Andre. I didn't mean—"

"We'll discuss this later. Right now, finding Lila is my priority."

Rosa sniffs on the other end of the phone before hanging up.

I glance at Marco, whose face has gone pale.

"He has her." I ball my hands into fists. My entire body is shaking, but I try to push the rage down so I can think rationally.

I can't afford to make any mistakes here, otherwise it may just cost Lila her life, if it hasn't already.

Dez moves. "Let us go and collect Rosa."

I shake my head.

"No, we all go. I need to see with my own eyes that she's safe."

Knowing that Xander let Rosa slip past him has severed all trust in my men when it comes to my sister.

"Andre..." Marco starts, but I shoot him a glare.

"It's not up for discussion. We need to leave *now*."

Every second that passes is a second too long that Lorenzo has Lila in his clutches. My stomach churns, and I fight the urge to vomit at the thought of what he might be doing to her.

As if Marco can sense where my thoughts are going, he places a hand on my shoulder and squeezes it hard.

"We'll get her back."

"I can't lose her too," I choke out.

"You won't." He nods. A promise. One he has no way of guaranteeing he can keep. "Dez, go get the car ready, we leave in five."

"Yes, sir." Dez disappears out of the room.

I punch the wall closest to me. "*Fuck*! How did he slip through like this?"

"We can worry about that later. Right now, we need to focus on making sure Rosa is safe and finding a lead on Lila. Only then can you let yourself focus on Lorenzo."

Marco's right. I'm wasting precious time.

I open up the hidden safe in the living room behind the TV and pull out enough weapons for all four of us. I don't plan on playing any other way but dirty.

"Let's go." I tuck another handgun into the waistband of my pants as I head toward the elevator. I pull out my phone as we step inside and try to track Lila's phone.

I look at Marco. "Rosa said Lila called an uber, right?"

"Yeah."

"Her location is saying she's on the side of route 26, but she's not moving."

"It's likely they tossed her phone out of the window if the car was intercepted." Marco frowns. "They would know you're tracking her."

"I say we head there once we collect Rosa."

"They'll be long gone, Andre."

"Do you have any better ideas?" The elevator doors open onto the underground garage. "For all we know she could be lying on the side of the fucking road!"

I slam my fist into the side of the elevator, my blood thumping in my ears as I try to ignore the images of Lila lying in a pool of her own blood.

My knuckles sting, and I rub them absentmindedly as I storm across the garage to where Dez waits in the driver's seat of the Hummer.

I climb into the passenger seat. "Marco, call your cop guy, and see if we can get a lead on the uber driver."

"On it." Marco climbs into the back alongside Sloan.

Dez taps a few buttons on the central screen. "I have your sister's location up now."

I groan. "Fuck, that'll take over thirty minutes to get to her."

Dez puts the car into reverse. "I can get us there in fifteen,"

As Dez races out of the garage and out into the open air, I turn in my seat to look at Marco. He has his phone propped between his cheek and shoulder, loading his weapons as he talks hurriedly into it.

I try to ignore the way his jaw is set and his eyes are filled with anger, which can only mean the information he's found out isn't what we were hoping for.

After he ends the call, he looks at me with regret in his eyes.

"Carlo traced the uber driver to route 26 also. There's been no activity on his phone for the past ninety minutes. It's not looking good, Andre."

Sloan looks at me. "You think they were run off the road?"

"It's possible." I try to sort through all the information we have.

"But I have no doubt that Lorenzo knows about Lila," and maybe even the fact she's pregnant, but I don't divulge that information. "He's using her as bait, just like he was planning to do with Rosa."

Marco nods. "Then we can only hope that he wants to keep her alive."

I turn back around in my seat, not wanting to see the look of sympathy on Marco's face.

Lila can't be dead. I refuse to believe that.

"Fucking step on it Dez." I grip the door handle so tightly my knuckles turn white.

Ten minutes later, Dez is swerving through a sea of ubers as we approach *Vision*.

The sight of my little sister standing outside in a black dress that leaves very little to the imagination has me seeing red. "Pull over."

Dez slams his foot on the brakes, and I throw open the car door, my body shaking as I storm over to Rosa.

"Get in the fucking car, *now*." I take her arm and drag her over to the Hummer.

For once, she doesn't fight me as Marco opens his door and Rosa climbs across to sit between him and Sloan. Her eyes are red and her cheeks are wet with tears, but I don't have the capacity to reassure her right now. *Especially* when none of this would have happened if she had never disobeyed me in the first place.

"Route 26," I order Dez.

He nods, pulling away from the curb and speeding through the sea of cabs.

I connect my phone to the central screen and load my tracking app so Dez can follow the directions to where Lila's phone is supposed to be. It's only ten minutes away, and I know Dez can get us there faster.

Part of me hopes she's not there, because if she is, it's likely that we won't find her alive. But the alternative may be so much worse.

It's happening again...

I screw my eyes shut, trying to ignore the feeling of dread building in the pit of my stomach. Images of Lila turn to images of Valentina, and then Rosa, and then my parents. So much death, and there's nothing I can seem to do to stop it.

Everyone I love is going to be taken from me.

"Oh fuck," Marco curses under his breath.

My eyes fly open to the freeway in front of us, and up ahead is a mangled silver car. Smoke is billowing out of the front radiator, and glass covers the ground around it from the smashed windscreen.

"Pull over!" I yell at Dez.

He swerves, slamming his foot on the brakes.

"Rosa, stay in the fucking car," I order as I throw open my door and start running toward the wreckage, reaching for my gun as I scan the surroundings.

Glass crunches beneath my feet as I slow my pace, pointing my gun at the car in case Lorenzo's planted a guy inside.

Tire marks cover the ground leading away from the car, so it seems whoever the uber crashed into managed to get away.

Sloan appears at my side. "Check the driver."

He nods, pulling a knife from his back pocket as he approaches the wreck. He leans into the driver's side and shakes his head. "Dead."

"Fuck. And Lila?"

I hold my breath as Sloan walks around to the passenger door and peers inside.

"No sign of her, sir." He shakes his head, bending down to pick up a cracked device. "But her phone is here."

"Lila," I breathe.

I sink to my knees among the shattered glass as my heart cracks in two.

Lorenzo has taken Lila and my unborn child right out from under my nose.

I thought I had already lived through my worst nightmare.

But it turns out I was wrong.

38

LILA

Where the hell am I? Why is it so cold here? I pat around for my sheets, but the bed feels off.

I open my eyes to an unfamiliar room.

As I glance down, I find myself stripped down to my underwear. My skin is covered in goosebumps, and a thick cuff is locked around my left ankle.

I scramble backwards off what I notice is a thin, stained mattress I must have been put on, but I can only go so far until the chain locks out.

"Not again," I breathe, as I pull against it. The chain rattles, the sound echoing around the damp cell and in my ears as it pulls against the heavy metal pipe it's connected to.

I pull again, and the muscles in my leg scream at me, as if I fought whoever it was who put the chain on me.

What happened?

I want to hope against hope that this is Andre's way of punishing me for leaving the house. But looking around, I know better.

This time, I'm in big trouble. But how? Why?

I screw my eyes shut and rub at my temples, wincing at the pain in my head as I try to decipher the last thing I remember.

I was in an uber, and there was a car. Oh, my god, he was trying to run us off the road. It passed us and swerved and then...fear...pain...nothing...

Holy crap. We crashed. My baby! My hands move to my abdomen as bile rises in my throat.

I need to see a doctor. I need to make sure my baby is okay.

I pull on the chain on my leg again and again. I need to free myself. I need to get out of here, wherever 'here' is.

I look around, trying to find a way out, other than the door, which I'm sure is either locked or has someone nasty on the other side.

Thick, iron bars block the window high above me.

My eyes flick to the door, and I notice more bars, orange with rust.

Two exits.

But no way out.

On the other side of the bars in the door, there's the top of a blond head—a guard who is sitting outside to make sure I don't escape? Not that I could, even if my life depended on it.

"Help," I croak.

My throat is bone-dry, and I'm desperate for water.

How long has it been?

My head's foggy, as if I've been asleep for days, and my stomach growls.

"Help!" Though my voice is barely above a whisper, the empty cell still carries the sound, but the guard makes no indication that he's heard me.

"Please!" I choke out, crawling onto my hands as knees as far as the chain will allow. "*Help.*"

My limbs shake with the effort, and they eventually give out, my body collapsing onto the cold, damp floor.

"Andre..." I whimper, as if somehow my voice will carry all the way to him. That I'll wake to the sound of him breaking down the door, where he'll rush to my side and lift me into his arms, whispering in my ear how he'll always keep me safe.

I let my eyes flutter closed, praying that Andre will come, because without him, I doubt I'll leave this cell alive.

———

I CAN FEEL HIS PRESENCE LONG BEFORE I OPEN MY eyes. I try to keep my breathing shallow, feigning sleep as I try to come up with a plan.

Even if I managed to unlock the chain around my ankle, there's at least one guard outside, and potentially more beyond the building where I'm being kept. There's no way I can fight them all off without a weapon.

So, that's what I'll need to find.

I peel my eyes open, ignoring the painful pounding of my heart as I take in the man crouched before me with a feral smile plastered on his face.

"It's a pleasure to meet you, Lila Morano."

His face is heavily lined, and his dark gray hair is neatly styled. He's wearing a pristine three-piece suit the same color as his hair. The man oozes wealth and power, and I know somewhere on his person he'll have a gun or a knife.

I take a steadying breath as I look into his dark green eyes.

"Who are you?" I fear I already know the answer.

"Andre hasn't told you about me?" He pretends to look hurt, pressing a hand to his heart. "I'm offended."

"Lorenzo," I whisper, my voice catching in my throat.

Lorenzo chuckles, rubbing his hands together as he eyes me.

"Very good. I was worried for a moment that Andre had tricked you, hiding his true identity and life for fear of scaring you off."

"I know who he is, what he does." I try to speak with confidence.

"Interesting…" Lorenzo climbs to his feet. "And what has he told you about me?"

I blink, trying to muster up a lie, to think back to that news article which linked Lorenzo and Andre together—the very one that revealed Andre's true life to me. But I come up short, and Lorenzo seems to realize it as he lets out a bark of a laugh.

"Well, I must say I'm surprised, Lila." He frowns. "I would have at least thought Andre would have told you of our history."

"We don't waste our breath speaking about scum like you," I spit, baring my teeth.

"Feisty." Lorenzo chuckles. "I can see why Andre likes you."

"What are you going to do to me?" The longer I keep him talking, the longer Andre has to find me. There's no way he hasn't realized what's happened by now. Rosa would have given in and called him when I didn't show up at the club—

Rosa.

My stomach churns at the thought of her alone at that club. I only hope that Andre got to her before anything bad happened.

"We're going to have some fun, you and I." Lorenzo crouches back down in front of me, reaching out to run a calloused finger along my cheek.

I flinch beneath his touch, cowering back against the brick wall, trying to shield my half-naked body from him.

"One thing you should know about me, Lila, is that I take great *pleasure* in torturing people. I like to inflict so much pain that my victims beg to die. I want to see their pale flesh stained red with blood." His eyes rake over my body, a wicked gleam in his eye.

I try to keep my face neutral, almost bored, but I can feel the blood drain from my face at the thought of what will happen to me if Andre doesn't make it in time. What will happen to my baby…

"Is that all?" I raise my eyebrows.

I see through Lorenzo's façade.

He's no different to any man whose masculinity is threatened, except he has the power to kill you and sweep you under the rug as if you never existed. He wants to instill fear, make me cower. This is already part of the torture, the psychological part of it.

It might be working, but I will do my best to not let it show. I just have to keep breathing until Andre gets here.

"Oh, no, sweet Lila. Once your skin is dyed red, I plan on chaining you by your wrists and ankles, spreading those soft thighs of yours, and fucking you, over and over until you finally scream my name with pleasure."

I have to swallow down the vomit that starts to fill my mouth at Lorenzo's words.

"And trust me, I won't stop until you do." He licks his lips as his eyes flick over my shaking body.

"No," I breathe, my armor faltering.

"Then, Lila, when I am finally done with you, I will

likely sell you at an auction to the highest bidder. And with a body like that, I'm guaranteed to make a small fortune. Though not as much as you would normally go for, considering you've already been sullied by a De Luca. In which case, I might just save myself the trouble and slit your throat while I'm still buried inside you."

My throat burns as I swallow back bile.

"Why not just kill me now? I have no information to offer you."

Lorenzo laughs, the grating sound echoing around the damp cell.

"I want nothing from you, Lila. All I want is to send Andre a message, and when he eventually finds what's left of your body, you will have fulfilled your purpose."

"You're a monster," I spit. "I've done nothing to you."

"Perhaps." Lorenzo shrugs. "But Andre has. And he must learn that his actions have consequences."

"He'll kill you!"

"He can try." Lorenzo chuckles. "But by the time he finds you, it'll be too late. My time of fun will be over, and I'll be long gone."

He rises to his feet. "He will learn his lesson. I'll crush him like the bug he is." He reaches out a hand to pick up a strand of my hair. "But that is not a problem for you, my sweet, because by then, you'll be dead."

39

———

ANDRE

THE WORLD STOPS TURNING AS I KNEEL IN THE shattered glass.

Lila...

This is all my fault. I should have never let her out of my sight.

I failed.

I wasn't able to keep her safe like I promised. And now Lorenzo has her, and time is running out.

"We'll find her, Andre." Marco rests a hand on my shoulder.

My fists clench, my knuckles turning white as I try to suppress my rage.

"I'm so sorry, Andre," Rosa sobs from behind me.

I close my eyes, the sound of my sister's sobs grating on my nerves. "I told you to stay in the fucking car. Why can you never do as you are fucking told?"

"Andre—"

"*Enough!* You've done enough for tonight. Get back in the fucking car. Now!"

Her sobs intensify, but her running footsteps are moving away from me. Good.

I have to think through our next steps. Part of me wants to go after her, snap at Rosa for being so fucking irresponsible. This is *exactly* the sort of thing I was afraid of happening. Did she think I kept her locked in the house for fun?

I grind my teeth together as I try to think through a plan.

"Marco, get Kyle on the phone." I climb to my feet, turning my back on the wreckage.

"What for?"

"We need something in our pocket to bargain with when we find Lorenzo."

"Can't we just kill him?" Marco frowns.

"It's likely he'll be keeping Lila somewhere separate and use her to bargain with us. We need to have something to offer in return if we have any chance of bringing her back alive." My stomach churns at the thought that we might already be too late, but we can't storm Lorenzo's hideouts without having a plan, otherwise *none* of us will walk away from this alive.

"I want names, Marco. Anyone we could use who might be close to Lorenzo. I don't care if it's his fucking dog, get me something!"

"On it." My brother pulls his phone out of his jacket pocket, dialing Kyle's number.

I let out a breath and walk over to the Hummer where Rosa is seating with tears streaming down her face.

She goes to speak, but I shake my head, not wanting to hear any more of her apologies.

My jaw is clenched tight and it's a struggle to unclench it enough that I can talk. "Jerry is going to come and pick you up and take you back to the main house. I'm assuming I don't need to reiterate my point of staying *in your fucking room.*"

Rosa hangs her head, her dark hair falling in front of her face as she nods.

"Once this is all over, Rosa, we're going to have a very serious conversation, do you understand?"

"Yes, Andre," she whispers.

"Good." I place a hand on her shoulder and squeezing once.

I know she blames herself, and at this moment, to a degree, I do too, though I would never speak the words out loud. She's clearly wracked with guilt, and I can only hope this will teach her to never defy my orders again.

But I know that ultimately, this is all my fault. I'm the one that failed at making sure they stayed in the fucking house as they should.

"Dez, Sloan." I walk away from Rosa.

The two men flank either side of me as we stand before the wreckage, waiting for my brother to get off the phone with Kyle.

If he has nothing to offer us, I'm at a loss for where to start. We have no leads as to where Lorenzo might have taken Lila, but we've already wasted too much time.

My hands are shaking as I run them through my hair, trying to sort through the chaos in my mind. All I can think of is all the ways Lorenzo might be torturing her, and with each second that passes, she gets closer to death.

And I refuse to lose her too. "Marco."

My brother hangs up the phone and turns to face me, a deep frown lining his forehead.

"There's a potential mistress that Lorenzo has been sending large amounts of money to each month for the past few years."

"A mistress?"

Marco nods.

"I'm assuming the money is to pay for her lifestyle?"

Marco shakes his head, his dark hair falling into his eyes.

"Kyle doesn't think so. It seems the chick comes from money."

Dez pipes up, "So, why does she need it?"

"He's buying her silence." My mind's racing as I try to think through each scenario.

Marco frowns harder. "What do you think she knows?"

"It could be anything, but it's clear that she's important to him, otherwise he would've just killed her. Is Kyle looking into an address?"

Marco nods.

"Good. In the meantime, I suggest we start working through all of Lorenzo's hideouts."

"You don't think he'd keep Lila at any of those, do you? He knows we know those locations—"

"He wants me to come to him, Marco. Why else would he have taken Lila? He's not simply sending a message. He wants to start a war."

"*Fuck*." Marco runs his hands over his face. "Where do we start?"

Dez tucks his hands into his pockets. "I suggest we start in East Harlem, at *Luciano's*. I know he's got a few guys making the rounds over there, so even if Lorenzo's not there, it would send a nice little message to him."

"Fine. We head there once Rosa has been collected."

THE MOMENT ROSA IS IN THE BACKSEAT OF JERRY'S Mercedes, heading safely back to Westchester, I climb into the front seat of the Hummer, with Dez driving, and we race toward Harlem.

This is going to be a bloodbath, but I won't stop until I'm holding Lila's warm body in my arms. I refuse to accept any other outcome.

I think of the baby she's growing, and I have to swallow down the acid in my throat. If Lorenzo knows...

"Andre." Marco snaps me out of my spiraling thoughts.

"What?"

"I know what you're thinking, so stop it right now." He leans across the center console of the car. "She's not dead. She's not Valentina."

I flinch at the mention of her name, my wounds threatening to burst open with each passing second.

Dez tightens his fists around the steering wheel. "We're going to get her back, boss."

I say nothing as we race toward the city, choosing instead to check each of my weapons.

Two handguns, each with seventeen rounds, four magazines, a six-inch blade and a nine-inch blade.

By the time Lila is safely back in my arms, I want each of these bullets embedded in the skulls of Lorenzo's men, and I want at least one of the knives buried deep in Lorenzo's chest cavity after I've run it across his throat. I want to wear his blood like a tattoo on my skin, a marker to any who think they can take what belongs to me.

"He's not getting out of this alive." I click the safety off my gun.

Luciano's is a dive situated in the center of East Harlem. At two in the morning, the place looks abandoned, with no lights on and the sign half hanging off the wall.

But I know better. Most of these places have hidden basements beneath the bars, left over from the prohibition, which are now used for drug deals and money laundering. It will no doubt be full of Lorenzo's men.

Dez pulls down a side alley and puts the Hummer in park. "Should we even bother going around the back?"

Marco's safety click echoes around the car. "No point in being discrete, Dez. Let's smash this fucking place up."

Sloan chuckles. "I like your style."

I open the car door and climb out. "Don't leave anyone alive. I want the floors flooded with blood by the time we leave."

Sloan leads the way, a baseball bat resting on his shoulders as we approach *Luciano's*.

I stand back beside Marco as Sloan lifts the bat and sends it straight through the glass front, shattering it into a thousand tiny pieces.

He steps to the side. "After you, boss."

I tighten my grip on my gun as I step through into the restaurant, the glass crunching beneath my feet as I creep across the floor. No doubt the sound of the glass shattering sent whoever is below into action.

"Dez." I signal for him to join me.

He climbs through the front window with expert grace, his machine gun pointed straight at the locked door behind the cash register. ∼

I glance over my shoulder at Marco and Sloan. "Ready?"

They both nod, sly grins on their faces as they point their weapons.

This is it. Time to teach Lorenzo the lesson he never learned.

He thinks he can mess with me? Touch my family? The woman I love? The mother of my child?

Those thoughts nearly have me crumbling. Because I do love her. As I do my unborn child.

And they need me more than ever. So, I stand taller.

Lila is counting on me.

I failed to keep her safe, but I won't fail again.

Lila, sweetheart, hang tight. I'm coming for you.

40

———

ANDRE

Dez storms the door leading down to the basement, his gun already firing before we've even reached the bottom of the stairs.

Gunfire rings in my ears as I fire my weapon at the dozen or so men huddled around tables, stacks of packaged cocaine surrounding them.

They barely have a chance to pull their own weapons before I embed bullets between their eyes and watch with delight as the light slowly drains from them before they hit the floor.

A few more appear from storage rooms to our left.

Before I have a chance to aim, an arm is around my neck.

I send my elbow back, knocking the wind out of the fucker before whirling and smashing my gun into the side of his head, knocking him out.

I put a bullet through his head before he even hits the floor, the blood spraying my skin like scarlet rain.

I glance behind me.

Sloan's in a hand-to-hand fight with a guy even bigger than he is.

He manages to get a few hits to Sloan's jaw, whose head snaps to the side.

Sloan's lip is split, and he has the start of a black eye forming, but there's such wildness in his eyes that I know that there's no way Lorenzo's guy is walking away from this.

"Need a hand, Sloan?" I release my empty magazine and load up a new one.

"I got this one, boss." He grabs the guy by the shoulders, rearing his head back and smashing it straight into his nose.

"Ouch." I chuckle as the guy groans, blood spurting from his broken nose.

He stumbles backwards, straight into Dez who wraps his hands around his head and twists, instantly snapping his neck.

The guy falls to the floor like a ragdoll, and Dez and Sloan grin at each other as they step over the body.

I glance to my left and see my brother crouched low in the corner behind one of the tables. "Marco?"

He's grunting with effort, and as I approach, I notice his hands wrapped around the neck of a guy, slamming his head repeatedly into the concrete floor. Blood spills out beneath him as his skull disintegrates, coating my brother's hands red as he takes every last ounce of life from the man.

"I think you made your point." I place a hand on my brother's shoulder.

"You wanted the place flooded with blood," Marco grits out. "Plus, the fucker tried to break my jaw."

Sloan chuckles. "And that's your best feature."

"Exactly." Marco slams the guy one last time against the floor before releasing his hold around his neck. "Did we get them all?"

Looks around. "Looks like it."

A phone starts ringing.

Marco climbs to his feet, pulling his phone out of his jacket pocket and handing it to me.

I glance down at the screen before answering.

"You better have an address for me, Kyle." I wipe my bloody hands on my shirt.

"I have something better," Kyle replies. "Turns out it wasn't a mistress Lorenzo was wiring all that money to."

"How is this better?" Fuck, if it turns out to be some lacky, it's likely Lorenzo won't give two fucks whether we take them hostage.

"It was an illegitimate son he had with a mistress two decades ago. The kid lives on the lower east side, some swanky apartment on Orchard."

I glance to Marco, who's switching out the magazine on his gun with swift efficiency. He glances in my direction with raised brows as I hang up the phone.

"Turns out Kyle got us something better than a mistress." A feral smile tugs at my lips. "He got us a descendent."

"An eye for an eye." Marco chuckles, cracking his knuckles. "This just got interesting."

I crack my neck and roll my shoulders before climbing out of the Hummer. "Dez, you and Sloan stay here."

I slam the door.

"What's the plan here, brother?" Marco falls into step beside me as we approach the apartment building.

"Climb the fire escape to the top floor, get the fucker in his sleep."

Marco grins.

"It's showtime." He reaches for his gun.

Soon enough the city will rise from its slumber to find the bloodbath we've left in our wake, but until then, we hide in the shadows as we quietly ascend the stairs to the top floor.

"This is it." I press myself against the red bricks.

No lights are on, and I only hope that means our target is tucked up in bed.

We're running out of time, and without this lead, I've got nothing to offer Lorenzo in exchange for Lila.

I glance over my shoulder at Marco. "Ready?"

He nods.

I slam the base of my gun into the glass window and climb through into a darkened living room.

"Rise and shine!" I call out, pointing my gun at the ceiling and firing.

I hear a thud off to the right in what I assume is the bedroom.

Making sure Marco is following, I charge in there.

Vince Rossi is waiting, his own gun pointing straight at my chest.

"Too slow." I point at his shoulder and fire.

He cries out, falling to his knees as he clutches at the wound.

Marco strolls over and picks up his weapon before sending it careening into the side of Vince's face, splitting his cheek and possibly cracking a few of his teeth.

"Fuck, you look just like him." Marco crouches down and gets to work binding Vince's hands behind his back.

Vince smirks, showing his blood-stained teeth.

Marco's not wrong.

Vince has the same dark green eyes as Lorenzo, and his hair is jet black and slightly curled. He can't be more than twenty, though he's got a fair amount of muscle on him. He's wearing nothing but a pair of boxers, which gives us perfect access to the one thing he will value the most.

"That's *not* a compliment." I lift his chin with the tip of my gun. "Now, I suggest you start giving us some information if you plan on keeping all of your limbs."

"I don't know anything." Vince throws his head back, spitting bloody drool at Marco.

"You *fucker*," Marco hisses.

"Marco. we need him alive." My eyes find Vince's. "Now, start fucking *talking*."

"I told you, I don't know anything." A thin sheen of sweat covers his forehead. He's losing a lot of blood from the bullet wound, but it won't be enough to kill him. Yet.

"I'm sure we can change that." I take a step back. "Marco, why don't you start with his right hand."

"I'd be happy to." Marco chuckles, pulling out a knife.

Vince's eyes widen at the sight of the six-inch blade.

"This might hurt just a little," Marco purrs.

"I've been working with him!" Vince splutters, his eyes darting between me and Marco. "But he tells me nothing. No specifics."

I frown. "He doesn't trust you? Why?"

Marco pauses, the edge of his blade pressed into Vince's wrist, ready to sever the limb at my command.

"I-I don't know."

Marco shakes his head. "Surely, Lorenzo would want his son knowing the ins and outs of his business. I don't buy it."

"I gave up the location of *The Vault*," Vince admits. "There was a mole, and I didn't realize it."

Marco barks out a laugh. "Sounds like you're a fucking liability. Seems to me, *daddy* would be glad to see the back of you." Marco turns to me and raises his eyebrows. "He won't be enough."

I let out a long breath as I look into Vince's eyes, *Lorenzo*'s eyes, and know what my brother says is true.

If Lorenzo doesn't trust Vince enough to tell him anything of use, then there's no way he'd give up Lila in exchange for him.

Marco scowls. "He's dead weight."

Vince squirms, shaking his head. "I could be a mole for you—"

My gun is already pointed between his eyebrows, my finger pulling the trigger before he even has a chance to finish that sentence.

"We've wasted too much time." I look down at Vince's body now slumped on the floor, his blood staining the cream carpet. I kick him, hard. "Fuck!"

Lila's been in Lorenzo's clutches for hours. Who knows what sort of pain he's inflicted on her? She's slipping through my fingers, the last few threads keeping us tied together are snapping.

A phone starts buzzing on the nightstand, and I freeze.

"Vince's phone." I walk around to the other side of the bed and pick it up.

It's an unknown number, but it's likely one of Lorenzo's guys calling from a burner phone.

"Answer it," Marco hisses.

I swipe the green call button and place the call on speaker.

"Why the fuck aren't you here yet?" a voice barks through the phone.

My breath catches as I realize it's Lorenzo.

I swallow, trying to stay calm. This could be the lead I've been searching for, so I can't afford to make any mistakes.

I keep my voice low. "Where?"

"Fucking Chinatown. Fuck's sake, Vince! Don't make me regret putting you on the payroll."

A woman screams in the distance, and the sound makes my blood run cold.

"On my way." I hang up the phone and throw it at the brick wall, where it shatters. "He has her." My teeth are clenched so hard I have no idea if Marco even understands me.

"Where?" Marco climbs over Vince's body to get to me. "Andre, what's going on?"

"He has her at that fucking warehouse in Chinatown."

"Oh, shit. The one where he killed..."

"Valentina."

41

LILA

"PLANS HAVE CHANGED, SWEETHEART," LORENZO PURRS as he stalks into my cell.

I cower in the corner, my arms wrapped around my shivering body as I try to read the expression on his face.

He left me alone to answer a phone call and hasn't come back for what seems like a few hours. The feral amusement in his eyes has turned to that of pure, unadulterated rage.

My heart rate quickens as he stalks toward me, brandishing a knife. "I'm going to have to kill you."

"W-why?"

"It seems your *boyfriend* is smarter than I give him credit for."

I flinch at the mention of Andre.

He will hurt so much if I die. If I let our baby die. I can't believe that I fell for him, that I came to love him. I think I've loved him from that first moment I looked into his eyes.

Is he trying to find me?

Please hurry.

"It seems he's been busy killing my people, so he's given

me no choice but to return the favor. Pity. I was hoping to spend more time getting to know you, *Lila*."

My name on his lips sends a shudder through my body. Not the good kind.

"Andre will kill you if you harm me." I have to buy myself some time.

"He can try." Lorenzo shrugs. "But I won't harm you just yet, princess. First, we're going to have some fun, you and I. Why don't I set up a little camera to give Andre something to watch before I kill him too? That way, he gets to endure the consequences of his actions, and he can die riddled with guilt, knowing your blood is on his hands."

My chest heaves as a sense of panic builds deep in my core.

Lorenzo is rattled, which means Andre is likely on his way.

If I can only keep him talking long enough for Andre to find me...

"I could be useful to you."

Lorenzo pauses, his eyes narrowing as he glares at me.

"Andre trusts me."

Lorenzo throws his head back and laughs, the harrowing sound echoing around the dank cell.

"Nice try, sweetheart, but I know about your little situation."

I frown. "What situation?"

"The fact that you're pregnant with Andre's child."

My blood chills as I look once more at the knife in Lorenzo's hands, my mind going to the darkest of places.

I have no idea what this man is capable of, but he seems to want to stop at nothing until he has Andre's blood on his hands.

"There's no way in hell I would trust you as a spy when

you're in so deep with De Luca. It wouldn't be worth the trouble. Besides, I'm very much looking forward to seeing his face when he realizes I raped the mother of his child and then cut open her womb to let her bleed out."

I can't fight the vomit that rises in my throat. I double over and empty the contents of my stomach on the floor.

"Please." I place my hands protectively over my abdomen as I look at Lorenzo. "Not my baby."

"Oh, yes. I like it when you beg." He crouches down in front of my cowering body.

He reaches out to run his fingers along my cheek, and I try my best not to show any fear, but I can't help but recoil at his touch.

I watch as Lorenzo's expression changes to one of fury. Pain sears my skin as his hand collides with my cheek, snapping my head to the side.

I whimper, fighting the urge to press a hand to my burning cheek, not wanting to seem weak.

"I'm the last man you'll ever feel inside you, so you might as well enjoy it, princess," Lorenzo purrs. "And the fact that you're pregnant with Andre's child only makes me harder."

"No woman would ever take pleasure from fucking you." I bare my teeth at Lorenzo.

His eyes flash, and he slaps me again on the same cheek.

I gasp at the pain, but I would rather the feel of his hand on my cheek then of his cock as he tries to fuck me.

"I'm going to take great pleasure in fucking you, Lila Morano." He wraps his hand around my neck, forcing me back onto the mattress.

I lash out, pounding my fists into his chest, but it only results in Lorenzo tightening his grip around my neck.

I gasp for air, clutching at his wrists as my lungs start to ache.

"There's no need for that," he purrs. "Now, let's get the camera all set up, shall we?"

Lorenzo releases his hold around my neck and climbs to his feet.

"If you resist me, Lila, you will render Rosa to the same fate. So, what will it be?"

"Rosa?"

She's here? The man at the club... He must have been one of Lorenzo's men, hoping to corner her and bring her to him.

The thought of this disgusting old man laying a finger on sweet Rosa has me swallowing down bile.

"Don't fucking touch her," I spit. "She's a child."

"That is up to you, now, isn't it?" Lorenzo shakes his head.

"I'll do whatever you want." I have to protect Rosa from this fate if it's the last thing I do. If Andre loses his sister too...

"Good, that's a start." He crosses the cell and opens the door, calling for the guard outside to come in.

The guard doesn't look much younger than me, and it chills me to think what happened in his short life to get him to this point.

I watch as Lorenzo reaches into his pocket and hands the guard his cellphone.

"Get ready to start filming."

The young guard looks at me, his expression cold and unmoving.

"Help me," I mouth, the taste of salt on my tongue as tears cascade down my face.

But the guard looks back to Lorenzo as if he never saw me, and I realize that I've exhausted my last option.

If Andre doesn't get here in the next few minutes, I'm going to pray that death claims me quickly, and that Lorenzo is satisfied enough to leave Rosa unharmed.

"I'm sure Andre will enjoy this very much." Lorenzo stalks toward me.

I keep my chin lifted, not wanting to cower away from my fate.

He smiles at me, as if sensing my thoughts.

"Tell me you want this." Lorenzo moves to sit beside me on the old mattress.

I swallow my disgust as he reaches out to run a finger along the curve of my breast.

I try my best not to flinch at the feeling of his calloused finger grazing my skin.

I swallow the acid in my throat as he devours my body with his eyes.

"Tell me that you can't wait to feel my cock inside you."

I glance to the guard who's moved closer, the phone pointing at us as he films.

I stare directing into the camera, hoping my eyes portray everything I will never get to say to Andre.

That I love him, that I'm sorry. That I was looking forward to having his baby. That I'm sorry that I couldn't save Rosa, but I'm trying hard nw. That my life only got better when he came into my life.

There are so many things I wish I could tell him, so many things I wish he could have told me back.

I love him, but now he will never have the chance to grow to love me back. He'll never have the chance to meet his baby.

The only good thing about it is that because he doesn't love me, he won't be as devastated as he was with Valentina.

I hope he knows this is not his fault. Was never his fault.

Lorenzo's voice snaps me back to reality. To the living nightmare my life has become. *"Say it!"*

I flinch. One last thought crossing my mind.

I'm sorry, Andre. I love you.

I close my eyes. "I want this."

Tears roll down my face.

Lorenzo strikes me across the cheek, but I barely feel it, I'm so numb.

"Say it like you mean it," he growls in my ear.

I cry out as he pushes down my bra and twists my nipple between his thumb and forefinger.

"I-I want this."

"I don't believe you, Lila."

"Please," I sob, keeping my eyes on the camera.

"Say. It."

"I-I..."

Guns firing outside the room have me looking at the door.

The guard falters, glancing over his shoulder, and I know it's now or never.

I let my lungs fill with air, throw my head back, and scream.

The sound bounces off the brick walls, and all I can hope is that it echoes through the open door.

To Andre.

Please let it be Andre.

"Oh no, you don't," Lorenzo hisses, clamping his hands around my neck so tightly my scream is cut off and black dots dance before my eyes.

42

ANDRE

Five years ago, Lorenzo Rossi murdered Valentina Magri. My fiancée.

There's no way in hell I'm about to let him take Lila and my unborn child too.

"Lorenzo is mine."

We approach the abandoned warehouse where my life was torn apart situated in the center of Chinatown.

It's derelict, with most of the windows broken or boarded up, the red bricks long since faded to a dirty brown. The perfect scene for the perfect crime.

"He took something from me a long time ago." I pull out my gun and flick off the safety. "It's about time he suffers the consequences."

We climb out of the Hummer and begin our approach.

It's likely Lorenzo has men stationed at the windows, so we keep to the shadows on the surrounding building, pressing up against the walls to shield ourselves from any unwanted attention.

The main entrance to the warehouse is a set of steel

rolling shutters, but they're rusted and practically hanging off the hinges.

I wave to Sloan and Dez to approach first while Marco and I stay in the shadows, our guns ready in case any of Lorenzo's men are waiting for us on the other side.

I don't realize I'm holding my breath until Dez sends his foot slamming into the steel, the sound of the impact making my teeth grind together.

"No turning back now," Marco mutters as he holds his gun out in front of him as he charges for the entrance.

I roll out my shoulders and let the red mist surround my vision as I ready myself for what I might find inside.

I'm coming for you, sweetheart.

We storm the warehouse and face immediate gunfire.

At least a dozen men are waiting for us with machine guns, but Dez is a quick shot and in less than ten seconds, takes out three.

Sloan darts behind a stack of wooden crates and starts taking out the men hidden on the balcony above.

Marco and I move to the right, crouching low behind old, rusted barrels covered in bullet holes.

We run the length of the main warehouse floor, bullets wheezing past us.

I glance above as stomping footsteps let me know that even more men are running across the metal grates.

I take aim above me, shooting one man in the thigh and another straight between the shoulder blades who goes crashing into the railing and topples over the edge, smashing into the stack of crates which are hiding Dez and Sloan.

Marco groans, "Fuck."

I whirl.

My brother's clutching his shoulder.

"Marco?"

He pulls his hand away, and it's covered in blood.

"No!" I run back to my brother. "Let me see—"

Marco brushes me away. "It's just a graze. You need to go. *Now*."

I hesitate, but Marco shoves at me with his uninjured arm.

"Fucking *go!*"

If I lose him too...

I shake my head and clear my thoughts.

Right now, I need to find Lila.

With one last look at my brother, I turn and sprint across the warehouse floor, dodging the fallen bodies of Lorenzo's men as I head toward a set of double doors.

My blood pounds in my ears as adrenaline courses through my veins, narrowing my focus.

Lila, where are you, baby?

I throw the doors open and take a set of stairs down to a basement, two at a time.

The place reeks of damp and mold, with barely any light to show me the way.

I nearly stumble at the agonized scream echoing from down below.

"Lila!"

I jump the last few steps and follow the sound down a dimly lit corridor.

At the very end, there's an open door with rusted iron bars in place of a window.

I creep forward, my gun aimed and ready as the back of a blond-haired man comes into view.

I freeze.

Did I take a wrong turn?

I look behind him, and my blood runs cold.

Lorenzo has his hands wrapped around Lila's throat,

chocking her, and the blond fucker seems to be filming the whole damn thing.

I want to make him suffer. Bleed, but there's no time. One bullet to the head has him collapsing to the ground.

Lorenzo doesn't loosen his hold on Lila.

I'll kill him!

Tucking my gun into my belt, I break out into a run, storming the cell.

I don't stop until I'm throwing Lorenzo at the brick wall.

He grunts, slumping down into a heap on the floor, but the impact isn't enough to knock him out.

I have maybe a few seconds before he's on his feet. But I need to make sure Lila is okay.

"Sweetheart." I crouch in front of her.

She's been stripped to her underwear, and she's shaking. There's dark purple bruising already forming around her neck.

I curse as I reach out to touch her cheek. "I'm going to make it all go away, okay, baby?"

She nods, a whimper escaping her lip as she glances over at Lorenzo.

"Andre..." she croaks.

I take a deep breath before climbing to my feet and stalking toward Lorenzo.

"I hoped I wouldn't ever have to step foot in this place again," I snarl, kicking Lorenzo hard enough to crack a few ribs.

He grunts but continues to try and climb to his feet.

I'm not going to let him.

"You. Sick. *Fuck*." Each word has my foot colliding with his ribs.

"She enjoyed it," Lorenzo coughs out, offering me a feral smile.

I roar as I reach for my gun and shoot a bullet straight into his thigh.

Lorenzo collapses against the concrete, howling like the fucking dog he his as he clutches his bleeding leg. "You *fucker*!"

"Trust me, this is only the beginning." I turn my back on Lorenzo, rushing back to Lila's side, tucking my gun in my back pocket.

I run my hands over her tangled hair, her cheeks, her shoulders, hating how cold she feels beneath my touch.

"The chain," she whimpers.

I frown.

Lila pulls her leg, and the rattling of the chain around her ankle has me gritting my teeth.

"That fucker chained you?"

And he was going to force himself on her for his own sick pleasure.

"I'm going to fucking kill him."

"Andre."

My name on Lila's lips snaps me out of my rage.

When I look into her ocean blue eyes and find nothing but fear, I almost crack in two.

"I'm going to get you out of here."

I get to my feet and stalk over to Lorenzo, who's leaning against the brick wall, his teeth bared as blood pools beneath him.

"I suggest you give me the fucking key before I put a bullet in your other thigh," I growl.

Lorenzo lifts his chin and looks at me with nothing but contempt in his green eyes.

"It's buried in my pocket, De Luca. I dare you to come and get it."

I wrinkle my nose as I crouch down in front of Lorenzo.

He reaches for my neck, but I pull my gun free and press it to the spot right between his eyes.

"I can't wait until I can watch the life drain out of your eyes," I whisper. "Now give me the fucking key."

Sweat beads on Lorenzo's brow, his breathing coming in shallow pants as he stares into my eyes, as if trying to call my bluff.

I click the safety off, which seems to be enough of a confirmation as Lorenzo reaches into his pocket and pulls out a small iron key.

"That wasn't so hard, was it?" I slam the barrel of my gun into the side of his head. Lorenzo groans as he slumps to the floor.

I climb to my feet and hurry back over to Lila.

"I need you to go and wait outside for me, sweetheart. Can you do that?" I make quick work of removing the heavy cuff.

"D-don't leave me," Lila sobs.

"Never." I slide the cuff off her ankle and slowly run my fingers over the bruised skin. "I just need to finish what I started."

"Make him suffer." Lila's eyes burn as she looks over to Lorenzo.

I wrap my arm around Lila's waist and haul her to her feet.

She wobbles, clinging to me as she finds her balance. She looks so fragile and breakable, her bare skin covered in bruises, but she's alive.

Lila's alive.

I got to her in time.

I take her face in my hands and press my lips to hers, needing her warmth against me just for a moment, to make sure that it's not all in my head.

"You're alive," I whisper against her lips.

"I'm alive." She rests her small hand on my cheek.

I lean into her touch for a second before pulling away. "Stay outside the door."

Lila does as I ask and I watch her every move as she leaves the cell and hides around the corner. I don't want her seeing this, but I can't risk her straying too far from me again.

I round on Lorenzo, who's desperately trying to drag himself into a seated position.

I almost laugh at the pathetic sight before I point my gun directly at his head.

"I was planning on dragging this out, wanting you to suffer like I suffered when you took Valentina from me."

Lorenzo huffs a painful laugh.

"Oh, I very much enjoyed taking her life. Especially when she begged so hard for me not to kill her—"

"Don't you dare talk about her."

"What about Lila?" Lorenzo smirks.

"You weren't clever enough this time, Lorenzo. Your son made sure of that."

Lorenzo bares his teeth as he attempts to pull himself up His wounded leg gives out before he makes it, and he collapses back onto the floor.

"He is no son of mine," he spits.

"Your blood runs in his veins, and I made sure to spill every last drop. Like I'm about to do with you."

"You don't have the fucking *balls*—"

My eyes close for a moment, and Valentina's beautiful face enters my mind. Her rich mahogany hair, her dark hazel eyes, her big beautiful smile.

"Do it for me, Andre," she seems to whisper, and I let the memory of her fuel my movements.

I let the memory of her drive my finger to squeeze the trigger and drown out the sound of the bullet releasing from the barrel.

My body jerks, and my eyes fly open.

Lorenzo's lifeless eyes stare back at me, the bullet wound in his forehead tricking blood down his face.

I'm frozen as I stare at Lorenzo.

He's actually *dead*.

After everything this man took from me, to have his blood finally on my hands helps to heal over the wounds. It's not enough to erase the pain, but I hope in time, I can come to live with it. I can let Valentina go.

I'm free to love Lila.

"*Andre*," Lila groans from outside the cell.

"Lila?" I pocket my gun, rushing from the cell without a backwards glance at the lifeless body of Lorenzo Rossi.

"Andre," Lila gasps, clutching at her stomach, her face contorted in pain.

She cries out, her legs giving out.

I barely catch her before she crumbles to the floor.

"Lila." I cradle her against me.

"Something's wrong...with the baby," she moans.

The air is sucked from my lungs as Lila arches her back, her body going rigid.

"Andre!" Color leaches from her face.

I blink, snapping out of whatever had me paralyzed.

I lift Lila into my arms and carry her up the stairs to where Marco and the rest of the guys are cleaning up.

When Marco spots Lila, his shoulders sag. He looks behind me. "And Lorenzo?"

"Dead."

Lila groans, and Marco's attention instantly shifts.

"What's wrong?" He rushes to my side, glancing anxiously at Lila.

"I need to get her to a hospital. *Now*."

He glances down at my blood-soaked clothes and Lila's half-naked body. "Take the Hummer. There's some spare clothes in the back for both of you." His eyes roam the room. "We still have some cleaning up to do around here. "

"Your shoulder—"

"It can wait. I've bandaged it well enough," Marco assures me. "Lila is the priority here, Andre."

I nod at my brother, silently conveying my thanks before I turn and start to hurry across the warehouse floor toward the entrance.

Lila's whimpers make my chest ache as I look down at her pale face.

Her skin is clammy, and her eyes are screwed shut.

"Hold on, sweetheart. Just hang in there."

43

LILA

Pain wrecks through me as I cling to the passenger door handle.

Andre races along the highway. I glance at the speedometer and nearly choke as I realize he's doing almost double the speed limit.

"Andre, slow down!" My heart races as he narrowly dodges a Prius.

"We need to get you to the hospital."

"I need to be alive for that."

He looks at me sideways for a split second before focusing on the road again.

My hand goes to my flat belly. "You can slow down, I think the cramping has stopped." I still feel a few twinges, but nothing compared to the agony that was tearing through me up until five minutes ago.

He slows down a bit. "That might not be a good thing."

"We're going to be okay," I state, not only to Andre, but to myself and the baby.

I take the opportunity to pull the gray sweatshirt Andre

found in the truck over my head and get to work pulling on a pair of sweatpants.

"I'm not taking any chances." He looks over to me.

I flinch at the pain in his eyes.

For losing me or his baby? I know he doesn't love me, but I love him. And maybe he can learn to love me.

Tears sting my eyes. I reach for his hand.

He squeezes my hand. "I can't lose you, Lila. I love you."

My breath catches, but I can't say anything because Andre stops the car in the ambulance bay, throwing open the driver's door and rushing around to help me out of my seat.

"Sir!" A nurse is running over to the car. "Sir, you can't park there!"

Andre ignores her as he wraps an arm around my waist and lifts me out of the car.

"Andre, she's right." I cling to his shirt.

He lets out a breath, his jaw rigid as he turns to face the woman who's charging toward us.

He adjusts me in his arms and takes something out of his pocket. He hands the nurse a wad of hundred-dollar bills. "Here. Park it and leave the keys at reception for De Luca."

"Sir, I—" The look on Andre's face and the blood stains on his hands and shirt probably have her thinking better of it, and she takes the money.

"That's probably more than her Christmas bonus," I mutter.

"I'll give every person in this fucking hospital a thousand dollars if it means ensuring you're safe, sweetheart," he murmurs into my hair.

My eyes close for a moment as I take in the feeling of his

strong body beside mine. "I thought I'd never see you again."

"I'll always come for you. Always." He presses a kiss to my hair. "Now, let's get you checked out."

***

"Everything looks good, Miss Morano." Dr. Peterson removes my blood pressure cuff. "Your blood pressure is a little elevated, but it's nothing to be concerned about."

"And the baby?" I cling to Andre's hand as I try to read Dr. Peterson's expression.

He seems to sense my anxiety as his kind face breaks out into a smile. "Your baby is fine. It has a very strong heartbeat, and seems to be progressing nicely."

"Oh, thank god." My eyes overflow with tears.

It seems as if they've been running tests for hours, checking vitals and running bloodwork.

I'm sure many of them were unnecessary, but Andre insisted that they run every possible test just in case, paid the doctors off to ensure I was receiving the best care, and from the size of my private room, it worked.

Andre wraps his arms around me and holds me tightly, gently stroking my hair as I sob into his shirt.

"I would like to keep you overnight just to monitor your blood pressure, but it's highly likely we can send you home tomorrow."

I'm barely listening, only caring that my baby is healthy and safe and that Andre is by my side.

Andre gets to his feet to shake Dr. Peterson's hand. "Thank you so much, doctor, for taking such good care of Lila."

Dr. Peterson nods and offers me one last smile before leaving the room.

I watch Andre with his back to me, and his shoulders are still rigid.

"Andre..."

He turns, his eyes constantly searching my face. As if he can't quite believe I'm all right.

"Sit with me." I tap the space beside me on the bed.

I shift across to make room, and he sidles in beside me, wrapping his arm around my shoulder.

"I thought I lost you," he whispers.

"I'm not going anywhere." I take his hand and squeeze it. "You're stuck with me."

"Forever?"

I look into his eyes. "Is that what you want? What you said in the car..."

"Yes. Forever. I love you, Lila Morano. So, what do you say?"

I smile, nodding, tears streaming down my face.

"Use your words, sweetheart, I need to hear you say it."

"Yes. *Forever*. I love you too, Andre. So much."

He beams. "Good. And I guess we should make it official..."

I blink, glancing up at his face.

"Is that supposed to be a proposal?" I tease. "Because your whole ensemble is really adding to it."

"Well, I wouldn't want to raise your heart rate by doing some big, romantic gesture." Andre grins, his shoulders finally relaxing.

This is a joke, right?

I laugh.

When Andre slides off the bed, I frown. Then he drops to one knee beside me.

"Oh, my god." My hand goes to my mouth as I stare at Andre.

His dark eyes are filled with nothing but warmth as he takes my hand and presses a kiss to my knuckles.

"For a long time, I thought I had had my fill of happiness." He takes a deep breath as he looks down at our entwined hands. "So, when you came along, I thought it was too good to be true. I thought the universe was playing some cruel trick on me. I didn't know I was ready for you, so I tried to fight it. I tried to suppress the feelings that were starting to grow, but no matter what I did, I couldn't seem to let you go."

"Andre..." My eyes start to sting with tears.

"I don't deserve you, Lila Morano, but I will spend every day for the rest of my life trying to make myself worthy of you. So, think you could accept me, flaws and all? Better yet, would you do me the honor of becoming my wife?"

Tears stream down my cheeks, my throat thick with emotion. All I can do is nod vigorously before throwing my arms around Andre, almost falling out of the hospital bed.

"Words, sweetheart. Is that a yes?" He chuckles, wrapping his strong arms around me.

"Yes, of course it's a yes." I take his face in my hands and kissing him.

"I love you, Lila," he whispers against my lips.

Those three words have my heart cracking open all over again, but this time from an overflow of joy.

"I love you too, Andre."

I WAKE UP A FEW HOURS LATER TO A KNOCK AT THE door. Andre is still beside me in the bed, though he's now wearing a crisp white shirt and slacks.

"What happened to the sweats?" I mumble.

Andre chuckles, tightening his hold on me.

"Marco and Rosa arrived an hour ago with some supplies. They're eager to see you, but I told them you were sleeping."

The knocking on the door becomes louder.

"I'm assuming that's them now?"

"I have a feeling that it might be." He kisses me softly before sliding off the bed to open the door. "And I was right..."

I push myself up to a sitting position as Rosa and Marco enter.

Rosa looks on the verge of tears as she looks at me, and I offer her a reassuring smile.

I know she feels guilty for what happened, but I don't want her to shoulder the blame. It's in the past.

"How are you feeling?" Marco moves to stand at the foot of the bed. His arm is in a sling.

I choose not to ask for the details. If anything, I want to try and forget that the past few hours ever happened.

"Great. Doctor says I'm all good and should be home tomorrow."

Rosa still hovers by the door, glancing anxiously at Andre, who's leaning against the door with his arms folded across his broad chest.

"Don't you *ever* disobey me again, you hear?"

"I promise," Rosa mumbles.

Andre drops his hands and pulls his sister into a tight hug, ruffling her hair playfully.

She wraps her arms around him.

I smile at the two of them before glancing at Marco, who is fidgeting from one foot to the other.

"Is everything okay, Marco?"

"I realized I never apologized." A blush creeps up his cheeks.

I frown. "For what?"

"You know, the whole kidnapping in the middle of the night thing," he mutters.

I bite the inside of my cheek to hide my laugh and glance at Andre, whose dark eyes are glittering.

He shrugs. "At least he apologized. My little brother is not usually one for such a gesture."

"Fuck off. I was only following your orders."

Andre smirks, tucking his hands into his pockets.

"This family is weird." Rosa plops down into the chair beside me.

"I appreciate the apology, Marco." I chuckle. "Though, if you *ever* try to kidnap me again, and that goes for you too, Andre, I will personally chop off both of your dicks and put them through a meat grinder."

Marco cringes. "Noted."

My eyes stay glued to Andre. "And from now on, no more thinking you know what's best for me. I want to be involved in every decision that affects me and my baby, you hear?"

I pause, realizing what I've just said.

Everyone is silent for a moment.

Rosa squeals, "You're pregnant?"

I cringe, but nod. "I am."

"Oh, my god!" Rosa cries, jumping up from her seat to launch herself at me.

Andre smiles. "We're also engaged."

"No shit!" Marco claps his brother on the shoulder with his free hand. "Congrats!"

"This is so exciting!" Rosa hugs me so tightly I almost choke. "I'm going to be an auntie!"

Overjoyed at her excitement, I hug Rosa back.

I'm so grateful that this baby is going to be surrounded by so many people who love it. Something I missed out during my own childhood.

Marco tilts his chin at me. "How far along are you?"

"About two and a half months, so it's still early."

Rosa is beaming. "Too early to know if it's a boy or a girl?"

I nod.

She gets a dreamy look on her face. "I hope it's a girl."

Marco groans. "Then we'll be outnumbered,"

"Exactly." Rosa chuckles. "Oh, think of all the cute clothes! I'll start making a Pinterest board for the nursery..."

I glance at Andre who's shaking his head.

I frown. "What?"

"See what you've done?" He tilts his head in Rosa's direction.

She sticks her tongue out at Andre before pulling her phone out of her back pocket.

"We could have a cute woodland theme, or circus theme. Oh, have you started making a list of names? Because I have a list somewhere in my phone of some really cute ones—"

Andre moves over to the bed and takes Rosa by the arm. "I think that's enough for now, little sis. Lila should rest."

"But—"

I smile at her. "I promise I won't make any decisions without you."

Rosa beams and let's Andre usher her toward the door.

Rosa waves as she leaves the room. "Welcome to the family, Lila!"

Marco chuckles as he follows behind Rosa. "Hope you're not regretting your life choices."

Andre shakes his head as he closes the door behind his siblings. "No turning back now."

He leans against the door looking so delicious I want to make love to him right here in this hospital bed. As if he can sense the tone of my thoughts, he smirks, reaching for the top button of his shirt.

"I say we make this engagement official."

EPILOGUE
LILA

Six months later

Family dinner has never been my thing. Ever. Because I never had a family. Just Aunt Maria.

Until Andre.

Now, here we are, all having dinner, like a proper family should.

I'm huge, now, a week away from my due date.

I put down my fork and turn to Marco. "Can you get me some water, please?"

He looks at Andre and Rosa. "You guys want anything?"

Andre shakes his head.

"Can I get a piece of that apple pie in there?"

Marco laughs. "Sure."

He gets up to go into the kitchen.

My baby is kicking a lot today and my back is killing me.

When Marco comes back in, he is doing a balancing act with my glass of water and two pieces of pie.

I get up to help him and something rips inside me. I

gasp, holding my huge bump as something warm runs down my legs.

I don't want to look. I'm too scared that it might be blood, that my baby might be dying.

Andre is up and beside me in two seconds flat. "What is it, sweetheart?"

Tears come to my eyes. I breathe, "I think there is something wrong with the baby."

Glass crashes to the floor.

My eyes lift to Marco as he points at my feet. "Oh, fuck!"

Andre looks down too. "Oh, fuck!"

My eyes follow theirs as Marco starts swaying on his feet and needs to hold on to a chair. I think he might pass out.

"Andre..."

He picks me up and carries me to the car. "We are leaving to the hospital now. Rosa, call Dr. Waite and tell him to meet us there."

"What, why?"

I look at her. "Because my waters just broke. It's time."

She squeals running to her phone, and Andre takes me to the car and has me in the hospital in next to no time. Only a couple of close calls this time.

As soon as we get there, someone is waiting for me.

I have to strip down and they put me and Andre in one of the private rooms.

Labor takes hours, and when pain starts to become too close together, I hold Andre's hand hard.

"What if I don't make it? What if I'm just like my mom?"

"Don't you dare, Lila. I'll ravage heaven and hell to get

you back. So, you just focus on breathing and pushing and I'll be right here with you the whole time. Deal?"

"Deal. I love you."

"I love you so much, sweetheart. Let's bring this baby to the world so we can ger it home."

My fear doesn't leave me, but it dims enough that I can do as he says, breathe.

And when the time comes, hours later, I push with all my might.

<hr>

"I can't believe she's finally here," I whisper.

"Me either." Andre climbs onto the bed beside me, wrapping an arm around my shoulders, pressing a kiss to my forehead. "You did so well, sweetheart, I'm so proud of you."

My eyelids close at the touch, savoring the moment I thought I would never get to experience.

The bundle in my arms starts squirming, and I open my eyes and smile down at my daughter.

She has Andre's dark hair and my blue eyes.

Her perfect rosebud mouth opens in a wide yawn, and both Andre and I laugh as she falls back to sleep.

"She's perfect, just like her mama." Andre reaches down to stroke his thumb across her pink cheek. "Now, I think Rosa and your Aunt Maria might combust if we don't let them in to meet their new niece."

I laugh.

Dr. Waite left thirty minutes ago after completing a few final checks, promising to be back in a few hours, after he's seen to his other patients back at the practice.

Andre offered to bring in both our families, but I

wanted some alone time, just the three of us.

"I bet Cassi is just as antsy. Fine, I think it's time this sweet girl met her aunties and uncle." I smile at the thought of them waiting downstairs.

I look up and grin at the look of pure pride on Andre's face.

Fatherhood suits him, and already I see us working hard at making many more mini us.

"I'll be right back." He bends down to kiss me on the lips.

I sigh at the taste of him, wanting nothing more than to stay in our little baby bubble forever. But Andre's right—I'm surprised the girls haven't already broken down the door.

Andre slips from the room, leaving me alone with my precious baby girl.

She's wrapped in a pink blanket, and I snuggle her against me, breathing in the smell of her as she sleeps peacefully in my arms.

"Mama loves you so much, sweet girl," I whisper before kissing her on the forehead.

I never knew I could love something so much until the moment Dr. Waite handed her over to me, screaming at the top of her lungs, her tiny limbs flailing as I reached for her.

The second I tucked her against my bare chest, she quieted down, and I thought my heart might burst.

My eyes start to blur as I think of my own mother, who never got to hold me like this, who never got to *love* me.

There's a soft knock at the door, and I hastily wipe my eyes as Andre opens the door.

"Ready?"

I nod, smiling as Aunt Maria leads the charge, followed by Rosa, who practically bounces into the room carrying a massive bouquet of pink peonies and an *It's a Girl!* Balloon.

Cassi is pulling a miserable Marco by his arm.

He looks uncomfortable, hands tucked into the pockets of his pants. He unhooks my best friend's arm from his as soon as they are inside to hovers by the door.

Rosa almost prances to the side of the bed. "Congratulations, mama!".

"Let me take these." Andre reaches for the flowers. "You'll knock someone out if you're not careful."

Rosa shrugs it off and perches beside me on the bed.

"Everyone." I glance between our family members. "I'd like you to meet your new niece, Holly Sofia De Luca."

"After Mom?" Marco asks, moving to stand at the end of the bed, his face a picture of awe as he looks at the baby nestled in my arms.

Aunt Maria's eyes widen slightly as she looks at me and the baby in my arms. Her bottom lip trembles slightly.

Andre moves to Marco's side and slings an arm around his brother's shoulders. "Holly for Lila's mother, and Sofia for ours. It seemed fitting seeing as they are no longer with us, and we wanted her to know where she came from."

"It's a beautiful name." Aunt Maria's voice is thick with tears.

I reach out and squeeze her hand. "Would you like to hold her?"

Aunt Maria's eyes light up, and she nods.

I place Holly in my aunt's arms before leaning back against the plush pillows, exhaustion threatening to pull me under.

Rosa and Cassi hover. I can tell they are dying to be the next to hold her.

Marco is shaking his head. "I still can't believe that you pushed a baby out of your—"

Andre looks a little green as he watches my aunt rock

the baby. "Let's not finish that sentence."

"For someone who's had a lot of experience with blood, labor really freaks you out, doesn't it?"

Marco shudders. "I don't want to talk about it."

"I think Marco's the real baby here, not Holly," Rosa mutters.

My aunt looks up and smiles.

"Here, I'm sure you want a turn too." She hands the baby to Rosa, who almost squeals, her eyes bright and shimmering.

Cassi is all but taking the baby from Rosa by now.

These will be some helicopter aunts for sure.

My baby is so loved. I smile.

At last, Cassi gets her turn and coos the baby for a couple of minutes before handing Holly back to me.

Andre grins. "You've got that right."

He catches my eye and flashes me a wink, causing my cheeks to heat.

With one look, I'm transported back to the night in the bar all those months ago where our paths first collided.

I smile, knowing that despite the journey not being perfect, I will never once regret it as it brought me here, to this room, surrounded by my new family.

"I love you," I mouth to him.

He whispers it back.

My life has been so full these past six months. I never knew how happy I could be.

And I can't wait to see the journey with the new addition to the family. The living proof or my love for Andre and his for me.

I look down at her. So beautiful. So peaceful.

Life waiting to happen.

"Welcome to the world, little one," I whisper.